Sharing with Spencer

HART'S CREEK STORIES - BOOK FOURTEEN

by

Suzie Peters

Copyright © Suzie Peters, 2025.

The right of Suzie Peters as the Author of the Work has been asserted by her in accordance with the Copyright, Designs and Patents Act, 1988.

First Published in 2025
by GWL Publishing
an imprint of Great War Literature Publishing LLP

Produced in United Kingdom

Cover designs and artwork by GWL Creative.

Apart from any use permitted under UK copyright law, this publication may only be reproduced, stored or transmitted, in any form, or by any means, with prior permission in writing of the publishers or, in the case of reprographic production, in accordance with the terms of licences issued by the Copyright Licensing Agency.

All characters in this publication, with the exception of any obvious historical characters, are fictitious and any resemblance to real persons, either living or dead, is purely coincidental.

ISBN 978-1-915109-81-1 Paperback Edition

GWL Publishing
Chichester, United Kingdom
www.gwlpublishing.co.uk

Dedication

For S.

Chapter One

Robyn

"It's all set up."

"Seriously? Everything?" I can't believe it. I'm pretty sure moving home shouldn't be this easy.

"Everything," Clark says. "I've even bought some new bedding for you, and I'll make the bed before I leave."

"That's stretching things a bit too far, isn't it?"

"No. There's nothing worse than arriving somewhere new and having to make up the bed, especially when all you wanna do is fall into it."

I wouldn't know. I've never moved house before, but I take his word for it.

"Thanks, Clark. I don't know what to say."

"There's no need to thank me. It's what cousins are for."

It seems cousins are also for helping to find you a new job, organizing your new apartment, and making the entire process go too smoothly to be believed.

"What would I do without you?" I say, unable to stop myself from smiling.

"Make your own bed?" he says, and I can hear him smiling, too.

"Is there anything left for me to do?" I ask.

"Well… I can't unpack for you," he says, chuckling. "I'll be in San Francisco by the time you get here."

"What are we gonna do about the key? If you're leaving Hart's Creek tomorrow, and I'm not arriving until the weekend, how are we gonna meet up?"

"We're not," he says. "But you don't need to worry." I wasn't aware I was. "Someone will be here. I've arranged it all."

He must be talking about the landlord… Tanner Pope. Clark's already told me what a great guy he is, so it seems there's nothing left for me to think about. Nothing at all.

"Okay… well, good luck in your new life."

"Thanks. I hope everything goes well with your new job."

We end our call, and I put the phone down on the nightstand beside my bed, wondering if I'd ever be brave enough to do what Clark's doing. It sounds romantic that he's given up his life here on the East Coast and is moving three thousand miles across the country to be with a woman he's only met a few times… but is it also reckless? Is it also crazy?

It seems that way to me.

But I'm the person who thinks she's taking a risk moving a hundred miles from Boston to Hart's Creek.

It's the biggest adventure of my life, so far… although that probably says more about my life than it does about Clark's and the things he's doing in the name of love.

Because I'm not moving for love.

There isn't a man waiting for me in Hart's Creek, like there's a woman waiting for Clark in San Francisco.

So, why am I going?

Because I'm *looking* for love, I suppose.

I've been doing it for some time now, and I'm reliably informed the right man for me is out there somewhere. The thing is, he doesn't seem to be here, and I can't see the harm in widening the search.

"Dinner in ten minutes, Robyn." My mom's voice filters up from downstairs, and I call out an acknowledgment, knowing that if I don't, she'll only come up to ask what's wrong. Then she'll sit beside me on the bed, and tell me for about the hundredth time this week that I don't need to leave… or in her words, that I'm better off staying here in Boston.

"But your dad and I love having you here," she said when I first announced that I'd got a job in Hart's Creek.

"And I'll come back to visit."

"How will you manage on your own?" Dad seemed confused by my decision, and doubtful of my ability to cope.

"I'll be fine. I'm twenty-eight years old, Dad. It's high time I stood on my own two feet."

They didn't appear to be convinced. The way they stared at each other for a minute and shrugged their shoulders gave them away, and since then, they've both done their best to persuade me that my place is here. To begin with, I wondered if there was an element of selfishness in their arguments. Were they hoping I'd change my mind and stay so I could look after them as they got older? It seemed perfectly possible. Except my parents aren't that old, and they're probably fitter than I am. They both play tennis, they're avid gardeners, and Dad also enjoys a round of golf most weekends. The closest I've ever gotten to regular exercise was the gym membership I took out a couple of years ago, which I cancelled after two months, because I'd only been twice.

It wasn't for me.

Having ruled out the idea that my parents were considering the prospect of imminent old age and frailty, I realized they meant what they said. They simply didn't want me to go.

And some of their arguments were pretty powerful.

"You can't cook," Mom said as she dished up one of her fabulous casseroles. "How are you gonna feed yourself?"

"I'll have to learn, I guess."

"But won't you be lonely? You've never lived by yourself."

She was right about that. Even when I was at college, I still lived here with them. That wasn't to do with me not wanting to leave, or with them trying to keep me here. It wasn't even about me not being able to cook. It was just convenient. The course I wanted to study was available right here in Boston, so why make life complicated?

"No," I said. "But I'm sure I'll be fine."

I didn't like to say that I was looking forward to it. They'd have been offended, and that wasn't my intention. They'd been amazing parents all my life, but I didn't think they'd understand that I needed to spread my wings.

"You don't know the first thing about maintaining a house." It was Dad's turn, and I looked across the table at him.

"Maybe not, but I won't be living in a house. And that's one of the advantages of renting an apartment. I don't have to know how to maintain it, because that's the landlord's problem, not mine."

I could tell from the look on his face that I'd thwarted his argument, so we got on with eating, and talked about something else.

Not that they gave up.

"How do you think you're gonna find your Prince Charming in such a small town?" Mom's latest attempt came just yesterday, when she was helping me pack.

"Because I don't think he's here."

"You think you'll stand more chance in a town with just a few thousand inhabitants than you will in a city the size of Boston?"

"I've kissed enough frogs in this city, Mom," I said, making her blush. "I think it's time I tried a different pond."

My answer embarrassed her enough to keep her quiet on the subject, which was a relief. It was also my intention. She was the one who'd convinced me Mr. Right had to be out there somewhere. She'd also raised me to believe in things like fairytale romances and Prince Charming, but as for me putting her theories into practice…? Let's just say she's always preferred to live in ignorance. Unless there's a chance of them working out, of course. Which hasn't happened so far.

I get up, put my phone into my pocket, and glance around my room. It's nearly all packed now. I've just got the last few things to deal with, and then I'll be ready to go. To be honest, I can't wait. The last couple of weeks have really dragged by… especially at work. That's mostly because they haven't given me anything new to do. I can't blame them for that. What would be the point, when I won't be there to see it through? But I wish they'd just let me leave, rather than making me work through my notice period, staring at the walls. It feels like such a waste.

Still, I've only got a few more days to go…

I make my way downstairs, the smell of Mom's meatloaf wafting up to greet me, as I join her and Dad in the kitchen.

"Dinner smells good," I say, sitting at the table.

"I thought I'd make meatloaf for you one last time."

"I'm not emigrating," I say. "I'm not even moving to the other side of the country, like Clark. Hart's Creek is a hundred miles away."

I may as well have said it was a hundred thousand miles, judging by the look on Mom's face as she sits opposite me.

"Don't mention your cousin," she says, dishing out the meatloaf. "You know your aunt hasn't forgiven him yet."

"He's moving to be with the woman he loves, Mom. Surely you can't disapprove of that."

"He's never brought this woman home to meet the family, though, has he?"

"It's kinda difficult when she lives in San Francisco. And I'm sure they'll come for a visit."

She looks less than convinced. "He still found you a job that means you have to leave home, didn't he?" she says, adding to Clark's list of crimes as she hands me a plate loaded with meatloaf and mashed potatoes.

"He didn't exactly find me the job, Mom. He helped, but his role was limited to telling me about the vacancy at the place where he worked. I did the rest."

I can still recall how nervous I was at the prospect of even putting in an application, but Clark assured me the company were great employers, and the process was a lot easier than I'd expected. My biggest problem was that when I went for my interview, Clark wasn't there. He'd gone to visit his girlfriend, Cerys, in San Francisco, so I had to find my way to the offices, meet the guy in charge, and get through the interview all by myself. I did it, though. And I did it well enough that they offered me the job.

When they called at the end of that week and made an offer I really couldn't refuse, I naturally said 'yes' without even thinking about it.

I'd enjoyed my time in Hart's Creek. It may have been a lot smaller than anything I was used to, but I liked it… and it was only after I put the phone down that I realized I'd made a mistake.

Not in accepting the job, but in accepting it without thinking about where I was going to live.

I could have kicked myself, but there was no way I was going to call them back and admit what a fool I'd been. Instead, I called Clark.

He was back in Hart's Creek by then, and immediately offered his congratulations, and listened while I pointed out the obvious problem.

"It's your lucky day," he said.

"It is?"

"Yes. Cerys and I have decided we're through with long-distance relationships."

"You're breaking up?"

"No. I'm moving out there."

I took a moment to recover from the shock. "But you barely know her."

"I know her well enough to know she's the one," he said. "I've already given in my resignation, and I'm leaving in a month."

"But that means I'll be moving to Hart's Creek just as you're leaving."

"I know."

"But…"

"Stop saying 'but' and think about what this actually means."

"Aside from the fact that you're abandoning me? It means you're crazy."

"About Cerys, yes. But for you, it means something a little more practical. It means you can move into my apartment."

"Can I?"

"I don't see why not. The rent is pretty reasonable, and the landlord is great. You'll like him."

I wasn't sure how Clark knew that, but the more I thought about it, the better it sounded.

"I've got some vacation time owing, so although I have to give two months' notice, I think I'll be able to leave my job in about five weeks' time. Is that gonna fit in?"

"Perfectly. You'll probably be able to move into the apartment just a few days after I move out."

Everything seemed to be slotting into place, and although it felt too good to be true, I accepted. That felt even more insane than taking the job. I'd never even seen Clark's apartment, but he explained to me that it was comfortable, and easy to keep tidy, and that it was above a bookstore.

"I remember the bookstore," I said. "I saw it when I drove through the town."

"Then you know where it is." That felt reassuring. "The guy who owns it also owns the apartment. His name is Tanner Pope. I'll talk to him about you moving in, if you like."

"Okay."

We left it at that, but things worked out just fine. My boss was a little confused when I handed in my resignation. Like most people, I think he'd expected me to stay in that job for the rest of my days – or at least until Prince Charming came along and whisked me away to a better life – and he looked up at me with a frown on his forty-something face.

"You want to leave?"

"Yes." I pointed to the letter in his hand. "I've got a few weeks of vacation time owing, so I've allowed for that in the final date I've given you."

He glanced down and then looked up at me again. "You're really going?"

"I am."

He shook his head, and I wondered if he was going to refuse to accept my resignation. I wasn't sure if that was possible, but I was already preparing my counter-arguments when he got up and came around his desk, offering his hand, which I took.

"We're gonna miss you, Robyn," he said. It was a kind remark, and I felt myself blush, which I did again when I recounted the story to my parents later that evening. They seemed just as surprised as I was by his reaction… although for different reasons.

"He didn't try to persuade you to stay?" Dad asked.

"No. There wouldn't have been any point. Everything's set now."

I could sense my parents' frustration, and that hasn't abated, even with the passing of time.

"You won't know anybody in Hart's Creek," Mom says, as we all start eating the delicious meatloaf. "Clark's leaving tomorrow."

"I know. We were talking just now. He's set everything up for me."

"Has he?" She seems a little disappointed by that.

"Yes. He's even bought me some new bedding, and he's arranged for someone to be at the apartment to meet me."

"Who?" she asks.

"He didn't say, but I imagine it'll be the landlord."

"And who might he be?"

"A man called Tanner Pope. He owns the bookstore in Hart's Creek. Clark's apartment is above it."

She huffs out a sigh, presumably irked that she can't find fault with Tanner Pope or his profession, and turns to my dad. He doesn't seem to have anything to say either, and she looks back to me again, reaching across the table.

"You can come back, you know? If things don't work out in Hart's Creek, our door is always open, Robyn."

I take her hand in mine and give it a gentle squeeze. "I know, Mom, and I'm grateful."

She manages a slight smile and sucks in a breath as she gets back to her meatloaf.

"Did I tell you about Georgia?" she says, taking a sip of water.

"No."

I recall the girl I went to school with, who used to live just down the street from us, until she went away to college, met the man of her dreams and wound up living in New Jersey. She had blonde hair, sparkling blue eyes, and no shortage of boyfriends. Not that any of them were serious. Not then. That came later…

"She's just had a baby," Mom says. "That's her second."

"Oh? Was it a boy or a girl?" I ask, pretending an interest I don't really feel.

"Another boy. She's named him Adam. Or was it Aaron? I can't remember," she says, and I have to smile, knowing Mom will have heard the news from Georgia's mom, who I have no doubt was keen to pass it on. She may have also rubbed a little salt in the wound that my mom is yet to bear the title of grandmother… but that can't be helped.

If I have kids, it'll be because I want them… not because I want to make my mother happy.

Don't get me wrong, I want my mom's happiness, and my dad's, too… but I'd like to find a little of it for myself along the way.

It's not much to ask.

It worked for Georgia. Just like it has for most of my other school friends.

They're nearly all married now, or at least living with someone. And I can't help feeling a little left behind… a little left out. They all know how to operate a washing machine, how to make meatloaf, and which end of a fitted sheet is which. None of them are still living at home, in the bedroom they had as a teenager, with their mom making their meals and doing their laundry for them. Georgia's up to her elbows in diapers, and so is April, who's also a mom now. Helena is more of a career woman, but she travels a lot, accompanied by her husband, Finlay. I know this because they post pictures all over social media of places I've never even dreamed of visiting.

I have no ambitions to travel, and as for becoming a mom, like I say, I'm happy to wait.

Because I want to find the right man first.

And I'm yet to do that… although it's not for want of trying.

"I've put some gas in your car and checked the tires, so you should be fine for the journey," Dad says, coming into the kitchen. We had breakfast ages ago, and I wondered where he'd gone to… although now I know.

"Thank you." I go over and give him a hug.

It's my last morning here, and I think if Mom and Dad could lock me in my room, they would. As it is, I've been persuaded to stay until after lunch, and when Dad first suggested it, I didn't mind agreeing to his plan, knowing it wouldn't take me long to get to Hart's Creek.

"You may as well have one last meal here," was Mom's comment, and I had to reiterate that I wasn't moving to the other side of the world. Just to New Hampshire.

Even so, I'm not sorry.

I think I'm going to be nervous enough about starting my new job on Monday, without having to spend the entire weekend by myself.

"Hopefully, you won't take too long to make friends," Mom says, like she's read my mind, and I glance over at her as she fixes us all a coffee.

"I'm sure I won't. They all seemed really friendly when I went for my interview… well, except for Bailey, maybe."

"Who's Bailey?" Dad asks.

"And what was wrong with her?" Mom fires her question immediately after his, and I step back a little to give myself time to answer.

"She's the woman I'm replacing in the surveying department, and she was just a little intimidating, that's all."

"Well, at least she won't be there when you arrive… will she?" Mom says, like there's a doubt about that.

"No. Mr. Andrews explained that she'd be leaving before I could start, so I won't even have to see her."

"Is Mr. Andrews your boss?" Dad asks.

"He owns the company, but my immediate boss is a guy called John. He's in charge of the department."

"And what was he like?" Mom asks. "Did you meet him?"

"Yes. He was nice enough."

"How old was he?" I can sense she's wondering if he might be 'Prince Charming' material, and I shake my head, letting her down gently.

"I don't know, Mom, but he's gonna be my boss." And he's really not my type.

"So? A lot of people meet their husband or wife at work. It's not unheard of, you know?"

She's got a knowing smile on her face, and it's directed at me. I remember seeing it before, when I've mentioned a guy I've met, or someone who's asked me on a date. It means she's plotting, and I'm even more relieved that I'm leaving home… at last.

That's not to say my mom has interfered in my love life, but she hasn't always helped it. My last boyfriend called her weird… and to a certain extent, I couldn't blame him for that.

It was pure fluke that they even met, and it certainly wasn't planned, but we'd been out for the afternoon one Sunday and had come back here to pick up a cardigan for me before going out to dinner. Mom and Dad were in the backyard, doing something with one of the flowerbeds, so I didn't see the harm in leaving Sean at the bottom of the stairs, waiting for me. We weren't at the stage where I felt comfortable inviting him up, and as my parents were in the vague vicinity, I knew it would be unwise.

When I came down, Mom was there with him, and they seemed to be deep in conversation.

"It was nice to meet you," Sean said as we left, and I assumed everything had gone well until we got back into his car and he turned to face me. "Did you set that up?" he said.

"Set what up?"

"Your mom. Did you ask her to talk to me?"

"No. I didn't even know she was gonna come in. Why? What did she say?"

He shook his head, starting the engine. "She wanted to know my thoughts on marriage."

I choked, unable to help myself. "Marriage?"

"Yeah." He glanced across at me, letting out a sigh.

"What did you tell her?"

He frowned. "That I thought it was okay… for other people."

"But not for you?"

"No. I've never thought of myself as the marrying kind."

"Sorry about that," I said. It was the only thing I could think of.

"About me not being the marrying kind? Or about your mom asking the question?"

"Both… I guess."

He shook his head, and as we reached a stoplight, he turned to face me. "It's kinda weird, Robyn."

"What is?"

"Your mom asking a guy those kinds of things… on a third date."

He had a point, and I apologized a second time.

The rest of our date was a little awkward, to put it mildly, and when he took me home, he didn't mention the prospect of a fourth.

And neither did I.

I can't say I was sorry things didn't work out between us. I felt like I'd reached a point in my life where I couldn't keep going out with guys, and even sleeping with guys, wondering if it might come to something.

I had to find 'the one'.

And that's why I'm hoping things will be different once I've moved out of here, to my new home… and my new job, and my new life in Hart's Creek.

Chapter Two

Spencer

"Why are you doing this, man?"

Clark turns around and looks at me, folding a pair of jeans, while I lie out on the couch in his bedroom.

"Do you need me to explain how love works… again?" he asks, clearly unable to stop grinning. He's been like this for some time, and it doesn't get any less nauseating.

"No." Please, God. "I need you to explain why you've given up a well-paid job, and a really nice apartment, to move three thousand miles for a woman you've only met a handful of times."

He sits down on the end of the bed and stares at me. "Because I fell in love with her. How many times do I have to tell you this?"

"As many times as it takes for one of us to realize it doesn't make sense."

"Except it makes perfect sense."

I don't know why I'm having this argument with him. He's already made his decision, and he won't be talked out of it, no matter how dumb he's being. Heaven knows I've tried.

Right from the moment he first told me, I've tried.

Back then, when he came home from his most recent visit to Cerys in San Francisco, I couldn't believe what I was hearing.

"You wanna move out there?"

"Yes."

He sat on the couch in the living room and looked up at me as I paced the floor in front of him.

"Are you crazy?"

"No. Cerys and I have talked it through. We can't keep doing this long-distance thing. We miss each other too much, and no amount of video calling is gonna make up for not seeing each other in the flesh, so I'm gonna give up my job here and move out there to be with her."

"But wouldn't it make more sense to do it the other way around? Cerys works in marketing, doesn't she?"

"Yes."

"Then isn't her job more transferable than yours? Unless I'm much mistaken, you can't just rock up in California and start practicing law."

"No. But Cerys has just been promoted. She's in charge of her department now, and believe it or not, she earns more than I do. She's happy to keep a roof over our heads while I sit my bar exam."

I sat down, feeling a little dizzy… although I don't think that had anything to do with the pacing. It was fear. Fear of the unknown.

That was an unusual sensation for me. I'm pretty familiar with the unknown, and having spent most of my life drifting, I've never had a problem with it before.

Except I've grown used to living here. Would I call myself settled? Probably not, but I like Hart's Creek. It's a great place to live.

And the last thing I wanted to do was change.

Clark and I might not have been lifelong friends, but we'd shared our apartment for over a year. For me, that felt like a lifetime, and his news left me in the lurch.

I wasn't just looking at losing a friend or a roommate; I was staring into the void of homelessness, because I'd already worked out there was no way I could afford to keep this place on my own. My salary as one of several minions in the finance department at Andrews and Son Properties was significantly less than his. We'd always known of the disparity, ever since the day we first moved in together, and for that reason, I'd offered to take the smaller of the two bedrooms. It seemed only fair, as I was contributing less to the rent.

Clark didn't mind. He liked the room on the top floor, even if it doesn't have a door. It has a curtain, shielding it from view, and enough space for a king-sized bed, a dresser, closet, and a couch. When I first saw my room, I was struck by the difference in size, but I knew I'd get by. It wasn't as though I intended to stay a minion for the rest of my life.

Which is why I applied for a promotion a few weeks ago.

I'd been planning to tell Clark about it, and maybe suggest that if I got it, we could look at getting somewhere bigger together. It's not that I don't like our apartment, and Tanner is a fabulous landlord, but a second bathroom would be kinda useful, and I felt pretty sure Clark would prefer the privacy of a door on his bedroom.

I'd decided to tell him when he got back from visiting Cerys, little expecting that he'd drop the announcement of his imminent departure on me.

It made going for the promotion seem a little pointless.

Even if I got it, and the pay rise that came with it, I knew it still wouldn't be enough to keep this place by myself, and as I sat, staring at the floor, and wondering what to do, I felt Clark move along the couch a little.

"You don't need to worry," he said, like he'd read my mind. "I get that staying here on your own is gonna be a problem, but I'm sure Tanner will find another tenant to share with you."

I nodded my head, although I wasn't sure I liked the prospect of sharing a relatively confined space with a complete stranger. Clark and I may have been just that when we moved in, but we had a lot in common. We both worked for the same company, and we were new to town. We also had shared interests in sport, food, and women, and even if Clark has dropped the ball on the last of those, by getting serious about Cerys, we still have some great times together.

Or we did, until now.

The silence between us has stretched to ludicrous proportions while I've been reminiscing, and I look up to find Clark staring at me.

"I love her, man," he says, like he thinks that justifies everything.

"How do you know?" I ask.

"I just do."

"Even though you've only known her for… what is it? Four months?"

"Four months, one week, and two days. And I don't think time really matters when you fall in love." It clearly does if he's practically counting the hours, but I don't comment. "It can take some people half a lifetime, and others half a minute. I knew Cerys was the one from the moment we first spoke."

"Before you even met her?"

"Yes." He nods his head, that stupid grin forming on his face again.

"And you're willing to give up everything you've got here, and move three thousand miles, so you can be with her?"

"I'd move to a different planet if she asked me to."

"I can't imagine ever feeling like that."

He studies me for a moment, tilting his head to one side. "No. You're not the type, really, are you?"

"The type to sacrifice my life, and my freedom, and everything I've worked for? No, I'm not."

He chuckles, getting to his feet. "I don't think of it as sacrificing anything, though. I think of it as gaining so much more than I'm giving up."

I shake my head, knowing there's no way he's ever going to change his mind, and that I really shouldn't be trying. He's happy. Cerys is happy. And when it comes down to it, that's all that matters.

As for myself…

Well, I'm certainly not about to follow in his footsteps. As we've just established, love and commitment really aren't my thing. But I'm a lot less worried about the future than I was.

That's not because I've suddenly inherited a fortune, or even because I've been given the promotion I applied for. I haven't actually heard about that yet, but the word around the office is that a decision is imminent, so I've got my fingers crossed.

No… the reason I'm less frantic than I was is because Clark has arranged for a cousin of his to move into the apartment. I've never met the guy, so I still have that slight trepidation about living with a stranger, but at least he's gonna be working for Andrews and Son, in the surveying department. Being related to Clark, I'm sure we'll find some way to break the ice… even if it's just discussing all of Clark's shortcomings.

He has a few… the worst of which is not concentrating. He's burned a few dinners that way, especially since he's been with Cerys, and has been prone to daydreaming.

"Don't forget, you agreed to be here next Saturday to meet my cousin," he says, wandering around the bed to resume his packing.

"I haven't forgotten."

"Thanks."

He checks the drawers in his dresser, and then the closet, and finally closes up his suitcase.

"Are you done?" I ask.

"Looks that way."

"Shall we go to MD's for one last drink together?"

He nods his head, and although I'll admit to feeling a little sad that this will be our last night out, I wander down the stairs to put on my shoes.

As I get to the bottom, a horrible thought occurs and I turn around, looking back up.

"Tell me your cousin isn't teetotal," I call out.

Clark chuckles. "Hell, no."

"That's good."

I wander to my bedroom, safe in the knowledge that I'll still be able to share a glass of wine over dinner, and a few beers on a Friday night after work. Clark and I have done that since our first week here, finding it helps to unwind. It also gives us an opportunity to talk about our week, and discuss our plans for the weekend. I'm not just talking about grocery shopping and laundry, either. Sharing an apartment needs a little give and take, especially when it comes to entertaining, and we've always used our Friday nights to ensure there were no clashes of interests.

It's worked well in the past, at least until he got together with Cerys and I stopped having to worry whether he might bring someone home on a Saturday night. Over the last few months, it's only been my own plans that have needed any consideration... although to be fair, that side of my life has been fairly quiet since Christmas. That's only two months ago, and I'm putting most of that down to stress over Clark's departure and worry about my promotion, which hopefully means normal service will be resumed pretty damned soon.

"Are you ready?" Clark calls as I grab my pea coat and close my bedroom door.

"As I'll ever be."

He smiles, shrugging on his jacket, and I pick up my keys from the breakfast bar. Clark probably has his, but we've learned the hard way that it pays to take both sets. I can remember the one and only time we didn't, and the memory still makes me smile.

"What's funny?" he asks.

"I was just thinking about the time when we went to the bar for the evening, and I didn't take my keys. You went home with that brunette…"

He chuckles. "Oh, yeah… and you and your blonde friend couldn't get in here."

"No."

We start down the stairs. "Remind me… why couldn't you go back to her place?"

"Because she still lived with her parents, in Willmont Vale."

"Yes. I remember now. You went to Tanner's place and asked to borrow a key from him, didn't you?"

"We did. Fortunately, it wasn't late, but it was embarrassing, and the walk down Maple Street and back kinda took the edge off of things."

He pauses, holding open the door at the bottom of the stairs and looking up at the ceiling for a moment. "Tess," he says.

"Tess who?"

"The brunette. She was called Tess."

"You remember her name?"

He chuckles as I let us out the back of the building, waiting for him to close the door behind us. "Of course I do. I get that just about every woman who passes through your life does so anonymously, but Tess was different. She was hot."

"I don't think you're supposed to say things like that anymore. You're practically a married man."

"I'm not. Not yet."

"But you will be?"

"It's something I'm thinking about," he says, surprising me.

"And you still think Tess was hot?"

"She was," he says. "She just wasn't as hot as Cerys."

I laugh, leading the way to MD's, which is just next door.

"You still haven't told me how old your cousin is," I say as we make our way around to the front of the building, on Main Street.

"Twenty-eight." He stops for a moment. "I think."

"You don't know?"

"Not precisely, but it's around that."

I shake my head, although twenty-eight sounds pretty reasonable to me. It makes the guy four years younger than me, and as far as I'm concerned, that's a good thing. Most of my contemporaries are married, or engaged, or most of the way there… like Clark. I've never even considered settling down, and there's every hope that a guy of twenty-eight will feel the same… so at least we'll have something we can agree on.

The noise coming from the bar seems a lot louder than usual, and I turn to face Clark as we round the corner onto Main Street.

"What's going on?" I ask.

"I have no idea."

"Do you wanna go somewhere quieter?"

"No. We're here now."

He pushes open the door, the noise ratcheting up even further, and we walk inside. The place is absolutely heaving with people, especially for a weekday evening, and we glance around, surprised there isn't a single free booth or table in the place.

"This is crazy," I say to Clark, raising my voice to make myself heard.

"I know."

I make my way to the bar, grateful for my height, so I can at least see where I'm aiming for, and once there, things become even more confusing.

There's no sign of Dawson. He's the guy who owns this place… along with his wife, Macy. Clark and I come here often enough now that we're on first-name terms with them both, and although I vaguely recognize the woman who's serving behind the bar, I can't put a name to her face.

"Can I help?" she asks when she eventually gets to me, and seeing her up close, I remember, she's one of the waitresses who works here. They only serve food at lunchtimes, but I've been in here once or twice – most recently when someone was leaving my department and we all came here for a farewell lunch. I must have seen her then.

"You can tell me what's going on," I say, waving my hand around, and she smiles.

"Macy's had her baby," she says, leaning in a little closer.

"A boy or a girl?" Clark asks from behind me.

"A girl," she says. "She's a couple of weeks earlier than expected, but she's absolutely fine, evidently. They're calling her Olivia."

It sounds as though she's repeated that line several times tonight, although she doesn't seem tired of it.

"That makes sense of why Dawson's not here," Clark says.

The woman nods her head. "As far as I know, he'll be back on duty tomorrow evening, thank God, but for tonight, your first drinks are on the house."

"Seriously?"

"Yeah. It was Dawson's idea… although I wish he'd thought through how quickly the word would spread before he left me here to manage this place by myself."

I can see her point and quickly order two beers, which she fetches without another word. The one advantage to our drinks

23

being free is that she doesn't have to hang around taking a payment from us, and she moves on to her next customers, while we step away from the bar.

"That's good news, isn't it?" Clark says.

"What is?"

"Dawson and Macy becoming parents." He makes it sound like the answer should be obvious, although it's not to me.

"If that's your kind of thing, then I guess so."

He shakes his head at me as I spy a couple vacating a booth at the back of the bar, and make my way over, letting Clark follow, and sit down, waiting for him to copy me.

"You've got no desire to become a father?" he says.

"No. Why? Have you?"

"Eventually. It's not something Cerys and I are gonna rush into, but we've…"

"Are you telling me you've had the children talk already?"

"Of course we have."

I stare at him, wondering when he changed, and why. The Clark I used to know would have run a mile from discussing anything as serious as having kids, and yet now it's a given.

"Don't look so shocked," he says. "Things like that are important."

"Are they?"

"They are when you find the person you wanna spend the rest of your life with."

"The rest of your life?" I say, echoing his words. "That sounds so… depressing."

He chuckles. "It's not. Honestly. I can't wait to wake up next to Cerys every morning, and go to sleep with her every night."

"You don't think it'll get boring? You don't think you'll crave a little variety?"

"No."

I can't agree with him, but rather than spend our evening discussing our differences, I ask how long he thinks it'll take him to find work in San Francisco.

"I've already put out some feelers," he says. "A guy I used to work with before I came to Hart's Creek moved out there about three years ago, and he thinks there might be an opening at the law firm where he works."

"A law firm?"

"Yeah. It's where I started out, before I came to work for a property developer, and I'm kinda looking forward to going back to it."

"Because there's more variety?" I ask, although I know practically nothing about what Clark does.

"Exactly," he says, grinning. "My job here is pretty mundane, and it'll be nice to do something a bit more exciting again."

"Why did you come here?" I ask. "You weren't following a woman. I know you weren't, and you weren't running away from one either. You've made it clear you were leaving a better job than the one you were coming to, so what brought you to Hart's Creek?"

"I wanted to escape from home," he says. "It's the same with my cousin." He sips his beer. "We both have fairly domineering mothers… to put it mildly. It's just that I got out first."

I chuckle, and he joins in, both of us glancing around the bar, which seems to be quietening down a little.

"Don't forget the shippers are coming tomorrow," he says.

"I know. It's in my diary. Your flight's at three, and the shippers are due at four-thirty. I've arranged to leave work early so I'm there when they arrive."

"Thanks," he says. "I appreciate it."

"I'd have taken you to the airport if you'd asked."

"No. It's just as easy to catch a cab."

He's probably not wrong about that, and besides, he needs me to be at the apartment for the shippers.

"Have you heard anything about your promotion yet?" he asks.

I told him about it eventually, once I'd recovered from the shock of his announcement, although I didn't mention my plan that the two of us could have found somewhere bigger to live. It seemed unnecessary.

"Not yet, but the rumor is that there's gonna be an announcement next week."

"You'll have to let me know. I'd hoped to still be here, so we could celebrate together."

"Assuming I get it," I say, sipping my beer.

"They'd be crazy to give it to anyone else."

"Oh, I don't know. The other candidates are pretty good."

That was one of the reasons I hesitated in applying… that and my fear of responsibility. The thing that persuaded me to try was the desire to find a bigger apartment with Clark, and while I know I could suggest it to his cousin, I don't think I'd want to commit to something like that with someone I didn't know.

Still, I guess we can see how it goes.

There's no rush.

We'll have to see how we get along first. Making friends with Clark was easy enough, but I know it's not always like that. At least, it hasn't been for me. In fact, I can honestly say, Clark is the first real friend I've ever had, and at my age, that's saying something. I guess that's the problem with living a nomadic life, though. You don't hang around long enough to get to know anyone properly. And I'll be honest, when I moved to Hart's Creek, I didn't intend to change my ways. I assumed I'd stay for a while, and then move on.

Except I like it.

I enjoy living here, and I've got my fingers crossed nothing changes now that Clark's cousin is moving in.

I really hope he and I can at least get along, and maybe even become friends, too.

Chapter Three

Robyn

I drive down Main Street, wondering why I'm suddenly so nervous.

I've been fine all the way here, but now my mom's words of farewell keep ringing in my ears.

"You can always come back if things don't work out."

"I'm sure they will."

"But if they don't… if anything goes wrong, you can easily come home again."

I wanted to tell her that home wasn't in Boston anymore. I was making a new home for myself in Hart's Creek, but I knew she'd be offended, and I turned to my dad instead, giving him a hug.

"There are bound to be things you don't know how to do, so just call if you need any help," he said, making me feel even more inadequate.

In the end, it was easier just to leave. So I did, with rather more mixed feelings than I'd hoped. I'd wanted to drive away feeling strong and confident, like I could conquer anything, and while I was still determined to make a go of things, my parents' negative comments had eroded any faith I might have had in myself.

Still, I'm here now, and feeling nervous about it won't help.

I need to embrace my new life and feel more positive about it. This is my decision, after all, and I've spent the last few weeks defending it. So, I smile as I turn my car onto Maple Street and immediately pull into the parking lot behind MD's, following the instructions Clark gave me.

"There's a parking bay behind the bookstore," he said, when he was explaining everything to me a couple of weeks ago. "But that's where Tanner leaves his car."

"Okay. So what do you do?"

"When he started renting out the apartment, Tanner arranged with Dawson that his tenants could park behind the bar."

"Who's Dawson?"

"He's the guy who owns the bar. It's called MD's. You can't miss it."

He wasn't wrong about that, and I find a parking bay near the back, alongside another Toyota. It's black, while mine is blue, and it looks to be a couple of years older, but who's counting? I'm not.

I'm trying to work out whether I should leave my things in the car, or take them with me.

Clark told me I only needed to bring clothes, as the apartment is fully equipped, and I managed to get everything into one suitcase… but it's an enormous suitcase, which Dad helped me squeeze into the trunk of my car.

Getting it out and into the building is going to be a challenge, but I didn't leave home for a simple life, and I pop the trunk and gaze down at it, hoping I haven't bitten off more than I can chew.

It's every bit as heavy as I expected, and I take a good few minutes to haul it from the trunk, relieved it has wheels and I can drag it along behind the back of the bar to the bookstore, which is right next door.

As expected, there's a car parked exactly where Clark said it would be, and I make my way past it, being careful not to scrape its paintwork with my case.

I'm a little out of breath, and I take a moment before glancing at the doorbells. There are two of them, and they look new, one having a label beside it that reads 'Bookstore', while the other is labeled 'Apartment'. That's the one I need, and I ring it, putting my car keys into my purse while I wait… and wait.

I'm wondering whether Clark was wrong. He seemed pretty definite that someone would be here to meet me, but did he mean I should ring the bell for the bookstore instead?

I'm absolutely certain he said I should ring the top bell… which is the one marked 'apartment', and I'm about to try it again, when the door is yanked open and I jump out of my skin, looking up at the man who's standing there, frowning down at me.

"Can I help?" he asks, his deep voice making my skin tingle as he tips his dark head to one side.

I'd like to think he could… especially with a body like that. He's got to be well over six feet tall, with muscles to die for… or certainly to dream about. They're muscles which are barely concealed by his tight-fitting t-shirt and thigh-hugging jeans, and even on this brief acquaintance, I can imagine this guy fueling my fantasies. I study him for a moment before raising my eyes to find he's still looking down at me through the most delectable brown eyes, which are set in an absolutely gorgeous face.

Yep… total fantasy material.

"That would be fabulous, if you don't mind," I say, coming back to my senses as I nudge my suitcase forward. "This thing weighs nearly as much as I do."

He smiles, showing off sparkling white teeth, while he pushes his fingers back through his thick, slightly untidy hair, and says, "I'm not surprised."

His comment has me a little confused, especially as he hasn't moved an inch, or even tried to lift my suitcase.

"What does that mean?" I ask.

"There's not very much of you," he says. "And there seems to be quite a lot of your suitcase."

"Oh. I see."

I smile up at him and step inside, although he does his best to get in my way, which seems like an odd thing to do.

"Excuse me," he says. "And please don't think I'm being inhospitable, but where do you think you're going?"

"Upstairs." I move toward the open door marked private. I can see stairs leading upward, and it seems the most obvious choice of the three doors down here, although once again, the man steps in my way, with a little more determination than earlier. He's not actually touching me, but he's blocking my way, and I stare up at him… doing my best not to drool as he shakes his head.

"Why would you wanna go upstairs?" he says. "That's my apartment."

"I know. I get that you're the landlord, and… oh, yes. Now I come to think about it, I'm supposed to give you this…" I rummage in my purse, finding the envelope I put there earlier and pull it out. "I've signed the rental agreement, but rather than sending it in the mail, I thought I'd just give it to you when I got here. Is that okay?"

The man's brow furrows, and he looks down at the envelope, although he doesn't take it from me.

"I'm sure it would be, if I were the landlord… but I'm not."

I lower my hand, taking a step away from him.

"Then who are you?"

"I'm Spencer Kidd."

"That may be your name, but it doesn't tell me who you are, or what you're doing here."

"I live here," he says. "Like I said just now, this is my apartment."

"No, it's not. It's mine. I'm renting it from Tanner Pope." I wave the envelope at him to prove the point.

"Yeah… oddly enough, I've got a rental agreement just like that one," he says. "Only it's got my name on it." I lower my hand again, confusion getting the better of me.

"I—I don't understand. My cousin arranged all this. I'm due to start work on Monday morning, and as he was leaving town, he said I could move in here."

The man in front of me lets out a long sigh, nodding his head. "I don't suppose your name's Robyn, is it?"

"Yes. Robyn Greene. That's Robyn with a 'y' and Greene with an 'e'… well, three e's if we're being precise, but—"

He holds up his hands. "Okay. That's enough spelling lessons for now," he says, putting his hands over his face, then dragging them down. "You're a woman."

"Hmm… I know."

"Sorry. I'm not being deliberately dense, but when Clark said you were called Robyn, I assumed I'd be sharing with a guy."

"Well, I assumed I'd have the apartment to myself, so it looks like we've both been kept in the dark. Which I guess means we need to speak to my cousin, doesn't it?"

We both pull out our phones, his from his back pocket and mine from my purse, but before he can do anything, I grab his arm and he stops and stares down at me.

"Sorry, but can I go first?"

"Sure," he says, lifting my suitcase inside as I look up Clark's details. I can't help but be distracted by the way Spencer's muscles flex, although I know I shouldn't be so superficial and I lean back against the wall, doing my best to concentrate on the situation, rather than the man in front of me, as I connect the call.

The lobby we're now filling is small, with white painted walls and three doors leading off of it. The open one, which leads up to the apartment, has the word 'Private' painted on it, as does the closed one opposite, while the one at the end has no markings at all.

Spencer is leaning against the open doorframe, with my suitcase at his feet, his arms folded across his chest, and his eyes fixed on me as I wait for Clark to pick up. He's taking his time, and I'm half expecting his voicemail to kick in when he eventually answers, sounding out of breath.

"I do hope I've interrupted something important," I say, rather than bothering with a 'hello'. I'm not in the mood for politeness, although he just chuckles at my comment.

"Nearly," he says.

"That's a shame."

"Well… I wasn't gonna take the call, but as you're moving into the apartment today, I thought I'd better, just in case something's gone wrong."

"Wrong?" I say, raising my voice just a little, which makes Spencer smile.

"What's happened?" Clark asks. He wounds worried now, and so he should.

"You forgot to mention I'd be sharing the apartment. That's what's happened."

"Did I?"

"You know you did."

"No… I'm sure I explained."

"Clark, you didn't say a word."

"Yes, I did. I remember now. I told you Tanner had arranged for his tenants to park their cars behind the bar. Tenants… plural."

"You think that made it clear?"

"Clear enough."

"Jesus, Clark. The way you phrased that made it sound like Tanner had made the arrangement for each of his tenants in turn, not for multiple tenants at the same time."

"Even so, you can't say I didn't mention that there would be more than one of you."

"Yes, I can." I wave my free arm in the air, ignoring the smirk on Spencer's face. He seems to be enjoying this, even though I know he's just as unhappy as I am with the situation. If he wasn't, he wouldn't still be holding his phone, ready to call my cousin when I'm finished.

"Okay," he says, sounding a little more contrite. "I guess it must have slipped my mind."

"How?"

"I've been a little preoccupied, Robyn… what with moving, and everything. And in any case, I can't see why it matters."

"Are you fucking serious?" I say, glancing at Spencer as he laughs out loud, his broad shoulders shaking.

He's really not helping the situation, especially as Clark laughs, too.

"Is Spencer there with you?" he asks.

"Yes."

"Then surely you can see you've got nothing to worry about. He's a good guy. He's really tidy, and he can cook even better than your mom. You'll be fine."

"It's not as though I have a choice, Clark. Not now."

He laughs again, and because I'm so angry, I hang up on him and turn to Spencer, who's still smiling.

"It's your turn," I say, although he surprises me by shaking his head.

"It sounded like you might have interrupted something." There's a sparkle in his eyes that makes my body heat, and although I do my best to ignore it, my pussy tingles with longing… reminding me it's been a while, although now is not the time for thoughts like that.

"Not quite, evidently," I say, and his smile widens.

"In which case, I'll leave it for now."

"You're more considerate than I would be."

He shrugs his broad shoulders. "Well… from what I could gather, this seems like more of a misunderstanding than a deliberate deception."

"Even so…"

"There's no point in ruining his afternoon… and as it looks like we're gonna be sharing the apartment, we may as well get on with it."

He has a point, and rather than stand around discussing the ways in which I'd like to punish my cousin, I step toward my new roommate, glancing down at the envelope I'm still clutching.

"Do you want me to take that?" he asks.

"Well… as you're not Tanner Pope, I guess not."

He frowns, and I wonder if my answer came across as abrasive. "I can easily pass it on to him," he says, and rather than refuse his offer, I nod my head.

"Okay. Thanks," I say, handing it over and watching as he folds the envelope and puts it in his back pocket, along with his phone. There's something confident, or at least assured about every movement he makes, but rather than dwell on that, I reach for my suitcase, although he beats me to it.

"Let me. You'll never get it up the stairs by yourself," he says as he nods toward the doorway. "After you."

"Thanks." I feel like I'm repeating myself, which I am, but there's no need to make a thing of my gratitude, and I head up the stairs, letting out a sigh when I reach the top. "This is lovely," I say as Spencer joins me, dumping my suitcase by my feet.

"It is pretty nice, isn't it?"

'Nice' feels like an understatement, and I take a moment to absorb the muted tones of gray and blue that decorate the walls, and the light wood flooring. That looks quite new, although I don't remark on it, as my eyes wander to the kitchen, which is at the far end of the open-plan space, overlooking Main Street, I guess. It's divided from the rest of the room by a staircase that leads to the floor above, and while there's no door at the top, there are two in the back wall of the room we're standing in.

"Are these the bedrooms?" I ask.

"One of them is. It's mine. The other is the bathroom."

"Okay. And my room?"

"It's upstairs," Spencer says, nodding toward the staircase.

I glance up at it again. "But there's no door."

"No. There's a curtain."

A curtain? That has to be a joke. "You're kidding me."

He shakes his head and picks up my suitcase, leading the way up. I follow, feeling a little nervous, although when I join him, I have to admit, the room itself is beautiful. It's also enormous, the decor being similar to the room downstairs, with the king-sized bed set against the left-hand wall, and a closet and dresser opposite. There's also a couch at the end of the bed, and Spencer puts my case beside it, turning to face me.

"I've always liked this room," he says, glancing around, and part of me wants to say he can have it, because I can't help feeling concerned about the lack of a door… the lack of any form of privacy.

Even at my parents' house, I had a door on my bedroom. My mom may not always have respected it, but at least it was there. It provided a barrier… a barrier I won't have here, and as I glance at the curtain and then back at Spencer, I revise my thoughts about him. Sure, he's ideal fantasy material, but it looks like I'll have to keep my imagination under control. I daren't let it run away with me. I mean, I may have perfected the art of coming quietly while I pleasure myself, but there's quiet… and then there's silent. And I'm not sure I'm capable of that.

"Is there a reason that the sleeping arrangements are this way around?" I ask, doing my best to put all thoughts of fantasizing about Spencer out of my mind.

"Yes. I pay less rent than you do, so I get the smaller bedroom."

"I see."

It doesn't seem fair to suggest a swap, and rather than embarrass him by asking any more about his financial situation, I wander over to the curtain.

"So, how does this work?" I say, running my fingers over the thick, gray material.

"You pull it across," he says with barely disguised sarcasm.

I didn't need that, or the smirk on his face.

"I get that, but it doesn't feel very secure, or very private."

"It is. Honestly." He sounds more sincere now… and maybe even a little concerned.

"But surely, you'll be able to hear everything I do."

He raises his eyebrows just slightly, and I wonder what's going through his mind, and whether I'm blushing. I hope not. That would be painfully embarrassing.

"Do you snore?" he asks, the sarcasm replaced with a hint of a tease, which I have to say is much more fun.

"No, but…" Where the hell am I going with this? Letting him tease me is one thing, but joining in is a really bad idea, especially as I have no idea what to say next.

As though he senses that, Spencer steps forward, and keeps coming until he's right in front of me, and I'm forced to crane my neck to look up into his chocolate brown eyes. That's not such a good idea. They make me want to melt… and I really shouldn't. At least not while he's still standing here, staring down at me.

"I spend most of my time in my room," he says. "So feel free to do whatever you want… I almost certainly won't hear you."

Did he guess what I had in mind? It's hard to tell, and I'm not about to ask. He doesn't give me the chance, anyway, and with a final, deadly smile, he walks around me and heads down the stairs, making me wonder what on earth I've let myself in for… and what kind of torture I'm going to inflict on Clark the next time I see him.

Chapter Four

Spencer

I've left Robyn with a 'y' to unpack her things, and as I get to the bottom of the stairs, I wonder if practically falling over my tongue was the best way of breaking the ice with her. Telling her she was a woman definitely wasn't. That was blindingly obvious, and certainly didn't need pointing out. Man, what a lame thing to have said. Even though her arrival here was a shock, I could have thought of something more imaginative than that… surely.

I'd like to say I was distracted… and I was.

After all, I was expecting a guy to knock on my door, not a beautiful redhead.

But is that really a good enough excuse for the way I've been behaving over the last few minutes?

I mean… why on earth did I ask if she snores?

Was it to hide the fact that she'd just remarked that I'd be able to hear everything she did, and that my brain had automatically switched to an image of her lying naked on the bed, her legs spread wide, while her fingers played across her clit as she brought herself to multiple screaming orgasms?

Probably.

But snoring? Really?

I tried to cover that dreadful faux pas by telling her I spend a lot of time in my room… because although I never have in the past, I think I will from now on. I think I'm going to need a little privacy of my own to come to terms with the fact that even thinking about her turns me on.

That's obviously not a problem I ever had when Clark was living here, but with Robyn…?

I guess it's something I'll have to get used to.

While going quietly insane.

Although speaking of her living here, I guess I'd better take her rental agreement down to Tanner, rather than let it burn a hole in my pocket.

Who knows… it might help the situation if I can put some distance between us.

And hell might freeze over in the next ten minutes, too…

I wander down the stairs, letting myself into the bookstore through the back door. Tanner's standing behind the counter, which is off to one side, and in front of him, deep in conversation, is Peony Hart. I know her because she's my boss's wife. For that reason alone, I don't feel I can interrupt them, although approaching doesn't feel out of place. It's certainly better than hanging around by the back door, hoping Tanner might notice me.

"Kane's still working for me," Peony says as I step closer. I have no idea who she's talking about, so I change my mind, assuming I'm interrupting a private conversation and hang back just slightly.

"Even though he's inherited all that money?" Tanner says.

"Yes. We discussed it in between making plans for their wedding, and he said he wanted to stay on at the apple orchard. I certainly wasn't going to argue. He's fantastic at what he does, and I didn't relish the prospect of finding another manager."

"What about Diana?" Tanner asks.

"She's given up her job at the deli," Peony replies, and I remember seeing someone new working over there… someone different to the pretty blonde, who used to make my sandwiches from time to time, or serve me with bread and milk on the odd occasion when Clark and I ran out and didn't want to drive to the grocery store. "They're renovating Laurel's old house, so that's taking up a lot of her time."

"Does it need that much work?"

Peony shrugs her shoulders. "It had been empty for quite a while, and I don't think the previous owners had done much with it."

"Bearing in mind how long it took Zara to get our place the way she wanted it, I'm sure that's keeping Diana occupied," Tanner says as Peony pays him for the books she's buying which mostly seem to be for a child… a very young child, and I recall someone telling me my boss has a little boy, which makes sense.

"Did you hear about Pierce and Harley?" Peony says as Tanner puts her books into a canvas bag.

"No. What about them?"

"They're back."

"For good?" He seems surprised, until Peony shakes her head.

"No, just for a visit. I haven't seen them myself yet, but I heard they're engaged."

"Well… I guess that was inevitable," Tanner says with a smile, and although – yet again – I don't know who they're discussing, it seems their news is welcome… and predictable. "Speaking of Harley, have you heard anything about this new doctor?" I'd expected Peony to leave, but Tanner seems keen to talk, and I move a little closer again, just to make my presence felt. I may have wanted to put some distance between myself and Robyn, but I don't want to be down here all day.

"He's proving a real hit, I think," Peony says. "And as he's married to Bronte now, I think we can assume he's staying."

"I wasn't doubting that. I just wondered if you knew anything about him."

"Why?" Peony asks. "Is something wrong?"

"No. Nothing's wrong. Not with me." Tanner smiles at her, and she tips her head to one side.

"Is it Zara?" Peony sounds worried, although Tanner's still smiling, and I imagine if his wife were sick, he wouldn't be doing that, which makes his reaction a little weird. Except Peony clearly doesn't think so, as she smiles, too.

"Are you saying what I think you're saying?"

"That depends on what you think I'm saying."

Peony leans in a little. "Is Zara pregnant?"

"Yes, but you didn't hear it from me, and I only asked about the new doctor because Zara called up yesterday to get an appointment and Doctor Dodds is on vacation next week, so she had to agree to see Doctor… Moss, is it?"

"Yes, it is… but this is so exciting," Peony says, grinning. "I take it you haven't told Nash yet?" That's a name I am familiar with. She's speaking of Tanner's son from his first marriage. From what I've gathered, it ended badly. I don't know the details, and they're none of my business, but I've met Nash a few times, and he's a great kid.

"No. We're gonna wait until things are a little further along."

"And Sabrina?" That's Tanner's ex-wife, who I only know by reputation… and it's not a good one.

Tanner shakes his head. "I'm putting that off for as long as possible. Maybe until after the baby's born… or when he or she graduates."

Peony chuckles. "Your secret's safe. I won't tell a soul."

Tanner looks up and finally notices me, his cheeks reddening just slightly. "Sorry, Spencer. I didn't see you there."

"Have we kept you waiting?" Peony asks.

"No. It's fine." I smile at her, and then look back at Tanner. "I won't tell anyone, either," I say, and he nods his head.

"Thanks."

Peony steps away from the counter, but then stops and studies me for a moment.

"Do I know you?" she says, tipping her head to one side.

"You might. I work for your husband… in the finance department. And I live upstairs, so you could have seen me around the town."

"No, I think I might have seen you at the office. I don't go there very often… not unless Ryan's forgotten some papers. But I'm pretty sure I saw you there once."

"You've got an excellent memory."

She nods her head, gives me a smile, and then turns to Tanner. "I'll see you soon," she says, and leaves with a wave of her hand.

Once the door has closed behind her, Tanner focuses on me again. "Sorry we kept you. I honestly didn't realize you were there."

"I kinda got that," I say, nodding my head. "And congratulations."

"Thanks. Like I say, it's early days…"

"And I promise I won't say a thing. Not to anyone."

He lets out a sigh. "It's a great feeling, you know?"

"What is?"

"Impending fatherhood."

I shake my head. "I'll take your word for that."

He chuckles. "It's not your thing?"

"Hell, no."

"You might change your mind one day."

"I doubt that… although I guess this explains why we haven't seen Zara around for the last few days."

He nods his head. "She's already getting the first signs of morning sickness, or at least nausea, and the tiredness has hit her really hard, so she's cut her hours at the store. I want her to rest as much as possible."

"I can understand that," I say, pulling the envelope from my pocket. "I only came down to give you this."

"What is it? Don't tell me you're leaving too."

I shake my head, smiling. "No. This is the new tenant's rental agreement."

"I see." He takes it from me. "And he couldn't bring it down himself?"

"I offered," I explain. "And your new tenant isn't a he. It's a she."

He drops the envelope onto the counter. "Seriously?"

"Yes, although I'm pleased to see I'm not the only one who didn't know."

He takes a deep breath, letting it out slowly. "What's she like?" he asks.

"My worst nightmare."

He frowns. "Is this gonna cause a problem?" he says, tapping the envelope.

"I hope not. I mean… she was under the impression she was gonna have the apartment to herself, and…"

"You mean Clark hadn't told her she was sharing?"

"No."

"And is she okay with the situation?"

"I think she's getting her head around it. Just like I'm getting my head around the prospect of sharing with a beautiful redhead."

"Ahh… it's like that, is it?" he says with a smile.

"Oh man, yes." I let out a sigh, and his smile widens.

"You might wanna watch yourself," he says, doing his best not to laugh.

"Why?"

"Sounds like you could be in trouble."

"Yeah… with a capital T."

He gives in to his laugh, and I take the opportunity to leave, going out through the back door, and up to the apartment. There's no sign of Robyn, and I notice she's pulled the curtain across the top of the stairs, which I guess means she wants some privacy. That's fair enough, and although I know I could offer her a coffee, it seems best to leave her to her own devices for now. That doesn't mean I'm not gonna make one for myself, though, and as I think I might need it, even if Robyn doesn't, I make a full carafe, my temper building as I watch it filter through.

My bad mood isn't aimed at Robyn. It's aimed at her cousin, and although I know I said I'd leave calling Clark for now, I'm feeling even more disgruntled than I did earlier. This may have felt like a misunderstanding, and maybe it is, but the fact that he didn't tell our landlord anything – that he didn't tell any of us anything – is really getting to me, and once I've poured myself a cup of hot coffee, I pull out my phone and connect a call to him, sitting down on the couch as it switches straight to voicemail… damn him. It would be easy to hang up, but I'm not about to go easy on Clark, and I take a breath before I leave a message.

"Call me back when you've grown a pair of balls. You're gonna need them."

I lean back, resting my head, as I sip my coffee and wonder what to make of my new roommate. It's a natural train of thought, considering she's only upstairs behind a curtain, but it's also a mistake. I shouldn't have started down this road, because thinking about Robyn makes me hard as nails… again. What's a guy to do, though? Especially when he's faced with someone so cute and sexy, with light green eyes, and long, wavy red hair that falls down over her shoulders to the middle of her back. How's a guy supposed to ignore such porcelain-pure skin, or a perfect hourglass figure? Even her jeans and sweater clung to her, and I honestly couldn't blame them. Given the chance, I'd do the same.

Ignoring her is impossible… and yet I have to try. I have to do more than try.

I have to resist her.

Although she's not making it easy. Not when she's everything I could ever want in a woman… if I were looking.

Which I'm not.

I'm really not.

Except I have to say, it's not just about the way she looks, as tempting as that is. It's about the way she is. It's about the way her eyes sparkle when she smiles… and positively glint when she loses it, like she did with Clark. I've never had a problem with women who speak their minds, and it seems Robyn could be just such a woman.

Which means she's more than trouble. She's deadly.

But man… what a way to go.

I smile to myself, just as my phone rings, halting my overactive imagination, and I sit up, seeing Clark's name on my screen, which is enough to distract me from my wayward thoughts as I turn my phone onto speaker and place it on the arm of the couch beside me.

"Don't tell me, you're calling about Robyn," he says before I can utter a word.

"Yeah, I am. Honestly, man. What were you thinking? Not only didn't you tell her I live here, but you neglected to point out to me that Robyn is a woman."

"I could have sworn I mentioned it," he says, doing his best to sound innocent.

"Well, you didn't. But you've been so fucking preoccupied with Cerys, it probably slipped your mind."

"Probably, but like I said to Robyn, it'll be fine. She's great, you know?"

"I noticed," I say. "Just like I noticed she's a redhead. You know my weaknesses. What are you trying to do to me?"

He chuckles. "I know you normally can't control yourself around anyone with even a tint of red in their hair, but trust me, in this instance you've got nothing to worry about."

"I don't?"

"No. Robyn isn't your type."

Out of nowhere, I have a sudden and strange hollow feeling inside me, like someone just sucked the life out of me, and I take a moment before I can ask, "Why not?"

"Because she's looking for Mr. Right," he says. "She wants a guy she can settle down with, not someone who just wants to fuck her and move on."

"Is that how you think of me?"

"That's who you are. We both know that, so don't pretend to be offended. You've always been proud of the fact that you're not the kind of man who does commitment."

"Yeah, but it's not all one-night stands."

"Who are you kidding? Can you remember the last woman you saw more than once?"

"Not off the top of my head."

"Can you remember the name of the last woman you slept with?"

I think for a moment. "No, but it began with an 'L'… maybe."

"Which is why you don't need to be concerned about living with Robyn. Like I say, she's not your type… or you're not hers. However you wanna look at it."

"How do you know?" I ask. "I mean, how do you know she's looking to settle down?"

"Because it's not exactly news in our family."

"You mean you all talk about it? You discuss the fact that your cousin is saving herself?"

"Did I say she was saving herself?" he says, confusing me.

"You mean she's not?"

"No. She's had boyfriends in the past, but for whatever reason, none of them have matched up to her expectations."

"Are they that high?"

"Who knows? I've never asked her. All I know is, she's looking for her Prince Charming… and you're not it."

"Thanks." I can't help feeling disappointed, and I guess it shows.

"Well, you're not," he says, bursting my bubble completely. "We both know you're not ready for anything long-term, let alone permanent, and if it's not for you, that's fine. No-one's saying you can't keep playing the field. Just don't expect Robyn to want to play along with you."

That hollow feeling intensifies, and I do my best not to sigh out loud, knowing he'll be able to hear me.

"You still could've told me," I say.

"I know, and it wasn't intentional. Honestly. Although now I come to think about it, you might be able to teach her a thing or two."

"Excuse me? You've just spent the last ten minutes telling me I'm not the man for her, and now…"

"I'm not talking about sex," he says. "I'm talking about practicalities."

"Such as?"

"Cooking, cleaning, doing the laundry."

"What the fuck? Are you telling me she can't do those things for herself? She's twenty-eight years old. That's what you said. Surely she's learned how to fend for herself by now."

"Not as far as I know," he says. "Aunt Amy still does everything for Robyn. She's even more domineering and claustrophobic than my mom… and that's saying something."

"I thought you were my friend."

"I am."

"Then why would you do this to me? Why would you send me a woman who's not only a redhead, but who's also incapable of looking after herself?"

He chuckles. "You don't have to pretend to be a knight in shining armor…" *Who was talking about pretending?* "Just show her how to use the dishwasher, and maybe teach her how to boil an egg."

"I'm sure she knows how to boil an egg."

"I wouldn't bank on it. Aunt Amy is very overbearing. She's never let Robyn do anything for herself."

"She sounds like the polar opposite of my mom."

"Maybe, but if you want me to be honest, I think that's one of the reasons Robyn left Boston and moved to Hart's Creek."

"She wanted to escape?" I say.

"Something like that. She's not cutting herself off from her parents as far as I know, but I think she wants to live her own life for once. She wants to find her own feet."

"And that includes settling down, does it?"

"Yeah, but on her own terms, and not her mom's… and I can't say I blame her for that."

"Neither can I."

I honestly can't. I'm just not sure about the wisdom of her doing it here… with me.

"Are you coming back to bed, babe?" I hear Cerys in the background, and can't help smiling.

"Duty calls," I murmur.

"It's not a duty," Clark says. "And don't worry about Robyn. You'll get along fine… just as long as you remember who you are, and who she is."

I'm not so sure he's right. Remembering simple things like who I am seems to be beyond me right now. My cock definitely isn't getting the message… although I guess it doesn't matter about my reactions, as I know they'll be one-sided. Robyn won't be interested in me, and there's nothing I can do about that, is there?

Clark ends the call, telling me he'll be in touch later in the week to find out about my promotion. To be honest, I'd forgotten all about that, and once he's hung up, I put my phone on the table again, sipping at my lukewarm coffee, although a creak on the stairs makes me look up, and I see Robyn coming down from her room.

Shit… did she hear what Clark and I were just saying?

I wish I hadn't put the phone on speaker now. It's a habit… something I'm used to doing all the time, because I rarely have anything private to say, but I can see I'll have to change my ways, and I get to my feet as she approaches.

"Are you okay?" I ask, surprised that the slight sadness in her eyes bothers me so much.

"I'm fine," she says, making it clear she isn't. Her voice is too monotone… too distant.

"Can I fix you a coffee?" I doubt she'd tell me what's wrong, even if I had the courage to ask… and I don't. She might just tell me she overheard my conversation with Clark, and I don't think I could bear that.

"I'll get it," she says, and the defiance in her voice makes me realize she must have at least heard her cousin tell me she's incapable of doing things for herself. That in itself means I can't offer to help, so I watch as she wanders into the kitchen, and then spends ages going through the cabinets, searching for a cup.

"They're above the microwave," I say in the end, and she goes over and grabs a white one, resting it on the countertop before she fills it with coffee. "Did you want milk?" I ask. "There's some in the fridge."

"No. I take my coffee black."

"Okay." She sips it and adds a little cold water. "Too strong, or too hot?" I ask.

"Too hot."

I nod my head and move a little closer, although the breakfast bar forms a natural barrier between us. "So you don't mind strong coffee?"

"No. The stronger, the better."

Her answers are informative, not detailed, and her tone is definitely on the chilly side. I hate that, between us, Clark and I seem to have offended her, although I think pointing that out will only make things worse. So instead I turn to more practical matters.

"Did you have any plans for this evening?"

She shakes her head. "No."

"I was gonna make some pasta, if you want to join me?"

"I don't wanna be in the way."

"You won't be. Honestly. If I'm cooking for one, I may as well cook for two."

"Are you sure? Only I don't have any supplies yet."

That's the most she's said since she came down here, and I lean over the breakfast bar, getting a little closer to her.

"It's fine. One thing we're never short of in this place is food."

She manages a half smile and then bites her bottom lip, which is way too distracting for my cock. It presses against my zipper to the point of becoming painful, and I do my best not to stare… and not to walk around the breakfast bar and free her lip, by kissing her.

Control yourself, man. Remember who you are, and who she is. She's not for you.

"What did you and Clark do about food?" she asks, giving me something else to focus on, and releasing her lip in the process… thank goodness.

"We used to write a vague menu and a shopping list to go with it on a Friday night or Saturday morning, and then we'd take it in turns to go to the grocery store sometime over the weekend, splitting the cost between us. Quite often we'd run out of bread or milk, but we could just pick those up from the delicatessen across the street. They sell cheeses and cold meats, and they make amazing sandwiches if you need something for lunch."

"Oh, that's good. I haven't thought about lunches yet. I guess I'd have to drive back here from the office, would I?"

"You would. But you might find there's someone in your department who's coming here anyway, and who'd be happy to pick something up for you. You can maybe take it in turns with them? That's what some of us do in my office… when we haven't been organized enough to take lunch in with us."

She nods her head.

"And the grocery shopping… taking it in turns…"

"What about it?"

"Who's turn is it this weekend?"

"Officially, it's yours. I went last weekend, because Clark was busy packing, but it doesn't seem fair to send you off by yourself."

"I'm sure I'll cope," she says, with that defiant edge to her voice again.

"No. I wouldn't hear of it. You probably don't even know where the grocery store is yet."

"Is it hard to find?"

"Not especially, but why don't I drive us over there tomorrow and show you around, and then you can go next weekend?"

"Okay. As long as you're sure. I don't want to cause any trouble."

"You're not, Robyn."

She startles at the sound of her own name… or maybe at me saying it. I can't be sure, and either way, I know her reaction means nothing.

"Shall we… Shall we make a list later?" she says. "Or have you already done it?"

"No. Unlike you, I knew I'd be sharing with someone, so I was waiting for him – or, as it turns out, her – to arrive."

"I see."

"We can work it out after we've eaten, if you like?"

"Okay. Is there anything you need me to do for tonight's dinner?"

I shake my head. "I'm happy to cook, although I suppose I'd better just check… is there anything you don't like?"

"Nothing I can think of."

"And you're not a vegetarian?"

"No."

"So tagliatelle with bacon and mushrooms would be okay?"

"It would be perfect," she says, rewarding me with a genuine smile that didn't seem to take too much effort this time.

That feels more promising, but before I can say anything else, she walks back past me and heads for the stairs, climbing slowly up them, and taking her coffee with her. Personally, I'd prefer her to stay down here with me, but I can't blame her for going… especially not if she heard my call with Clark.

I could kick myself for that, and for hurting her, and although I know I shouldn't let it worry me, it does.

And I don't think that's just because she's a cute and sexy redhead.

Chapter Five

Robyn

I lay out three skirts on the bed, wondering which one will be best. They're all pretty similar, but I want to make the right impression on my first day. The gray one is perhaps a little short, so I dismiss it and focus on the other two, trying to remember what everyone else was wearing when Mr. Andrews showed me around the office after my interview.

John had on pants and an open-neck shirt, which isn't very helpful, and I remember Bailey wore a short black skirt and a revealing top that I'd never be able to carry off… not at work, anyway. There was another woman there, though. I can't recall her name, even though I'm sure Mr. Andrews introduced me to her. I do remember she was wearing a black skirt and white blouse… and I decide to go with that, pushing the navy blue one aside and settling on the black one.

At least that's one decision made. Now I've just got to choose a top.

I have several that will fit the bill, and after about twenty minutes of indecision, I choose a blouse with three-quarter length sleeves. I used to wear this at my old office, and although it's a little tight across the bust, no-one ever objected.

I can't help the way I'm made, can I?

I clear away all my clothes, leaving out only the things I'm going to wear tomorrow, and place them on the couch at the end of my bed, along with my underwear. It seems best to be organized about this, rather than panicking in the morning… because, to be honest, I'm panicking enough already.

I don't know why. It's not as though I'm not qualified to do this job, so I should just swallow down my nerves and get on with it.

If only I could…

I can hear Spencer moving around downstairs, which is hardly surprising when there's only a curtain between me and the rest of the apartment. I haven't gotten used to that yet, but I'm sure I will. Well… I hope I will.

As it is, I stand and listen for a moment, trying to work out what he's doing, the clink of a glass suggests he may be fetching himself a drink, but then I hear the clang of something metallic and realize he's probably still clearing up after dinner.

I offered to help. Honestly, I did. It felt like the least I could do after he'd cooked us such a lovely chicken dish… which was every bit as good as the pasta he made last night. But he seemed to have sensed my nerves and declined my offer.

"Why don't you get your things ready for the morning?" he said. "I can deal with all this."

The kitchen looked like a mess, but even when I offered a second time, he still said 'no', and I wondered if he wanted some time to himself.

He hadn't been expecting me to move in with him anymore than I'd been expecting him to be here, and it was perfectly understandable that it would take us a while to adjust, and that we should probably both allow each other to do that… in our own way.

That said, going to the grocery store with him this afternoon was a lot more fun than I expected… the biggest surprise of all being that the Toyota beside mine in the parking lot belonged to Spencer. We spent the journey to the store discussing the things we like and dislike about our cars before he steered me around the aisles, wheeling the cart, and making light of practically everything. I don't know why that surprised me. Fun is probably Spencer's middle name if that conversation I overheard him having with Clark is anything to go by.

I'm still reeling with embarrassment about that, and I can't believe my cousin went into so much detail about my life. I've been tempted to call him up to ask what he thought he was doing, but I refuse to give him the satisfaction… or embarrass myself any further by admitting I overheard practically every word they said.

Or that it hurt so much.

Or that he was so damn accurate in just about everything he said.

Except, accurate or not, why on earth did he think it was okay to share so much information?

Did he really think Spencer needed to know that I'm looking for Mr. Right? Or that I haven't been 'saving myself', as he put it. I wouldn't have used those words myself. They sound like something my mother might say… or maybe even her mother, now I come to think about it. But even if the sentiment behind them is right, do I really need my new roommate knowing that much about me?

Admittedly, he still doesn't know precisely how many men have been in my bed, but that's only because I've never told my mother about them. That's where Clark's getting his information. It's obvious to me, although he's not getting it directly from Mom, you understand, but from my aunt. Mom and her sister like to trade gossip like it's going out of fashion, which makes me grateful that while Mom knows about some of the frogs I've kissed, she has no idea that Joe, Dominic, and George, made it further into my pond than any of the others.

And she never will.

Because, even though I thought they might be 'the one', it turned out that none of them were right for me.

Although that had nothing to do with me having high expectations, which is what Clark implied. It had everything to do with me realizing – maybe a little too late – that we just weren't suited.

I don't regret what we did. In all three cases, it felt right at the time, and at least I have a better idea of what I'm looking for now.

Or I thought I did until I met Spencer.

Because he's my idea of the perfect man… at least to look at.

And looking is as far as it can go, I'm afraid, because as well as hearing my cousin tell my roommate that I'm looking to settle down, that I'm no longer a virgin, and that I'm practically incapable around the house, and specifically in the kitchen, I also overheard them discussing Spencer's sex life. He sounds like a player of the worst kind… the sort of man who has one-night stands like the rest of us have hot dinners, and who can barely remember the names of the women he's slept with.

That's definitely not what I'm looking for. It's the polar opposite. Although having heard Clark tell Spencer he could continue playing the field, I can't help wondering how many women are likely to pass through the apartment while I'm here.

That thought makes my heart sink a little. I don't relish the prospect of hearing everything that goes on in his bedroom. Who would? I don't think anyone enjoys hearing other people's intimacies.

Except this is more than that.

It's about me wanting Spencer for myself.

Which I know sounds crazy, given everything I've just said about him being a player of the worst kind, but there's no point in denying how I feel about him, or what he does to me, even if I know I can't have him.

The man is irresistible, and every time I'm near him, I get the urge to do something about it… like throw myself into his arms and kiss him… or drop to my knees and worship him in the best way possible. Heaven knows what he'd do if I did. After his conversation with Clark, he'd probably run a mile.

Because we're incompatible. I'm not his type… and he's not mine. And that means I have to resist.

He doesn't want the same things as I do. So, no matter how hard it is, I have to leave him alone. I have to pretend he hasn't gotten under my skin. That shouldn't be too hard at all.

I set my alarm for six this morning, just to be sure I'd have plenty of time to get ready. It won't take me that long, but I don't want to rush. I don't want to feel flustered on my first day at my new job, and once I've stopped the shrill beeping, and come to my senses in the darkness, I switch on the lamp beside the bed, just so I don't fall over anything as I get up.

I'm sure it'll be better and easier to do this in the summer, when the sun will be up, even at this unearthly hour of the day, but for today I'll have to make do with floundering around while I find what I need… which right now is my bathrobe. There's no hook on the back of the door, because there's no door, so I left it over the arm of the couch. It's not the best solution, but it's okay for the time being, and I pull it on, and grab a towel to take with me. As I draw back the curtain, I realize the prospect of falling down the stairs into the darkness below is very real, and I leave it open, just so I have a clue where I'm going.

The furniture is in shadow, but I can see my way to the bathroom, and as I switch on the light, I'm surprised to see that Spencer has already been in here. His presence is obvious… not because the room is a mess. Far from it. No, I know he's been here because the mirror above the sink is all steamed up.

I don't mind that. I'm not in any hurry to look at myself. My hair is nearly always a mess first thing in the morning, but that can't be helped, and I take off my bathrobe and hook it up behind the door before stripping out of my chemise. There's nowhere to put it, so I close the toilet seat and dump it there for now, stepping into the shower.

The water is lovely and warm, but I remind myself not to take too long, and as I shampoo my hair, I study Spencer's body wash, which comes in a large brown bottle, and says it has a scent of citrus and sandalwood. Unable to resist, I pick it up, hold it to my nose, and inhale. It's divine… just like the man who uses it, and I have to smile when I remember how he showed me where to put my things in here on Saturday night.

"Clark always used the right-hand side of the cabinet," he said, opening it to show me. "And there should be enough space on the shelf in the shower, but if not, just put my things on the floor."

"I wouldn't dream of it."

He smiled, and I got the feeling that if I didn't do as he suggested, he'd do it for me. Although I didn't need to worry. The shelf is more than big enough for both our needs, and I replace his body wash and get on with taking my shower… because time is moving on.

Once I'm finished, I brush my teeth and make sure to wrap my bathrobe tight around myself before I exit into the living room. There's no sign of Spencer out here. Not even in the kitchen. So I hurry through and up the stairs to my room, closing the curtain behind me.

The first job of the day is to put on my makeup, which doesn't take long as I don't wear very much when I'm working. I hate applying it in electric light, though, and just hope it doesn't look too unnatural. It's not light enough outside to find out yet, so I hope for the best and dry my hair. Giving it that extra bit of time while I did my makeup means it doesn't take as long as it might, but even so, by the time I've finished, there's a definite smell of bacon wafting up the stairs.

Bacon? For breakfast? On a Monday morning?

I could get used to this, and as my stomach growls, reminding me how hungry I am, I hurry through getting dressed, relieved I left my clothes out last night, and that all I have to do is put them on.

I probably should make my bed, but I'm so hungry now, I can't wait a moment longer, and I draw back the curtain, suddenly remembering I don't have any shoes on my feet, and that my coat is still hanging in the closet.

I tut at myself, going back and slipping into my black pumps, which I left at the end of the bed, and then I wander to the closet, pulling out my long black coat. My parents bought this for me, not last winter, but the one before that, and I love how it looks and feels. It's made of the softest wool, and is double-breasted, coming down to just below my knees… which is perfect when it's as cold as it is at the moment.

Still, I don't need to put it on yet, and I fold it over my arm, carrying it down the stairs with me.

Spencer's in the kitchen, and I take a moment to absorb how different he looks today. Over the weekend, he dressed casually, in jeans and t-shirts, or sweaters, but today, he's wearing dark gray formal pants, a white button-down shirt and a blue tie… and he looks heavenly. It's tempting just to stand and stare, but I don't want to be caught doing it, so I dump my coat over the back of the couch, and wander across to him, surprised when he turns around and lets out a slight gasp.

"Sorry. I didn't mean to startle you."

"You didn't," he says. "It's just… you look lovely."

I'm surprised by his compliment and do my best not to blush… or to take him too seriously. He probably just means I look different… like he does. After all, he's only seen me in jeans and sweaters, too, and in any case, I have more pressing problems.

"Will this be okay for the office?" I ask, glancing down at my skirt and blouse.

"It'll be fine." He studies me for a moment longer and then steps up to the breakfast bar. "As it's your first day, I thought I'd make you a proper breakfast."

"You mean you don't eat like this every day?"

"No. Usually I just grab some toast, but today it's bacon and scrambled eggs. Is that okay with you?"

"It's perfect. Thank you."

He spins back around again, and I watch as he dishes up the eggs, adding the bacon, which he's been keeping warm, and places a slice of toast at the edge of each plate.

"Do you want me to do anything? I can fix the coffee, or…"

"No, it's fine. Everything's under control."

He brings over the plates, placing one before me, and pours the coffee before he comes around the breakfast bar and sits up beside me.

"This is really kind of you, thank you," I say as we both start eating.

"It's my pleasure… although, like I say, it won't be an everyday occurrence."

"That's okay."

"Are you looking forward to your first day?" he asks.

"I would be if I wasn't so nervous."

He turns slightly, so he's facing me. "What is there to be nervous about?"

"Oh, I don't know… not knowing anyone, wondering if I'm really good enough to do this job."

"Of course you're good enough," he says, surprising me, and I put down my fork, turning to face him properly.

"You can't say that."

"Yes, I can."

"But you don't even know me."

"I don't have to know you. I know Ryan Andrews… at least well enough to know he's not gonna jeopardize his organization by employing someone who can't do their job. Especially not in the surveying department. It's pivotal."

"Don't say that. It makes me feel even worse."

"I didn't mean it like that. I just meant that Ryan's not the kind of guy who'd get it wrong. That's all."

"You call him Ryan?"

"Yes. Everyone does. It's a first-name kind of company… which means you've got nothing to worry about."

I nod my head, giving him a smile as my stomach settles slightly. I don't think that's because of the delicious scrambled eggs, either. It's more likely because Spencer's put my mind at rest, and because he cared enough to bother. I know I shouldn't read anything into what he's said, but he's made me feel like I belong… and that I'm not about to fall flat on my face on my first day.

Which is something.

He finishes eating before me, swallowing down his coffee before he gets to his feet.

"I hate to cut and run, but I've got a meeting this morning."

"Is that why you got up so early?" I ask, watching as he stacks his plate and cup beside the sink.

"Partly… but I also wanted to fix breakfast for you."

I don't know what to say to that, so I don't say anything, and just finish eating while he gathers up his things, which include a dark gray jacket that matches his pants. He looks so damn sexy in a suit, but I put that thought out of my head as he wishes me good luck and dashes out the door.

I had been going to ask if we should drive to work together, but he's obviously starting earlier than me… at least for today, and I guess he might have plans for after work, too. Maybe with one of his many women…

I shudder at the thought, a pang of regret flaring in my gut.

"Stop it," I say out loud. There's no point in regrets. Spencer isn't the man for me… no matter how gorgeous and kind and friendly he is, and I need to remember that.

I also need to clear away these dishes, and once I've finished my coffee, I get up and wander around to the other side of the breakfast bar. There's a dishwasher, which Spencer has filled on every other occasion, but it can't be that hard, and I open it, relieved to find it's empty… which gives me plenty of choice where to put things.

Fortunately, it doesn't take too long, and once it's done, I pull on my coat, grab my purse, check I've got my new set of keys that Spencer gave me on Saturday, and head off.

Main Street is pretty busy, but I'm at the office five minutes early, which seems like a wise move on my first day, and having parked my car, I make my way into the reception.

The woman behind the desk doesn't recognize me, even though she was here when I came for my interview. Still, she probably sees dozens of people in a day, and once I've introduced myself, she apologizes.

"You'll need to go to the planning office," she says. "Can you remember where that is?"

I nod my head. "Through these doors, along the hall, right to the end?"

"That's it." She smiles up at me, and having returned the gesture, I follow my own directions until I reach a sturdy-looking wooden door, which I push open. John's standing on the other side, next to his desk, and he turns to face me, clapping his hand to his forehead.

"Oh, Robyn… I'm so sorry."

"What for?" I ask, pulling off my coat. It's warm in here, and the sooner I remove it, the better.

"I should have come to greet you," he says. "And I would have done, only we've got a minor crisis going on."

"Oh?"

"Yeah." I dump my things on the nearest chair and step a little closer, just as the door opens behind me, and Ryan Andrews walks into the room. He's accompanied by another man, who has reddish-brown hair, the two of them deep in conversation. "That's Gabe Sullivan," John whispers. "He's Ryan's right-hand man."

I nod my head, waiting as Ryan comes over.

"Hi, Robyn," he says. "It's your first day, isn't it?"

"Yes."

"In that case, let me introduce you to Gabe." He turns to face the man beside him, who holds out his hand.

"Nice to meet you," he says. "I'm sorry I wasn't here when you came for your interview."

"That's okay."

I hadn't expected him to be, but I don't mention that, and I stare at the two of them, wondering why they're here. It can't be just to greet me, so I imagine it must have something to do with this crisis John mentioned.

"Have you had time to show Robyn the plans?" Ryan asks, turning to John.

"Not yet."

Ryan nods his head, looking back at me again. "In that case, I'll explain what's happened."

"Okay."

"We're developing a property on the other side of Concord," he says. "Bailey completed the initial plans before she left, and while it should have been a simple process to get it through the planning stage, they've now said we've got to make it more environmentally friendly if we want it to pass."

I can't help smiling, although Gabe seems a little downcast. "It's not as easy as it sounds," he says. "The building is quite old, which gives us a few headaches anyway, but it was being used as offices, and the new owner wants to convert it to a hotel."

"Okay."

Ryan chuckles and turns to Gabe. "What you don't know is that one of the reasons I hired Robyn is that environmental design is a speciality of hers."

"Oh?" Gabe's face lights up. "So you know what you're doing with this?"

"I've got a few ideas," I say, and he lets out a sigh of relief.

"Thank heavens for that."

Ryan chuckles, turning his attention to John. "Can you take Robyn through Bailey's plans?" he says, looking back at me again. "I hate to do this on your first day, but I'm gonna leave you in charge of this one… and if you can get me something by Thursday?" He glances at Gabe, who nods his head.

"That should work."

"It's not much time," John says, speaking for me, even though I don't need him to.

"It's all we've got," Gabe says, and everyone turns to look at me.

"It'll be fine."

I do my best to sound reassuring, and Ryan thanks me before he and Gabe leave.

I feel a little like I'm being thrown in at the deep end, but I like that they trust me to do this, and once we're alone, I turn to John, who smiles down at me.

"Shall we get ourselves a coffee and look at these plans together?"

I don't remember the last time I felt so tired, but it's gone six by the time I leave the office, and I would have stayed on longer if I could. Except I couldn't. I had to leave when Ryan did, because I don't have a key.

"How's it going?" he asked as he walked me out to my car.

"Not too bad. As Gabe said this morning, it's a little more complicated than some jobs. It would certainly be easier if we were building from the ground up, rather than dealing with something that's already there, but I think we'll work it out."

He smiled down at me. "Thanks for doing this, Robyn."

"It's what you pay me for."

"This is a little above and beyond… especially on your first day. But it won't always be like this. I promise."

I nodded my head and got into my car, watching him drive away in his black Mercedes before I let out a sigh of relief and slowly made the journey home. I had to take it slow, because I wasn't used to driving around here at night, but I was happy to park up in the space beside Spencer's car, and let myself into the apartment.

He's already here… standing in the kitchen and stirring something on the stove, although he turns the moment he hears me come in, and I stop in my tracks, noticing how he's already changed out of his suit. That ought to be a shame, but he still looks incredible in his faded jeans and t-shirt, his muscles on full display, and I do my best to ignore the way he makes my skin tingle with desire as I stroll over, dumping my coat and bag on the couch.

"How did it go?" he says, abandoning the pot he's stirring and coming to the breakfast bar, where I sit and look up at him.

"It was great." He smiles over at me.

"I said you didn't need to worry… although I was starting to think you must be enjoying yourself so much you weren't gonna come home."

I chuckle. "It wasn't a case of enjoying myself, but of being up to my neck in work."

"They've given you that much to do? On your first day?"

I nod my head. "I've been tasked with updating some plans that my predecessor was working on."

"Did she screw up?"

"Not as such. She didn't realize the planners wanted the building to be as environmentally friendly as possible."

"So you're having to make the adjustments?"

"Yeah… by Thursday."

"Is that a tall order?"

"Fairly, but I think I'll make it. I've already redesigned and strengthened the roof structure to accommodate solar panels, and tomorrow I'm gonna look at how we can incorporate rainwater harvesting, and using gray-water systems to recycle the wastewater from the bathrooms."

He stares at me for a second or two, his lips parted slightly. "Is this what you do?"

"Most of the time."

He lets out a sigh. "I'm impressed."

"I'm sure I'd be impressed with what you do, too."

"I doubt it," he says, smiling. "I just move numbers around."

"Ahh… you work in the finance department?"

"Yes. Math is the only thing I've ever been any good at."

"And cooking," I say. "Because something smells delicious."

"That would be the beer-braised pork steaks."

"Is that what we're having tonight?"

He chuckles. "You were there when we wrote out the menu… right?"

"Yes, but I've had a busy day."

"In which case, do you wanna change out of your work clothes while I finish off?"

"Are you sure? I don't mind helping."

"No, it's fine."

I could hug him, but he wouldn't want me to, so instead I jump down from my seat and grab my coat and purse, hurrying up the stairs. As I go, I try to remember what was on the menu for tomorrow. I have a feeling it was chicken and rice, which doesn't sound too difficult, and as my day at work shouldn't be as crazy as it was today, I resolve to get back here in time to cook it.

Today has been even better than yesterday.

The plans are taking shape, and I'm confident I'll have everything ready by Thursday. I'm so confident, I left the office just a little earlier today. John said it was okay, as I'd worked late last night, and I took advantage of his generosity and hurried home.

Luckily, I've beaten Spencer back here, and I waste no time in changing into jeans and a top before rushing down the stairs so I have the chance to start the dinner before he gets back here.

It feels like the least I can do after that incredible meal he cooked last night.

The pork was so tender it didn't even need a knife, and as for the mashed potatoes… I thought I'd died and gone to heaven.

All I need to do now is make something that's just as good… but given my inexperience, I'll settle for edible.

Chicken and rice sounds easy enough, but even I'm not so stupid that I'd try cooking it without a recipe, and I take a few minutes searching on the Internet, finding a couple of options, and settling on the one that looks simplest, and for which I know we have all the right ingredients… because I remember buying them on Sunday.

The first thing I need is the chicken, which we bought ready-diced. That makes my life easier, so I pull it from the fridge, along with an onion.

The recipe says to marinate the chicken, but not which ingredients I'm supposed to use to do that, and although I read through the list twice, I still can't work out what I should do. On the whole, it seems best to skip that step and just get on with cooking, so I scroll down, noting that the instructions are to heat some oil in a heavy-based pan.

What the hell does that mean?

I search the cabinets, finding the one that provides a home to the pans, and pull a few out. They all seem pretty damn heavy to me, but allowing for the fact that I have to fit the chicken and rice into it, I choose the largest one and put the rest back.

The next thing I need to work out is how to light the stove, which takes a lot longer than it probably should, although once I've done that, it only takes a second or two to add the oil, and open the pack of chicken.

I don't feel comfortable touching raw meat, so I just tip it all in, hoping for the best, although as it sizzles, it also clumps together, which doesn't seem quite right. I guess that means I'm supposed to move it around a bit, and I find a wooden spoon, nudging the chicken around the pan, and feeling quite pleased with myself.

"Who said this was hard?" I mutter, leaving the chicken for a moment while I search for the rice.

We bought a new pack at the grocery store, because Spencer said he and Clark had used the last of it, so I know we've got some. I just don't know where it is. I put away the chilled things, while Spencer dealt with everything else. It can't be far away, though, and I check the cabinets, finding it on the fourth attempt. It's a large bag that's quite heavy, but I get it over to the stove, where the chicken is starting to smell.

I turn it over, surprised by how quickly it's blackened underneath… although I guess that'll add to the flavor, and once that's done, I check the recipe again.

I'm still unsure what I'm supposed to have done with the onion, and it says something about minced garlic, but I decide to focus on the rice, as that's a main component of the dish, and as it says I need two cups of it, I go over to the microwave and open the cabinet above, pulling out a couple of cups.

I duly fill them with rice, leaving the rest of the bag on the side for now, and then add it to the chicken.

The instructions say I'm supposed to stir constantly while adding the stock, but I have two problems with that. One is that it's kinda hard to stir when the chicken is in the way, and the second is that I don't have any stock.

"What's going on here?" Spencer's voice makes me jump, and I drop the wooden spoon and turn to face him. He's taking off his jacket and loosening his tie as he comes over, looking confused.

"I'm cooking… or trying to, although it doesn't seem to be going very well."

He stands right beside me, peering into the pan. "Is this supposed to be chicken and rice?" he asks.

"Yes."

"Are we expecting visitors?"

"No."

"Are you especially hungry?"

"No."

"Then why have you made so much?"

"I haven't. I just followed the recipe."

"What recipe?" he asks, looking around, until I hand him my phone, which he studies for a moment before he looks back at me. "This says it serves six people."

"Oh, shit. Really?"

He chuckles. "Yeah." He glances at the cups beside the stove. "Did you use those to measure the rice?"

"Yes."

The smile doesn't leave his lips as he shakes his head. "This just gets worse. Have you never heard of measuring cups?"

"No."

He reaches into the drawer to his right, pulling out a set of what appear to be miniature saucepans, although each of them has markings on the side.

"This is a cup," he says, holding out the largest.

"Oh." I study the cup I used, which is quite a bit bigger, my heart sinking. "I've screwed up, haven't I?"

"Well… we won't have to worry about lunches for the next couple of days, but it's nothing that can't be fixed," he says, putting down the measuring cups and picking up the onion. "Although I think you forgot to use this."

"Hmm… I had a feeling that should have gone in somewhere, and the recipe said something about minced garlic as well."

He chuckles, rolling up his shirtsleeves. "Would you like me to salvage this?"

"Do you think you can?"

"I'll do my best," he says, and although I'm grateful, I can't help feeling completely inadequate. It's not a first for me, and as though he senses something's wrong, he leans in to me and says, "It was nice of you to try."

"Yeah… and fail."

"We've all gotta start somewhere, Robyn, and maybe next time I can show you what to do."

I remember Clark telling Spencer he could show me how to boil an egg, and while I know Spencer thought he was exaggerating at the time, I guess he may be revising his opinion. It seems I should probably revise mine, too… because while it's embarrassing to be thought of as incompetent, I have to face the truth. I'm utterly useless when it comes to anything practical, and I shouldn't look a gift horse in the mouth.

"Would you mind?" I ask.

"Not at all."

"And do you think you could show me how to use the washing machine, too?" I may as well swallow my pride and admit how inept I am.

He nods his head, smiling down at me. "Of course. I'll take you through it after dinner, if you like."

"Thanks."

He tips his head by way of acknowledgement and before our dinner is completely ruined, he gets on with cooking it… properly.

"I'd have marinated the chicken before cooking it," Spencer says as he clears away the dishes. The dinner wasn't too bad in the end, despite the burned bits of chicken. They were my fault, not his, and considering what he had to work with, he did an amazing job.

"The recipe said something about a marinade, but didn't make it very clear."

"No. I don't think you could have chosen a worse recipe if you'd tried."

"You'll have to show me yours."

He raises his eyebrows, smiling slightly. "I don't have a recipe… not for chicken and rice. In fact, I don't have a recipe for most of the things I cook."

"Then how do you know what to do?"

"I've just worked it out for myself over the years."

"It sounds like I've got a lot to learn."

"Well… it's never too late to start," he says, and I sip at the wine I opened earlier, because I thought we could both do with some. It seems I wasn't wrong either. Spencer's day had been even busier than mine, and while he finished cooking and we ate our meal, he explained that his department is a little rudderless at the moment.

"My manager left last week," he said. "And even though the job was advertised over a month ago, Ryan still hasn't gotten around to filling the post yet."

"Is there a reason for that?"

"None that I'm aware of."

"Did you go for the job yourself?"

"Yes. I heard there's an announcement due this week, but in the meantime, we're trying to plug the gap as best we can… which basically means I'm doing two jobs instead of one."

He was obviously tired and stressed, which made me feel even more guilty about messing up the dinner… although he didn't seem to mind, and I have to say, we've had a lovely evening together.

"Do you want me to show you how to work the washing machine?" he asks.

"Oh… yes please."

I fetch some laundry from my room, bringing it downstairs with me, and watch as Spencer shows me what to do… from putting the detergent in, to selecting the program.

"My mom has one where the clothes go in at the top," I say as the drum spins around.

"Yeah, so does mine… or she did when I last spent any time at home with her and Dad, but this is a washer-dryer, which makes it so much easier." I nod my head, and although I'd like to sit and have a coffee with him, he insists he's gonna take a shower instead. "It's been a long day," he says.

"Not helped by my attempts at cooking."

"You did okay."

I know I didn't, but it's kind of him to say so, and I watch as he heads for his bedroom, before making my way upstairs to mine.

I lay out my clothes for tomorrow and make my bed, resolving that I'll do my best to make it in the morning in future. Coming home to do it in the evenings isn't ideal… although I'll need to be more organized. It seems that's the key to keeping house, and it's not my strongest suit. It's one I'll have to learn, though, because I can't keep relying on Spencer.

Even though I'd quite like to.

I shake my head, and wonder what it might be like to learn to cook with him. We'll be forced to spend time in a confined space, and there's bound to be some touching involved… although I really shouldn't think about him like that.

He's not for me.

He really isn't.

So why does he make me feel like this?

Whatever the reason, I need to stop it, and I also need to go to bed. First though, I need the bathroom, and I make my way back down the stairs.

There's no sign of Spencer, and no sound coming from the bathroom, so I try the handle, wishing I hadn't when I realize it's locked.

Hell… he must still be in there, and he'll know I've tried to get in.

I'm torn between standing here and waiting, or bolting back up to my room. Either seems ridiculous, and I wonder if I should just sit on the couch, or maybe at the breakfast bar, when the door springs open, a waft of steam billowing out as Spencer appears, wearing nothing more than a minute towel, wrapped low around his hips.

Oh, my…

It's all I can do to breathe, let alone speak, and he stares at me for a moment, pushing his fingers back through his damp hair as I watch the drops of water drip down onto his toned chest and do my very best not to reach out and touch…

Man… he's glorious. He's even more glorious than I'd expected, and I bite on my bottom lip just to stop myself from groaning out loud.

"Are you okay?" he asks, his eyes dropping to my lip before he raises them again, and I notice a slight sparkle behind them.

Heaven knows what that means, but I have to say something… anything will do.

"I—I'm fine."

"Did you wanna use the bathroom?"

"No. I mean, yes." *For crying out loud, woman. Stop behaving like an idiot and get your brain in gear.*

He smiles, stepping out. "Well… I'm sorry for holding you up."

"You didn't. I—I mean, it's not a problem."

He nods his head, still smiling as he turns and walks to his room, opening the door, although he stops and looks back at me.

"You can go in if you want," he says, nodding toward the bathroom, and I feel myself blush.

"Yes… thanks."

I dart inside, closing the door, unsure whether to laugh or cry. Could that have been any more embarrassing?

I doubt it, and before I give way to either laughter or tears, I brush my teeth, studying my reflection in the mirror as I wonder why life has to be so complicated.

It only takes a few minutes to clean off my makeup and moisturize my face, and once I'm finished, I open the door, relieved to find Spencer hasn't come out of his room. At least I don't have to face him again, and I dart up the stairs, pulling the curtain closed.

What's wrong with me?

It's not as though I've never seen a naked man before… and he wasn't even naked. The important parts were covered, I'm sorry to say, and I smile, pulling off my clothes, before I climb into bed. It's impossible not to smile when I think about Spencer… especially when I think about him standing there in nothing but a towel.

My skin tingles at the thought of what could have happened… at the idea of pulling away that towel and dropping to my knees before him. I wonder if his cock is as impressive as the rest of him, and what he'd do if I took him in my mouth… the thought heating my body. I push away the covers, my hands making their way slowly over my breasts, my nipples tight and hard, before I let my fingers wander down to my parted legs.

I haven't masturbated since I got here, and although I'm kinda wary about the fact that there's no door between me and the rest of the apartment, I can't wait any longer.

My body's on fire now, and I need the release.

My fingers delve between my soaking folds, and I let out a hiss of pleasure, keeping it quiet as I rub my clit, parting my legs even further while I think about Spencer lying between them, gazing down at me, right before he enters me…

"Oh, fuck…" I whisper, feeling that familiar quiver deep inside me.

I don't usually come this quickly, but I guess that's what happens when your fantasy is just downstairs, and as I imagine him thrusting deep inside me, I let out a low moan, my body curling in on itself as I succumb to pleasure.

Coming back from the heady heights of that indulgence is like nothing I've ever felt before, which is why, as I pull up the covers and turn over, I'm surprised by how disappointed I feel.

I shouldn't be. I've never had an orgasm quite like that, and usually after I masturbate, I feel quite satisfied. Except tonight,

I don't. Tonight I just feel downhearted… probably because the fantasy that just made me come so hard can never be a reality.

Chapter Six

Spencer

We've made it to the end of our first week, and as I let myself into the apartment and climb the stairs, I sigh out my relief, because there have been times when I thought we wouldn't get here.

But we have.

And not only that, I was told this afternoon, that I've got the promotion. I was honestly starting to doubt, and maybe even give up hope. I hadn't heard that anyone else had got it, but the silence was deafening, until Ryan called me into his office just after lunch and sat me down at his desk.

"I'm so sorry it's taken this long," he said, sitting opposite me. "We've had so much going on, but I really shouldn't have left it until now to tell you the job is yours."

"Thanks," I said, unable to think of anything more coherent.

He smiled. "I gather you've been practically running the department this week, anyway, but I want you to know, you were always our first choice. I've just been too busy and too wrapped up in other things to tell you. So, I apologize for that."

"It's okay."

He placed his hands flat on the table. "You'll be reporting directly to Gabe now," he said. "Unfortunately, he's not here this afternoon. He's had to take his wife to the hospital."

"Is she okay?"

"She's fine." He leaned a little closer. "She's having her twenty-week ultrasound."

"She's pregnant?"

"Yes. I think she's a little over twenty weeks, but these things don't always run to schedule." I shook my head, unwilling to let him see I had no idea what he was talking about. "Gabe will be back in the office on Monday, but I know he's snowed under with work, so you'll have to catch up with him when you can. Not that you need to worry. I'm sure you'll manage just fine. You'll be in charge of the department on a day-to-day basis, and I'll send out an email to everyone concerned, letting them know."

That all sounded a little scary, but also quite exciting.

It was what I'd expected when I'd applied for the job, but hearing it put into words made it so much more real, and it was certainly the most grown-up thing I'd ever contemplated…

Except falling for Robyn, of course.

The difference was, that wasn't planned.

It happened quite by accident.

I've spent my entire adult life actively railing against love, and everything that goes with it, citing it as dull, restrictive and boring… and yet, it caught me.

It caught me completely unawares.

And I can even pinpoint when it happened, almost down to the minute.

It wasn't when she first arrived, even though the sight of her blew me away. I mean, who doesn't need a beautiful, sexy redhead in their lives? Admittedly, I could see the complications. I voiced them to Clark, and to Tanner, but I was thinking with my dick, not my heart, so love didn't come into it.

Not then.

As for later that night, after my phone call with Clark... well, that was a little different, I guess.

I felt guilty for hurting her, because I was pretty sure I had, and that was a new experience for me. I've never cared about anyone else's feelings before, but I cared about Robyn's.

It still wasn't love, though.

I knew that much.

It wasn't love on the night she burned the chicken, either. Okay, so she looked incredibly cute when she was trying to explain what she'd been doing, and even more so when I told her where she'd gone wrong.

But that was a physical attraction. It was one I was getting used to by then. Let's face it, she'd been turning me on like no-one else ever since she arrived.

And she did the same thing later that night when she practically barged into the bathroom just after I'd finished my shower.

The look on her face was a picture, and as for her inability to string a sentence together... it was all I could do not to laugh out loud. Except that would have been unfair. She obviously hadn't been expecting me to be there. She wouldn't have tried the door if she'd thought I was still inside... so I had to be kind, despite the obvious temptations.

And believe me, Robyn is a walking temptation.

Especially, it seems, when I'm teaching her how to cook.

That's what we did the next night. I'd told her we would, and it had seemed a fairly harmless suggestion at the time.

If only I'd known...

I thought I'd keep it simple, sticking to a pasta dish that Clark and I used to have quite a lot, and rather than just letting her help, I got her to do the work.

"You'll learn better if you do it yourself," I said when she realized my plan.

"Can we order in if this goes wrong?"

"No. Because it's not gonna go wrong."

"Okay. If you say so… but tell me you've chosen something really easy."

I nodded my head. "We were supposed to have a curry tonight, but I've ditched that idea."

"Because it's too complicated?"

"Because I think we should start simple and work our way up."

"So we're starting with you teaching me how to boil water?" she said, and I had to laugh. She joined in, and the sound made my cock harden. That wasn't at all unusual. Just the sight of her turned me on, so her laugh, or her giggle, or the sound of her voice did really weird things to me. Fortunately, she hadn't noticed, and on that occasion, she was more preoccupied with cooking than with me.

"We are, actually. We've gotta cook some pasta, and that requires boiling water… although first we need to prepare the sauce that's going with it."

"You're already making this sound complicated."

"It really isn't." I grabbed a rectangular dish from the cabinet and handed it over to her. "There are some cherry tomatoes in the fridge. You need to put them in there."

She nodded and did as I said.

"Now what?"

"There's also a pack of garlic and herb cheese."

She turned, opened the fridge door, and took a moment to find what she was looking for. "This?" she said, pulling it out and holding it up.

"That's it. Unwrap it, then make a space in the middle of the tomatoes, and tip it out."

"Okay."

I watched as she followed my instructions, disposing of the wrapper.

"Now… we need some seasonings."

"Such as…?"

"What do you feel like?"

"I don't know. My culinary knowledge is nonexistent, Spencer. You must realize that by now."

"No, it's not. You know what you like and what you don't like. So… do you feel like basil, rosemary, thyme…?"

"Thyme. That would be nice."

"Okay."

I went over to the cabinet and returned with some dried thyme, along with the salt and pepper.

"Do I just sprinkle this on?" she asked, picking up the jar of thyme.

"Yes. As much as you want."

She added a little, and then a bit more, grinding over some salt and pepper before she looked up at me again.

"Is there anything else?"

"You need to drizzle a little olive oil over the top."

"Drizzle? That sounds kind of technical."

I laughed. "It really isn't. Especially as we have a dispenser bottle that either sprays or pours… and when it pours, the oil comes out quite slowly."

"So it drizzles?" she said with a smile.

"Exactly."

I handed her the bottle and showed her how it worked, watching as she carefully drizzled just enough oil over the tomatoes. She was very precise, but that was probably born of inexperience. I hoped it wasn't born of nerves, anyway. I didn't like the idea of her being nervous around me, and once she'd finished, I said she could put the dish into the oven.

"I've already pre-heated it," I said, and she nodded her head, lifting the dish from the countertop into the oven.

As she turned back, she glanced around the kitchen. "What do we have to do now?"

"Put some water on to boil, and pour some wine."

"But didn't you say something about making a sauce?"

"We already did. It's in the oven."

She stared at me. "You mean it was that simple?"

"Yes."

She seemed surprised, and maybe a little skeptical, but she persevered, putting some water into a pan and placing it on the stove, while I poured us a glass of wine each. With that done, I measured the pasta, and once the water was boiling, tipped it into the pan. I left Robyn to stir it, though, while I laid out the silverware on the breakfast bar.

"How will I know when this is ready?" she asked, looking across at me.

"It takes ten minutes."

"But I didn't make a note of the time when you poured it in."

"I did. It was six-thirty."

She sighed out her relief, rolling her eyes. "It's just as well you're paying attention."

It probably was. "You've only got two minutes to go. Do you want to drain it, or shall I?"

"I'll try," she said, and I had to smile as I fetched the colander from the cabinet, placing it in the sink for her.

"Just tip it into there, but be careful of the steam."

"Okay."

She did as I said, and I lifted the colander back onto the pan. "Now, leave that for a minute and use the oven mitt to take the dish out of the oven."

I watched her closely, making sure she didn't burn herself, and then smiled as she leaned in, inhaling deeply.

"That smells fantastic."

"It tastes even better."

I handed her a fork. "What's that for?" she asked.

"You need to squash the tomatoes and mix them in with the cheese. It'll be soft, so it won't be too difficult."

"Okay."

She pressed down on the tomatoes, seemingly surprised by how easily she was able to crush them, and then she mixed in the cheese, forming a creamy sauce.

"That's amazing," she said, looking up at me.

I brought over the pasta, tipping it in. "Now, give that a good mix."

I left her to it while I fetched the bowls and a spoon to serve it with, and by the time I returned, it was ready.

"Do you want me to dish it out?" she said.

"Of course. You made it."

She smiled right at me, her eyes locking with mine for a second, and then she got on with serving our food, piling it into the bowls.

We sat, adding some grated Parmesan, and I waited, letting Robyn taste it first.

"Oh, my God," she said, swallowing her mouthful. "That's so good."

"I know." I took a forkful, nodding my head. "And it's really versatile, too. You can add all kinds of things to it."

"Like what?"

"Almost anything you can think of… cooked chicken, spinach, bacon, chorizo, mushrooms. I didn't wanna complicate things, so I stuck with the basic recipe for tonight, but now you know how to do that, you can adapt it however you want."

"Thank you," she said, leaning in to me, and I shook my head.

"You don't have to thank me. I enjoyed it."

"So did I." She took another mouthful of pasta, the smile of triumph on her face a sight to behold… but it wasn't enough to make me fall for her.

Not then.

Because I was saving that for last night.

Robyn was late home, and because of that, I'd made a start on the dinner without her. I couldn't be sure when she'd get back, so I didn't feel as though I had any choice, but all I'd done was to chop an onion, and I was just in the process of peeling some garlic when I heard her footsteps on the stairs.

"What time do you call this?" I said, glancing over, my words dying on my lips when I saw her expression. It was one of utter despair, and I dropped the garlic and went straight to her. "What's happened?" I asked, surprised by the pain in my chest. It wasn't like anything I'd ever felt before, and I knew it wouldn't go away until I saw her smile again.

"It's just work," she said, which came as something of a shock. She'd been enjoying it, from what I'd been able to gather, so what had gone wrong? "Do you remember me telling you about the plans I had to amend?"

"Yes."

I took her hand in mine and pulled her over to the couch, sitting down beside her, even though she hadn't yet removed her coat.

"Well… I submitted them to Ryan this afternoon, only to be told that almost none of my suggestions could be implemented within the budget."

"Had no-one mentioned the budget?" I asked.

"No. And now I've got to start from scratch. Not only that, but I feel so… so stupid for not realizing there would be financial restrictions."

"How were you supposed to know if no-one told you?"

She shrugged her shoulders, and I longed to pull her into my arms. I wasn't sure I could make anything better, but I didn't see how a hug could hurt. Although I didn't get the chance to find out. Robyn got to her feet with a sigh and looked down at me.

"Do you mind if I don't join in with the cooking tonight? I really don't feel like it."

"That's okay. Do you want to just sit and watch?"

"I'll get changed first."

I nodded my head, my eyes fixed on her as she trudged up the stairs, before I returned to the kitchen. The look on Robyn's face kept haunting me, as did the pain in my chest. It was still there by the time she returned, looking just as dejected, and as I dished up our chili, I realized something had changed.

I couldn't work out what, but while we were eating, and she was doing her best to appreciate my cooking, it suddenly came to me.

I didn't care whether she liked my food, just as long as I could see her smile. Because her happiness was more important than mine.

It meant everything to me.

And that was when I knew.

I knew I'd fallen for her.

It was more than a physical attraction… more than that aching need to be inside her that's been with me ever since I first set eyes on her. What happened last night went deeper than anything I've ever felt before, and although I kept expecting to hear a voice telling me to snap out of it, there were no words.

And even if there had been, I'd have ignored them… because believe it or not, I like being in love. It's a weird, crazy, mixed-up kind of feeling, but that doesn't mean I want to turn back the clock and change things to how things were before.

I just want her. I want Robyn with a 'y', and no-one else will do.

Naturally, I can't tell her how I feel. I wouldn't know where to start.

But keeping my feelings to myself doesn't make them any less real. Or any less intense.

I hear the door close downstairs, my heart flipping over in my chest as I realize I'm still standing in the middle of the living room. I haven't changed my clothes, or even put the breakfast things in the dishwasher.

Is this what love does to you?

It makes you lose your mind, and forget all the things you usually do as a matter of course?

Clearly.

Robyn appears at the top of the stairs, glancing over at me, and although she takes a moment, her eyes raking up and down my body, I can't blame her for that. Not because she finds me irresistible, but because by the time she comes home, I've usually changed into something a lot more casual than a suit.

"Have you been home long?" she says.

"No."

That's not true at all, but she doesn't need to know I've spent the last twenty minutes daydreaming, and I put my keys on the coffee table as I shrug off my jacket and loosen my tie.

"How did your day go?" I ask, watching as she walks over, adding her coat to my jacket on the back of the couch, before she kicks off her shoes. Now that she's nearly a foot shorter than me again, she cranes her neck, looking up.

"It was a lot better than yesterday," she says, flopping down on the couch.

I decide the breakfast dishes can wait and join her. "Did you work out the plans?"

"Yes. The major problem was the alterations I'd made to the roof. There was no way they could be done within the budget, but once I'd accommodated that, and made a couple of other minor amendments, everything else seemed to be fine."

"That's good. Has Ryan approved everything now?"

"He has. I still feel a little foolish for not realizing there would be financial restrictions, but he said it's not my fault."

"Because it's not." I twist in my seat so I'm facing her, noting the doubt in her eyes. I can't ignore it, and I let my arm rest along the back of the couch. "Did you find out why no-one mentioned the budgeting problems?"

"No. I haven't had time, and it wasn't a priority… not compared with getting the plans completed, anyway."

"No, I guess not, but now I'm in charge of the finance department, I can do some digging, if you like?"

She leans back slightly. "You're in charge of the finance department?"

"Yes. Don't sound so surprised."

She reaches over and rests her hand on my leg, and although it's an act of innocent contrition, I can't help the way my body tenses, or that my cock hardens against my zipper.

Fuck… I need her.

"I'm not," she says, the smile on her lips making my heart sing silently in my chest. "But are you saying you got the promotion?"

"Yes. Ryan told me this afternoon."

She sits forward, positively bouncing with excitement. "But that's fabulous news, Spencer."

I love her enthusiasm… almost as much as I love her, and I take my chance, placing my hand over hers.

"Shall we go out tonight? I feel like we should celebrate. I've been promoted, and you've made it to the end of your first week."

That sounds like a reasonable excuse to take her to dinner, although she tips her head to one side, like she's unsure.

"Is surviving a week a good enough reason to celebrate?"

"It is if you didn't break anything."

She laughs, nodding her head. "Okay. Let's do it."

"Where would you like to go?"

"I don't know. What's on offer?"

"If we're staying in Hart's Creek, there's the French restaurant a couple of doors away, or the hotel at the end of Main Street. But if none of that sounds appealing, we can go to Willmont Vale… or there's always Concord."

"No. Let's stay here. I'd rather walk so we can both have a drink and celebrate in style, and I like the sound of the French restaurant, if that's okay with you."

"It's perfect."

Frankly, I don't care where we go, as long as we're together, and I bend in a little closer, reaching behind her.

"What are you doing?" she asks, pulling her hand from mine, and leaning away.

"Getting my phone. It's in my jacket pocket."

"Oh… sorry."

"It's okay."

It's not. I hate that she pulled away from me the moment I moved closer, but she's not to know how I feel, and I get to my feet so I can't be accused of crowding her, or doing anything else that might make her feel uncomfortable.

"I'd better check they've got a table for tonight," I say, and she nods her head, waiting while I look up their number.

It takes a while for anyone to answer, and when they do, I can hear people talking and glasses clinking in the background. It sounds busy, and my heart sinks.

"Do you have a table for two available for tonight?" I ask.

"What time?"

"In around an hour?" I tip my head at Robyn, asking her as well as the guy on the end of the phone, and she nods.

"That should be okay," he says, and I tell him my name, and give him my cell number when he asks, before ending the call.

"Is it booked?" Robyn says.

"Yes. We've got an hour… or just under."

"In that case, I'll take a quick shower… unless you want to go first?"

Personally, I'd rather we showered together, but given her reaction just now, there's no way I can suggest that, so I tell her it's fine. She can go ahead, and she does, dashing up the stairs to grab her bathrobe, before she wanders into the bathroom, leaving me to think about what it's like to fall in love with someone who doesn't love you back… and that maybe being in love isn't as much fun as I thought it was.

"The food here is fabulous," Robyn says, taking a second bite of her slow-baked salmon, which is served on a bed of ratatouille.

I have to agree. My lamb shank is delicious.

I've already explained to her about the fire they had here last summer, and that this place only re-opened in the fall, the conversation giving us the chance to get through our appetizers with no awkward silences.

Now, I take the chance to sip at my wine and re-live that moment when she came down the stairs.

I'd followed her into the shower, but even then, I was ready before her, having selected a pale gray suit and white shirt, while she was in the bathroom. A tie didn't feel necessary, and I'd been wearing one all day, so getting dressed didn't take too long. I even found the time to call Clark, just to let him know about my promotion. He was pleased for me, just like I thought he would be, although I decided against telling him I was going out for dinner with his cousin. I wasn't worried about how he'd react, but I was still a little mad at him for keeping us both in the dark.

As it was, he had plans of his own, so we couldn't talk for long, and by the time I left my room, there were still a few minutes to spare before Robyn and I were due to leave.

I was just thinking I might have to call up the stairs to remind her of the time, when she opened the curtain, and came down… blowing my mind.

I kept telling myself not to stare, but how could I do anything else?

She'd left her hair hanging loose around her shoulders, and although she'd put on a little makeup, it wasn't too much. All it did was enhance, not disguise.

As for her dress…

What can I say? Only that I was relieved I'd fastened my jacket, so all I had to do was pull it down slightly to hide my erection.

The combination of her short, figure-hugging black dress and high-heeled pumps was enough to drive any man crazy. And I was already crazy about her.

Even so, I couldn't just stand there with my mouth open, and I stepped forward, taking her coat as she reached the bottom step, and then helping her put it on. I'll admit, I rested my hands on her shoulders for a little longer than was necessary, and as I did, I leaned in and whispered, "You look beautiful."

She turned, looking up, and honored me with a smile. "Thank you," she said. "Shouldn't we be going?"

She had a point, and although staying at home had suddenly become a lot more appealing, I led her down here.

Our table is by the window, so as well as discussing the fire and the food, we've spent the first part of our evening talking about the town. I've pointed out the various stores she hasn't yet visited, and told her the names of the people who work in them… although I doubt she'll remember.

I know I will. I'll remember every second of this evening.

But I guess my motives are different.

She's here to celebrate. I'm here because I'm in love with her. Although I've realized that's a one-way street.

It's become clear to me over the last hour or so that, while she's friendly and cheerful in my company, there's no chance of her returning my affections.

She's far from being aloof, but there's a detachment in her… in the way she looks at me, and the way she sits. It's like she's keeping her distance.

I wish she wasn't, but she is, and I can't change the situation, can I? I can't make her love me, anymore than I can make her want me… and I sure as hell can't fall out of love with her. Which means I'm in a lose-lose situation.

"Where are you from?" she asks, breaking into my thoughts. That's probably a good thing. They're not the best thoughts a man can have, and I put down my wineglass and gaze across the table at her, doing my best to forget my feelings and just focus on our evening.

"All over the place."

She frowns. "Is that even possible?"

"It is if you've lived a life like mine."

She takes a bite of salmon, and I watch her lips, my imagination working overtime before I get back to my lamb. "What does that mean?" she asks eventually, and I look up again.

"It means I've led a nomadic life."

"Okay, but you must have been born somewhere."

I smile at her. "I was born in Colorado. My dad was stationed at Fort Carson, although I have no memory of it at all."

"Stationed? Your dad was in the military?"

"Yes. He eventually became a major, serving in the US Army."

"I see. And is there a reason you don't remember Fort Carson?"

"Yes. We left there when I was about a year old and moved to Virginia, and then to Germany. After that, I think it was Norway, and then Poland… but it might have been the other way around."

"Seriously? You can't remember?" She seems surprised, but I nod my head.

"One army base is like another when you're a child."

"I guess," she says, sounding doubtful.

"I spent most of my teenage years in the US, but even then we didn't stay still."

"What about your mom? Did she work?"

"No. With us moving around so much, it would have been impossible for her to hold down a job."

"I can imagine," she says, shaking her head in disbelief. "Did you go to college?"

"Yes, although I found it weird staying in the same place for so long."

"Good weird, or bad weird?" she asks.

"Just weird," I say, and she laughs. "I used to travel during the summer recesses, just so I didn't feel too tied down."

She frowns. "Tied down?"

"Yeah. That was how it felt."

"And you didn't like that? You didn't enjoy feeling as though you belonged somewhere?"

"No." I can't lie to her. "I hated every second of it."

"And after college?" she says.

"I drifted around for a while, going from one job to another, refusing to put down any roots."

"I see. So does that mean you'll be moving on soon?" she asks.

"No," I say, noting her slight sigh of relief. I'd like to think the idea of my imminent departure had worried her, but I know it hadn't. She was probably just wondering who would move into the apartment in my place, or whether she could afford to keep living there by herself… and who would do the cooking in my absence. Even so, I think I need to qualify my answer. "I came here for the job, but I'll be honest… I really like it," I say, gazing into her eyes, and wishing I could say more… wishing I could tell her why Hart's Creek has suddenly become so much more appealing than it already was.

"Well, now you've been promoted, I guess you've got every reason to stay," she says, and I nod my head, even though work has nothing to do with my motivation for wanting to remain here.

We both finish eating, and as neither of us wants dessert, I ask for the check, and while Robyn tries to pay half, I refuse.

"It was my idea, so it's my treat."

She shakes her head. "That's not fair."

"Yes, it is."

"Then I'll pay next time."

I nod my head, relieved she's thinking of a next time, although I know she's not thinking of it in the same way I am. To her, it would just be about two roommates finding an excuse to share a meal. To me, it would be so much more, and as I help her on with her coat again, I can't help feeling a pang of regret that our evening is coming to an end.

Ordinarily, if she'd been anyone else, I might have suggested taking things further. But I can't do that with Robyn… not when I know she doesn't want me. So, I escort her back to the apartment, and watch as she goes up to her room, turning at the top of the stairs to thank me for a lovely evening.

"It was my pleasure," I say, and she rewards me with a smile.

I'd like to say that's enough to satisfy me, but it's not. I want more, and I feel like my hopes have been dashed… not just for tonight, but for the future, too.

*

I'd like to say things have gotten easier… that I've grown used to being in love with Robyn, and that living with her in a purely platonic way is going just fine.

The reality is, of course, that our situation was never going to be easy, and I was kidding myself if I thought it would be.

The last couple of weeks have proved that.

Far from getting easier, things have gotten so much worse.

In fact, it's been torture.

I've continued to help her learn to cook, guiding her through various recipes, watching her moments of triumph, and the way she laughs when she gets things wrong. I've longed to pull her into my arms while she does it… knowing, of course, that I can't.

I've hated her moments of sadness, wishing I could do more to help without giving myself away. Except I can't seem to work out how.

It's like when her period started at the end of last week. She didn't tell me about it. We don't have the kind of intimate relationship where she'd want to share that sort of information with me… although I wish we did. I worked it out for myself, though, just from the clue of the pack of sanitary pads she'd left on the bathroom shelf. They hadn't been there before, and it didn't take a genius to work out what they meant. She gave me another hint, by spending the weekend lying on the couch, clutching a hot water bottle to her stomach. The pain seemed fairly intense, and I longed to hold her… to do anything I could to make it better. Except there was nothing I could do for her. Nothing at all.

I made a note of the date, though, so I can be better prepared next month. I might add some ice cream to the shopping list, or get in a supply of chocolate.

That would be something.

It'll certainly be better than nothing.

Either way, I want to do more, and as we've survived another week, and made it to Friday again, I can't help wondering if I could suggest we do something together. I can't make it sound like a date, but there must be something we can do. We don't have an excuse to go out to dinner again, but maybe we can just spend an evening here together. I could make us something nice for dinner, and we could sit and watch a movie over a glass of wine.

It's an idea… and I'm just wondering how to bring it up when Robyn walks up the stairs, a broad smile on her face.

"You look happy," I say as she dumps her purse on the couch and pulls off her coat, revealing her navy blue skirt and white blouse.

Fuck… she looks good.

"I feel happy," she says. "It's the weekend."

She kicks off her shoes as she's speaking and flops down on the couch.

"Would you like a glass of wine?" I ask.

"Oh, God… yes."

I chuckle, going over to the kitchen and pouring us one each, bringing them back. I sit beside her, and we clink glasses as I turn to face her, my suggestion for our evening poised on my lips.

"I've been meaning to ask," she says, getting there before I can. "How does it work if we want to date?"

My brain shifts out of kilter, my heart following it. Did she say what I thought she just said? Did she just ask me out? If she did, it's a weird way of going about it, but I can handle weird if it means I get to date Robyn. Hell… I can handle anything.

"Date?" I ask, needing to know if I'm right.

"Yes. You know, if I wanted to bring someone back here."

My heart lurches in my chest as everything else returns to normal, and I'm overwhelmed with disappointment, relieved I didn't put any of my thoughts into words. At least I don't have to face the humiliation of admitting my misunderstanding.

"I—I didn't realize you were seeing anyone," I say, taking a gulp of wine.

She does the same, almost emptying her glass in one go. "I'm not. Not yet." *Thank fuck for that.* "I'm just asking for future reference. If I wanted to bring someone back here, what would you do?"

Probably kill the guy.

I shrug my shoulders, keeping that thought to myself. "When Clark lived here, we used to make our plans in advance, whenever we could, so the other one could vacate the apartment for the night… although if that wasn't possible, we'd just kinda ignore each other. There isn't anywhere to hide in here, really."

She blushes. "I'm not talking about someone staying the night." *Good.* "But what if I wanted to bring a guy back here for dinner?"

"You'd probably have to be able to cook it first," I say, and as she smiles I wonder about sabotaging her attempts at learning.

"Yes, I would," she says, nodding her head. "But what would you do?"

"If I didn't have plans to go out, I guess I'd just stay in my room. It's what I used to do if Clark brought someone back here on a whim, and I didn't have anywhere else to be."

She lowers her head and lets out a sigh before she finishes her wine and gets to her feet.

"I'll just go upstairs for a while," she says, leaving her glass on the table before she turns to go. I'm not sure what I did wrong, but I feel dreadful, wondering what I'll really do when the time comes, because I can't bear the thought of sitting in my room while she's out here with another man.

I can just about tolerate the idea of her not loving me… but watching her fall for someone else? How the hell am I supposed to do that?

Chapter Seven

Robyn

I pull the curtain across the top of the stairs, wondering what on earth possessed me.

I only asked Spencer that question because I felt the need to move things forward. Did I achieve that? Not really. But I can't keep bringing myself off every night. I can't keep fantasizing about him, and all the things I'd love to do to him… and for him to do to me. It may be an inevitable end to each and every day, but the result is always the same. Sure, I come like never before, but that's accompanied by a wave of disappointment and regret that gets worse every time.

Why?

Because everything I've been imagining can never be real.

It can never happen. I know that.

Especially after our romantic dinner at the French restaurant.

Because it was romantic… even though it wasn't. The romance was a fiction. It was just the candles and the atmosphere that made it feel so intimate. That, and the company… and my vivid imagination.

Except that was just a façade. Which was why I did my best to keep my distance. I made sure I sat back in my seat and kept our conversation as neutral as I could. It would have been so easy to lean in to him, to gaze into his eyes and turn things around, to let him know what he does to me… but I couldn't be sure how he'd react, and as I pull off my clothes and get changed into jeans and a sweater, I recall that nagging doubt I had in the back of my mind, that no matter how sexy he looked, sitting across the table from me, or how much I was enjoying our evening, being with him wouldn't get me anywhere.

Hell, he made it perfectly clear that he'd always led a nomadic life, right from the moment he was born, and even though he said he liked Hart's Creek, that doesn't mean he'll stay here forever, does it? He'd leave in the blink of an eye if something better came along.

He's that kind of man.

When we got back here, I longed for him to kiss me… but I knew he wouldn't, and before I made a fool of myself, I went upstairs, only remembering at the last minute to thank him for a lovely evening… because it had been lovely. The fact that it hadn't ended in the way I wanted wasn't his fault. And it's just as well, really. We're all wrong for each other, and as I got undressed, I realized I needed to put my fantasies to one side, and get back to reality… the reality of finding the right man for me.

Which meant I needed to know what would happen if I did… and if I wanted to bring Mr. Right back here.

All I had to do was pluck up the courage to ask the question.

The problem is, now that I've done it, I'm not sure how I feel about having Spencer in the apartment while I'm entertaining another man. How am I supposed to concentrate, knowing he's in his room, and that I want him so much I can barely breathe? I know it's just lust, and that I'm looking for love, but I can't do that without a little privacy.

It was hard enough when I was at home, but at least Mom was on my side… rooting for me to find my forever man. And speaking of Mom, I guess I ought to call her.

I shake my head, feeling guilty. Not because I haven't called her before now. I have. I've made it a fairly regular thing. No, I feel guilty because it's starting to feel like a duty, rather than something I'd do for pleasure.

Even so, it's got to be done, and as I've got a few minutes to spare, I connect a call, sitting on the edge of my bed and then lying back with my head on the pillows, listening to the phone ringing, as I wonder whether they might have gone out. They don't usually on a Friday night, but I guess they may have done, and I'm about to get my hopes up, and decide what kind of message to leave when my Mom answers, sounding a little out of breath. I highly doubt it's for the same reason as it was when I interrupted Clark the other day, so I don't make any comment and just say, "Hi, Mom."

"Hello," she replies. "Sorry it took me so long to answer. I was down in the basement with your father, and I left my phone in the kitchen."

"What were you doing in the basement?" I ask, wondering if I want to know.

"We're thinking of turning it into a home cinema, and…"

"You are?" I can't disguise my surprise, or prevent myself from interrupting her. Why couldn't they have done something this exciting when I lived at home? I'm not saying it would have prevented me from leaving, but it would have made my time there so much more entertaining.

"Yes. Dad got a bigger bonus than he was expecting, and having a home cinema is something we've always wanted."

"It is?"

"Yes," she says, like I should have known that.

"I didn't realize."

"Well… we didn't used to talk about it very much because we never thought we'd get the chance to do it, but we've been taking the measurements, and we think we can make it work."

"That's exciting."

"Nothing's set in stone yet," she says, with a typical note of caution in her voice. "We've got to see how much it's gonna cost first."

"Even so…"

"I know," she says. "It is kinda thrilling, isn't it?" I don't think I've ever heard my mom so enthralled, and I can't help smiling as I turn over and face the window. "How's everything going with you?" she asks, putting a slight damper on the conversation.

"Not too bad." I'm as evasive as usual.

"And your apartment? Are you settling in okay?" she asks.

"Of course."

I haven't told her about Spencer. To start with, I couldn't work out how. Then I realized it was best not to. She'd have over-reacted, as only she can, and I feel like I've got enough to think about as it is.

"How are you managing?" she asks. "You haven't poisoned yourself yet?"

"Obviously not."

"And you haven't met anyone? Any men, I mean?"

"I haven't had the chance."

I can hear her disappointed sigh, even from here, and I shake my head, wondering how to put that right… not her disappointment, but my own.

There's no getting away from it; sitting around here with Spencer every evening isn't helping my situation. He's far too distracting, and I need something else – or someone else – to fuel my fantasies.

"You need to make your chances," she says.

"I know. That's why I'm going out tonight."

"Oh?"

I can hear the excitement in her voice, and I hate to crush it. "Don't start planning the wedding just yet, Mom. I'm only going out with a couple of friends from work."

"Female friends?"

"Yes."

"Maybe they can introduce you to some of the men in the town," she says, and I shake my head, relieved she can't see me.

"Maybe."

That's not the purpose of our outing, but now I've raised the subject, it seems reasonable to use it as an excuse to end our call.

"I've just seen the time, Mom. If I'm gonna get ready, I'll have to go."

"Okay… we'll speak again soon."

"Sure. Let me know about the home cinema, won't you?"

"I will… and let me know if you meet anyone."

I won't.

We end our call as I realize that I should have told Spencer of my plans for tonight… and I would have done earlier, when I got home, if I hadn't been so wrapped up in him.

Still, it's not too late, and once I've added my high-heeled black pumps to my outfit, I hurry back down the stairs, where I find Spencer sitting on the couch. He's still wearing his work clothes, looking like he hasn't moved a muscle since I went up to my room.

"Are you okay?" I ask.

He startles, looking up at me. "Sure. I was just thinking."

"You don't wanna do that. Not on a Friday. It'll spoil your weekend."

He chuckles, getting to his feet, and although he takes a moment, studying me just briefly, he soon comes to himself. "Did I just hear you talking?"

"Yeah. I called my mom. My duty's done for the week."

He smiles and nods his head, stepping toward the kitchen. "We're supposed to be making chicken casserole tonight," he says, sounding a little fed up.

"I know, but I meant to tell you, I'm going out."

"You are?" He spins around, looking down at me. "With whom?"

"Just some friends from the office."

"Anyone I know?" he asks, putting his empty wineglass on the breakfast bar, while I fetch mine from the table in the living room, where I left it earlier.

"I don't know. One of them is called Jodie, and the other is Alisha."

He tilts his head to one side, sucking in a breath. "There are a couple of people called Jodie that I know of. But I've never heard of anyone called Alisha. Where are you going?"

"Just to MD's."

"So you'll be here for dinner?"

"Yes, but I'm due to meet them at eight. Will that give us time to make a chicken casserole?"

"Not really. I guess we can switch things around, though, and have tomorrow night's pizzas tonight."

"That would work," I say, and he nods his head, going over to the deep freeze.

"We can look at the menu for next week while we're eating, if you like?"

"Okay."

"And then I'll go shopping in the morning."

"It's my week, isn't it?" I say, watching as he unwraps the pizzas.

"Yes, but you probably won't feel like getting up early… not after a girls' night out."

He has a point, and I nod my head as he turns and looks at me. "Thanks. I'll make it up to you."

"You don't have to," he says, switching on the oven, and I gaze at his back, admiring the way his muscles flex, and wishing things could be different.

*

"Is it always this busy in here?" I ask, raising my voice slightly.

"It can be. Especially on a Friday night." Alisha spots a group of four people getting up from a booth, and we make our way over to claim it before anyone else can. We've been standing by the bar since we arrived here, and I think we could all do with taking the weight off our feet.

Jodie slides in first, flicking her long blonde hair over her shoulder. She's followed by Alisha, who's fixed her dark brown hair in a complicated updo that I could never hope to emulate. The two of them stare across the table at me as I take my place opposite them, and we all take a sip from our second drink of the night... although in reality, it's my fourth. Spencer persuaded me to have a second glass of wine with our pizzas, and I didn't see the harm in accepting. Not that I'm worried. It's not as though I have a long journey home.

"How long have you worked for Ryan Andrews?" I ask now we're away from the noise of the bar and are able to make conversation.

"Just over two years," Jodie says, and I glance at Alisha.

"About the same."

"Do either of you know Spencer Kidd?"

Where on earth did that come from? Maybe I should have been more worried about how much I've been drinking... although it's too late now.

Alisha shakes her head. "I don't think so," she says.

"He works in the finance department, doesn't he?" Jodie's reply makes me sit up straight. She knows him?

"Yes," I say, an inexplicable fear rising inside me.

"I thought so. I don't know him very well," she says. "He's more of a name than a face. How do you know him? You work in surveying, don't you? Not in finance."

"I do, but I've wound up sharing an apartment with him."

Alisha smiles. "Oh? How's that going?"

It's confusing the hell out of me. "Pretty well," I say, hiding my actual feelings of relief that neither of them has slept with him. Was that why I asked? I can't be sure… about anything, it seems.

"Did you know him before you moved here?" Jodie asks.

"No. Not at all. My cousin used to share the apartment with him, and when he left and I got a job here, he said I could take over his room."

"Your cousin?" Jodie frowns across the table at me. "That wouldn't be Clark Baxter, would it?"

"Yes."

She nods her head. "I used to work with him."

"Of course you did." I remember Jodie works in the legal department, while Alisha is in sales… although I don't know in what capacity. We haven't discussed that yet. We met at the delicatessen, all of us there to buy our sandwiches, and wound up having lunch together when we got back to work.

"He was such a lovely guy," Jodie says, sounding a little wistful, and although I'm intrigued by her response, I'm not going to inquire any further. It's no business of mine what Clark did in his spare time.

Just like Spencer's extra-curricular activities are nothing to do with me, either.

They're really not.

Although that feeling of relief hasn't abated. I don't want to think how I'd have reacted if I'd discovered that either of my newfound friends had been intimate with him… but I don't think it would have been pretty.

"He changed so much when he met that woman in San Francisco," Alisha says.

"You knew him, too?" I ask.

"We all did."

I dread to think what Clark has been doing, but that was then, and this is now. "He seems very happy with Cerys," I say, and they both nod their heads.

"He was devoted to her from the moment he met her," Jodie says. "He never even looked at another woman again."

"It's kinda cute, really," Alisha says, sipping at her drink.

"Yeah." Jodie chuckles. "If only we could find a man like that. I don't know about you, but every guy I meet just wants to have sex and walk out the door."

"I know." Alisha rolls her eyes as she speaks. "Although I'm not really complaining."

Jodie laughs, and I join in, trying to look like my sex life is as exciting as theirs sound, especially as they're both staring at me.

"The last guy I went out with didn't get that far," I say, and they lean in a little. "We were on our third date when my mom started talking to him about marriage…"

"No. Seriously?" I can hear the surprise in Alisha's voice, and I nod my head.

"Yeah. I'd only gone back home to get a cardigan, and she cornered him at the bottom of the stairs."

"How did he react?" Jodie asks.

"He told me it was weird." *And that he wasn't the marrying kind.*

"He wasn't wrong," Alisha says, shaking her head and frowning. "Who wants to think about marriage at our age? Although I guess that's one of the problems with living at home. Parents can be difficult… and interfering. You're better off without them."

I'm surprised by her response, but before I can say anything, Jodie beats me to it. "What are you talking about?" she says, nudging in to her. "Your mom goes on more dates than you do."

Alisha giggles, nodding her head. "That's true." She glances across at me. "My parents are divorced, by the way. My mom's not cheating."

"Oh... I see."

She laughs and gets up to fetch us all some more drinks.

"Don't take too much notice of Alisha," Jodie says in her absence. "I'm sure your mom didn't mean any harm. She was probably just making conversation."

She wasn't, but it's nice of Jodie to smooth the waters.

When Alisha comes back, I stare down at the glass of white wine she's placed in front of me and let out a sigh.

"I really need to stop after this one. I can barely think straight."

"You're a lightweight," Alisha says, and I bridle against her remark. I may get on okay with Jodie, but I'm not sure about Alisha, and I lean back slightly, sipping my drink, my mind drifting to Spencer. It feels like the natural place for my mind to be, and I wonder what he's doing... whether he's sitting upstairs by himself, or whether he's gone out for the evening, too... and if so, who with.

I don't like the thought of him with someone else, or how that makes me feel, and I sit forward again, my hand around my glass.

"Are there any places in the town where I might meet someone?" I ask outright. Thinking about Spencer and what he's doing won't get me anywhere, will it? So I may as well focus on something positive.

"A man, you mean?" Jodie says.

"Yes."

"Well... you could try getting in line, right behind me." I laugh at Jodie's response, just as Alisha grabs my arm, taking me by surprise.

"Or you could try right here, right now," she says. She's looking over my shoulder, and I turn to see three men approaching our table.

I'd say they're all slightly younger than us... well, me at least. I'd put them in their mid-twenties, and while they're handsome enough, I'm really not interested. They certainly don't look like they'd want to settle down, and regardless of that, none of them do anything for me. I do my best to look indifferent, which isn't easy after this much wine, and they sidle up, staring down at the three of us in turn.

"Hey, ladies," says the taller of the three. He's standing closest to me, and gazes down into my eyes. I turn away, unwilling to encourage him, although Alisha clearly has other ideas.

"Hey," she says, shifting along the bench, and forcing Jodie to do the same.

One of the men sits beside her, while the taller man stares down at me expectantly. It would be rude to make them wait, so I move into the corner, the two of them falling over each other to be the one to sit beside me.

I stare across at Jodie and am surprised to find she's absorbed by the man who's sitting at the far end of my bench. She can't be interested, surely?

And yet, it seems she is.

"My name's Zane." I startle, turning to face the man beside me – the taller of the three – as I realize he's just spoken.

"Oh."

"What's your name?"

"Robyn."

He frowns. "That's a guy's name."

"Sometimes."

I may have had too much to drink, but I know when I'm out of my depth, and as Alisha shifts closer to the guy beside her, and Jodie licks her lips, staring at the man opposite, I realize the time has come for me to leave.

"I really should go," I say, loud enough for everyone to hear.

"So should we."

I hadn't expected Alisha's reply, but it seems everyone is in agreement, and the three men get up, stepping aside so we can all stand, too.

"We're gonna walk," Jodie says, giving Alisha a smile, which is returned.

"Why don't we come with you?" The man who was sitting at the end of the booth beside Zane steps in closer, taking Jodie's hand in his. The other man stands beside Alisha, and although I'd have expected my friends to object, they don't. In fact, they positively beam their acceptance. Personally, I feel that might be a mistake, and before they go, I quickly swap numbers with Jodie… just in case. She reassures me they'll be fine, glancing at Zane, who's still hanging around, the look on her face telling me she thinks I'll be fine, too.

I'm sure I will be… but not with Zane, and as I watch the four of them leave, hand in hand, I turn to him and say, "Goodnight."

"Goodnight?" he says. "I haven't seen you home yet."

"I don't need you to."

I make my way to the door, letting myself out, even though I'm aware he's following.

"I can't let you go home all alone," he says.

"It's not a problem. I only live next door."

He smiles, looking up at the night sky. "That's good."

"It is?"

"Yes. It means we don't have far to go," he says, smirking.

I shake my head and turn away, going around the back of the bar.

"Wait for me," he calls out.

"I'm fine by myself." The track is dark, and I'm starting to wish I'd gone for flatter shoes, or maybe had a little less to drink, especially as I'm aware of Zane's footsteps behind me, and I turn, nearly falling over. "Why are you following me?"

"Because I need to see you home."

"No, you don't."

"Yes, I do."

There's something in his voice that scares me, and rather than argue with him, I pull out my keys, and spin around, relieved that my feet are still working as I walk a little faster.

When I get to the door, my hands are shaking so much, I can't get the key into the lock. I try, over and over, aware that I'm panicking when I need to be calm, and as I take a deep breath, I feel Zane step up right behind me. He presses his body hard against mine, and all thoughts of calm abandon me.

"Leave me alone," I say, raising my voice.

"I just wanna help." He reaches for the key, but I pull my hand away.

"I don't need your help."

"I think you do," he says, flexing his hips so I can feel his erection pressing into me.

I turn around and push him, but he doesn't move. He's not going anywhere, and he just smiles down at me as he grabs my arms.

"Stop it… please."

I'm cornered, terrified, and am about to scream, when the door behind me opens and I turn my head, surprised to see Spencer standing there.

"What's going on?" he says, his eyes darting from me to Zane, and back again.

"I—I can't get my key to work."

I realize how much I'm slurring as I speak, and he frowns. "I heard," he says. "Who's this?" He nods toward Zane, and I realize he's still holding on to me. I try to pull free, but he's not letting go, and he just moves closer, staring up at Spencer.

"I could ask you the same question," he says.

"You could, but I got there first." There's a harshness in Spencer's voice I've never heard before, and I gaze at him for a moment, until Zane pulls me closer again.

"I'm her date," he says. "So, if you don't mind…" He tries to push past Spencer, dragging me with him, but I pull back, just enough to stop him.

"You're not my date," I say. "You just followed me here."

"Is that true?" Spencer darts forward. "He followed you home?"

"Yes."

Before I can say another word, Spencer steps outside and yanks Zane away from me, making it look easy, before he grabs my arms himself, holding on to me as he stares down into my eyes.

"You don't want this guy here?" he says, sounding a little desperate.

"No."

He nods his head and looks away again, facing Zane. "Go home," he says.

"Are you gonna make me?"

"If I have to." Spencer releases me and steps up to Zane, who glances up at Spencer, studying his shoulders for a moment before he backs down.

"She probably wasn't worth it anyway," he says, and turns away, hurrying down the track.

Spencer watches him go, while I heave out a sigh of relief, and as he turns back to me, I smile up at him.

"Thank you," I say, and he nods his head.

"Are you okay?"

"I think so."

He steps closer, looking down at me. "Sure? He didn't hurt you?"

"No. He just scared me."

"And you didn't call?"

"I don't have your number," I say, and he sighs, shaking his head.

"We'll have to do something about that. I'm just glad I heard you trying to unlock the door."

"So am I."

He puts his arm around me. "Let's get you inside," he says, and I nod my head, letting him help me through to the door, which he closes behind us. "Can you manage the stairs?"

"Sure." I kick off my shoes, picking them up, and then I glance up the stairs, wondering if this was such a good idea. They're swaying slightly, but I can't back down now. I'd look like a fool, so I struggle up them, taking my time, and stopping halfway to catch my breath. "Made it," I say when I reach the top, turning to find Spencer is right behind me.

"There's another set to go," he says, nodding toward the stairs that lead up to my room, and I shake my head.

"As much as I need my bed, I'm gonna take a break before I attempt that."

I'm still slurring slightly, and before I even think about making my way to the couch, I reach out for the wall beside me, misjudging the distance and stumbling over my own feet. Spencer catches me, holding me in his arms for a moment as we gaze into each other's eyes. There's something about him… something strong, and powerful, and even sexier than my fantasies, and as he stares down at me, I lose myself for a moment. I forget all the reasons I should keep my distance, and close the gap between us, leaning up and letting my lips brush against his. He feels so good, and as I moan in to him, I hope he'll respond and kiss me back. Except he doesn't. His lips don't move at all, and even in my drunken state, I know that's not good, and I pull back, releasing myself from his grip.

"I—I'll go upstairs," I say, faltering over my words.

"Not like this, you won't." He bends and lifts me into his arms, completing my humiliation as he makes his way through the living area and then carries me up the stairs to my room, staring straight ahead the entire time, rather than at me.

Once there, he puts me down on the edge of the bed and immediately turns away.

"Thank you," I say.

"You're welcome."

I want to say more. I want to ask him to stay… but I can't. Not because I don't want him, but because he didn't kiss me back.

And even I know what that means.

It means he's not interested.

That shouldn't bother me, should it? It shouldn't surprise me either. After all, I've been telling myself over and over that he's not the man for me… and how unsuited we are.

So why do I feel so rejected?

I thought my hangover would be worse, but even though my head has been feeling fragile since the moment I opened my eyes, that's nothing compared to the rest of me.

After all, what does a hangover matter when you're faced with the embarrassment of having your kiss dismissed by a man who's renowned as a player?

Does it get any worse than that?

Yes, it does… when the player concerned is the man of your dreams.

Oh… and you live with him.

I haven't been able to get past that all morning, and my only solace is that Spencer wasn't here when I woke up. He'd left a note on the breakfast bar to say he'd gone to the grocery store, and I took advantage of having the place to myself and made my way to the bathroom, taking my time over my shower.

He still wasn't home when I came out, and I'm already dressed and drinking my second cup of coffee by the time I hear his footsteps on the stairs and turn to see him reach the top, carrying two large bags of groceries.

"Can I help?" I ask

"No, I'm fine."

He dumps the bags on the breakfast bar and goes back down the stairs again. I can't sit here doing nothing, so I get up and wander into the kitchen, delving inside the first bag. It's got frozen food inside, so I get on with unpacking it, jumping out of my skin when Spencer returns and puts down two more bags.

"That's it," he says, dropping his keys on the countertop before he shrugs off his pea coat, throwing it over the back of the couch.

"I can handle this if you want to put your feet up."

He shakes his head. "No, it's fine."

That's the second time he's said that, but I get the feeling everything is far from fine… and that it's my fault. As we both reach into the bag, grabbing either end of a pack of spaghetti, I turn to face him.

"I'm sorry," I say. "About what happened last night. I was drunk, and I shouldn't have…"

"It's okay." He drops the spaghetti, holding up his hands to stop me talking.

I won't be beaten, though, and I lean a little closer. "I don't know what I'd have done if you hadn't rescued me."

He looks down, staring into my eyes for a moment, and then shrugs his shoulders, like it meant nothing to him… which I guess it didn't, and to cover my embarrassment, I get back to unloading the groceries.

That must mean he wants to forget the whole thing… and while I hate to admit it, he's probably right.

Chapter Eight

Spencer

"I'll pick you up at seven."

"Okay. I'll text you my address."

"Fine. See you then."

I end the call and lean back in my seat, staring down at my desk as I wonder if that was a good idea. It must be, mustn't it? After all, it's not as though Robyn's interested in me. Not when she's sober, anyway. That much was obvious from her drunken kiss the other night, and the way she reacted to it the following morning.

Okay… so she kissed me, and while I know I should rejoice about that, I can't. It's impossible when I couldn't respond to her. Not in the way I wanted. She could barely stand at the time, so responding was out of the question.

My only option was to take her up to her room and leave her there, no matter how tempted I was to stay and make something of it.

And I was tempted.

Especially after I'd seen that guy manhandling her by the back door. I'd been confused, hurt and angry when I'd first opened the door. Seeing her in the arms of another man was more complicated than I'd ever imagined.

But when she told me she didn't want him there…?

I felt triumphant… and madder than hell.

Who did the guy think he was?

Not who I'd feared, that was for sure, and once he'd gone, my only concern was Robyn. I had to be sure he hadn't hurt her, which he hadn't. Although I didn't like the idea of her being scared, or that she hadn't been able to call me. The thought of what could have happened…

It was too much to contemplate.

Did I expect her to kiss me? No.

But like I say, there was nothing I could do about it. To kiss her back would have been all wrong, so I took her to her room, and went to mine… on my own.

I was hard as nails, just thinking about how soft her lips had felt against mine, and although I'd avoided jerking off since Robyn moved in, I had no choice. I couldn't resist, and I stroked my cock, thoughts of her naked body beneath mine driving me insane with need.

It didn't take me long to come, and when I did, I whispered her name into the darkness, longing to make the dream a reality.

It felt more likely than ever. She'd kissed me, after all, with no prompting, and even if there hadn't been anything I could do about it, I wanted to see what we could make of it once she was sober… so I got up early the next morning with a plan in mind.

I'd go to the grocery store, get back as quickly as possible, and hope to find the time to talk to Robyn about what had happened. I'll admit, I factored in the possibility of another kiss… but talking seemed more important.

It was a loose plan, but it was better than nothing… and it all went smoothly, right until her apology.

I didn't see that coming.

I didn't realize how humiliating it would feel, either.

Okay, so she was grateful for being rescued, but as for the kiss? It had clearly meant nothing to her. She may not have said so in as many words, but the fact that she reiterated how drunk she was told me everything I needed to know. It's taken me a couple of weeks to get my head around that, and while I can't say I've succeeded, I've decided the best way to get over Robyn is to get back in the saddle… metaphorically.

I can't imagine sleeping with anyone else, but I can't sit around here moping over someone I can't have, either. It seems love isn't for me, after all, so I guess I have to accept that and move on.

Which is why I've just arranged to take Gina out to dinner.

I've never actually met her before, but we've spoken over the phone more times than I can remember… several times a week for the last year, to be precise. Although we haven't spoken since my promotion. She works for one of the company's suppliers, and her calls usually get put through to the main finance office, and not my direct line, but having talked so much – and flirted from time to time – I know a little about her. For example, I'm aware that she lives in a rented apartment in Concord, along with her cat, Pepper. I also know she likes action movies and hates romantic comedies, which I found refreshing in a woman. With the memory of Robyn's apology still ringing in my ears, when Gina's call was put through to me today, I decided to take the plunge. I didn't go out of my way. I didn't call her up and ask her out, but when she got in touch late this afternoon about an invoice she'd sent us by mistake, I thought, why not?

"Tonight?" she said, like that might be a problem, and I wondered if she'd given me a way out… and why I was looking for one.

"If you're not free…" I said, wondering if she'd take the bait.

"No. I'm free. I always keep my Friday nights free, just in case."

I knew she was kidding, and I had to smile, asking where she wanted to go. She suggested an Italian restaurant in Concord. I'd been there before, but didn't mention that. It didn't feel like a good idea… just like this dinner. Although it's too late to back out now.

We've made our plans… and I need to get on with my life.

I also need to go home so I can get ready to go out, so I close my computer for the day and switch off the lights before leaving the office. It's a mild night, but as spring is on the verge of blooming, that's hardly a surprise, and I don't bother putting on my jacket, and just throw it onto the passenger seat before climbing in behind the wheel, wishing I could feel more cheerful about the prospect of a night out. It's been a while, and I should feel more excited.

I would too… if I were seeing Robyn.

Except I'm not.

And I never will be.

And thinking like that won't get me anywhere. It's not fair to Gina, either, and I make the drive home, trying to focus on her… even though I've never met her.

That makes it a little tricky, but she's got a pleasant voice, and we seem to get along okay, so what's the harm in spending an evening together?

I mean… what's the worst that can happen?

I climb the stairs to the apartment, my jacket slung over my shoulder, and stop at the top, surprised to find Robyn is already home. That's unusual, and I'll admit, I'd hoped to sneak in, get changed, and sneak out again without her knowing. I'd have left her a note, but I didn't relish having to explain… although I'll have to now.

She's clearly been home for some time, and has changed into jeans and a blouse, and as she notices me for the first time, she leaps to her feet, a smile touching at her lips.

"Thank God you're home," she says.

"Why? Has something happened?"

"No. It's just that I finished work a little early, and I've been sitting here waiting to open the wine."

"You could have opened it by yourself," I say, pointing out the obvious as she heads for the kitchen and pulls open the fridge.

"I always think it's kinda sad to drink alone. Having someone with you makes it so much more fun."

I hate the thought of her being sad, but what can I do? What can I say?

"I'm sorry." The words fall from my lips, and she turns to face me, the bottle already in her hand.

"What for?"

"I'm going out."

Her face falls. "You are? I didn't realize."

"No. That's because I only arranged it this afternoon. I'm going to dinner."

"Oh? With whom?"

I can't hardly refuse to answer, having asked her exactly the same question when she went out with her friends the other week, but this feels different. It's a date. Still, she won't mind that, will she?

"Her name's Gina," I say, like that'll mean anything.

"Is she someone from work?"

"Not directly. She works for one of the suppliers I deal with."

"I see."

She puts the wine bottle down on the countertop and because I can't think of anything else to say, and I need to get ready, I wander to my room, although I stop on the threshold and look back, surprised to find Robyn is still standing where she was, staring into space.

"Are you gonna be okay?" I ask, and she looks up, nodding her head.

"I'll be fine. I'll heat up a pizza. It'll be safer than trying to cook."

That wasn't what I meant, but it just goes to show how little I mean to her. She's thinking about practicalities. I'm thinking about us… except there isn't an 'us', is there, and the reminder of that cuts deep. I let myself inside my room, leaning back against the door for a moment or two while I let that thought wash over me, and wish it was easier to get over loving someone.

Because this really fucking hurts.

I've never known pain like it. It seems to touch every inch of my body, and for a moment, I contemplate calling Gina to cancel. I could say I'm not feeling well. It wouldn't be a lie. I feel like shit. But I don't think staying here with Robyn will solve anything.

It'll probably just make me feel worse… if that were possible.

So I may as well go out.

By the time I exit my room again, wearing black pants and a white button-down shirt, both Robyn and the bottle of wine have moved to the living area. She's on the couch, and the wine is on the table in front of her, alongside a glass, which is half empty.

I could just leave, but something draws me to her, and I sit down alongside her, leaning in a little closer as I say, "I thought you said it was sad to drink alone."

"It is… but you're going out, so I'll have to make an exception."

I feel even worse about leaving her now, but she's not mine to leave, is she? "I've been meaning to say, we never got around to exchanging numbers, did we?"

She looks up, her brow furrowing with confusion. "Exchanging numbers?"

She was probably too drunk to remember our conversation, and for a moment, I can't think how to remind her without bringing up what happened that evening. "We said we would, in case you needed to call me for anything."

That's vague enough. It's so vague, she just frowns at me and says, "Like what?" and I wonder if she realizes how much that hurts.

"I don't know… if a situation arises, like the other night, when that guy followed you home from the bar."

There… I've brought it up. She didn't give me much choice in the end, and, in a shock to absolutely no-one, a blush creeps up her cheeks. Is she recalling what followed that scene at the back door? Or her regrets the following day?

"I guess…" she says, like she's still not sure, but she pulls out her phone anyway, and I do likewise. We swap, the two of us putting our numbers onto the other's device before handing them back again.

She hasn't mentioned going out tonight, and the fact that she's sitting here nursing a bottle of wine suggests she doesn't intend to… although the thought that she might, and that I'll be in Concord, and too far away to help if she gets in trouble doesn't sit well with me.

Even so, there's nothing I can do.

I can't ask her, can I? It's none of my business what she does… and the thought that she might tell me that, in those precise words, is enough to keep me silent on the matter.

Robyn's her own woman.

She's made that very clear, and she flicks on the TV to prove the point, dismissing me in the process.

"Enjoy your evening," I say, getting to my feet.

"It should be me saying that, shouldn't it?"

She smiles up at me, clearly oblivious to my feelings. If she asked me to stay, I would, but she couldn't care less what I do, so I leave and drive to Concord, feeling very disgruntled with life.

As it transpires, Gina is very pretty indeed.

Okay, so she's not exactly a redhead, but her hair is strawberry blonde, which is the next best thing, as far as I'm concerned. Not only that, but she has sparkling blue eyes, and generous lips… and if my brain wasn't otherwise occupied, I know I'd be thinking about what they'd look like wrapped around my cock. As it is, I'm struggling to concentrate on anything other than the sight of Robyn, sitting alone on our couch…

"It's lovely in here, isn't it?" she says as the waiter brings our appetizers. Gina's chosen a beet salad with goat's cheese, while I'm having the gnocchi.

"It is." I glance around at our elegant surroundings… the white linen tablecloths, and sparkling glassware, and then return my gaze to her. It's no hardship, and she smiles across at me.

"Can I let you in on a secret?" she says.

I'm not sure we know each other well enough for secrets, but it would be rude to say no. "Sure."

"I've been hoping you'd ask me out for ages."

"Really?"

"Yes." She smiles. "Don't take this the wrong way, but I was really disappointed when you were promoted. I thought we'd never get to speak again."

"We probably wouldn't have done, but someone put your call through to me by mistake."

"I wondered," she says, tipping her head. "But I'm not complaining. If they hadn't, this might never have happened."

She's not wrong there, although I shrug my shoulders. "Oh… you never know."

"Yes, I do. I'm leaving my job in two weeks' time."

"You are?" That's one thing about her I didn't know.

"Yes. I'm sick of working in finance. Everyone seems to yell at me."

"I hope I never have," I say, putting down my fork.

"No." She smiles across the table at me.

"If you're giving up the wonderful world of finance, what are you moving into?"

"It's just an administrative role," she says. "It pays less, but hopefully I won't have so much stress in my life."

I nod my head, contemplating my own stress levels over the last few weeks, which have been pretty crazy. That's had nothing to do with my promotion. So far, that's gone pretty smoothly. No, my stresses have all been about Robyn, and I let out a slight groan, wishing I hadn't let her get back into my head… although, to be fair, she's never really out of it.

I glance down at my gnocchi, recalling how we made a dish fairly similar to this last Wednesday night, and I can't help wondering if Robyn's okay… whether she's managed to heat the pizza, or has maybe given up and gone out somewhere. I hope not. Obviously, she's entitled to do whatever she wants, but the thought of her being out on her own after what happened the last time…

"Is everything okay?"

Gina's voice brings me back to reality, and I look up, surprised by how concerned she seems. It would be easy to lie and say everything's fine… but it's not.

"No," I say, and she puts down her fork, leaning in a little closer.

"This isn't working for you, is it?"

Oh, God… I feel just awful now. She's seen right through me, but again, I have to be honest.

"No, it's not. I'm sorry."

She shakes her head. "Don't be. I knew it was too good to be true." That just makes it worse. "Is it me?" she asks.

"No. It's someone else."

She frowns. "You mean you're seeing someone else, and you asked me on a date? That's…"

I hold up my hand. "That's not how it happened," I say. "I'm not seeing her."

Her face clears. "Oh… but you want to. Is that it?"

"Yes. Only she doesn't."

"Is she mad?"

"No," I say, shaking my head. "She just doesn't see me as boyfriend material."

"Well… more fool her."

That's the nicest thing anyone's said to me in ages, but I can't see the point in prolonging this. "Shall we call it a night?" I say, and she nods her head.

"I think it's for the best."

I call the waiter, who's surprised and not best pleased that we're leaving, although Gina saves the day, telling him she doesn't feel well, which seems to help.

"Thanks for that," I say as I put away my wallet and help her with her coat.

"That's okay. I guess you could see his point, but I don't think either of us wants to be here anymore, do we?"

"No."

Fortunately, her apartment is only a short walk away, and we get back there without exchanging another word. She has every right to be mad at me, but when we arrive at her door, she turns and looks up at me with a slight smile on her lips.

"Thank you for being honest," she says.

"Thank you for understanding."

It's a shame. In any other life, I think she and I might have been good together. But this isn't another life. It's mine… and right now, it's not working out very well.

Gina and I say goodnight to each other, both of us perhaps relieved that between my promotion and her new job, we almost certainly won't have to speak again, and I make my way back to Hart's Creek.

I've only been gone for ninety minutes, or just under, but when I get up to the apartment, I'm surprised to find Robyn exactly where I left her. Surprised and relieved. She's watching a movie, and the bottle of wine is half empty in front of her. There's a plate beside it, with just a few crusts of pizza to show for her dinner. She's eaten more than I have, but I don't care about that. I just care that I'm here… with her.

"Hello," she says, smiling up at me.

"Hi."

I remove my jacket and sit beside her, taking my wallet and phone from my pocket and placing them on the table.

"How was your date?" she asks.

"Not great."

"Oh… I'm sorry."

"I'm not."

She tilts her head and grabs the bottle, holding it in my direction. I take the hint and get up again, fetching myself a glass, which she fills with wine, topping up her own glass while she's about it. "What went wrong?" she asks, taking a sip.

"We weren't right for each other."

"That's the story of my life," she says, rolling her eyes. "I've yet to meet a man I'm right for."

Me! You're fucking perfect for me. If you'd only realize it.

"I find that hard to believe," I say, because it's the closest I can get to telling her how I really feel.

She frowns, glancing at my glass. "How much of that have you had tonight?"

"This is my first. I was driving. Why? How much have you had?"

"This is my third."

"Does that mean I'll have to carry you up the stairs again?"

She licks her lips, taking her time over it, and my cock hardens, pressing against my zipper. "I don't think so." *That's a shame.* I wonder if she's thinking the same thing, as her eyes wander, and although I know I should do something to hide my erection, I can't think what… not without making it obvious. In any case, why should I bother? I want her so much it hurts… so why should I hide it? She clearly notices, her eyes widening as they linger for a moment or two, before she raises them to mine again. "Are you saying your date didn't… appreciate you?" she asks a little randomly.

"No. It wasn't that. She said she'd wanted me to ask her out for ages."

"And who can blame her?" she says, a blush creeping up her cheeks.

I can't ignore that… not the blush, but her words. I can't misinterpret either. Not this time. Her meaning is clear, and I put down my wine and shift along the couch, getting closer to her.

"How sober are you?" I ask.

"Sober enough to know what I'm saying… and what I'm doing." She puts her glass next to mine as she's speaking, and stares right at me, making me breathless with just a blink of her eyes.

"Why? What are you doing?" I say, surprised by the rasp in my voice.

"Fulfilling a fantasy."

She reaches out, undoing my belt and pulling it from its loops before she drops it to the floor, her eyes never leaving mine, even as she unfastens the button and zipper on my pants. I don't say a word. In fact, I barely breathe, unwilling to break the moment, and unable to believe this is her fantasy. Other than that drunken kiss – the one she regretted the next morning – she's never given me any reason to believe it might be, or any hint she could be interested… and yet, here we are.

She's breathing hard as she delves inside my pants, rubbing my shaft through my trunks, biting on her bottom lip as she lets out a slight moan of satisfaction.

Man, that's hot. But it's nowhere near as hot as what she does next, because just as I'm getting used to her touch, she pulls back and tugs on my pants and trunks. I help, raising my ass from the couch, and between us we free my cock from its confines.

She gasps, studying me for a moment, and then wraps her hand around me, leaning in even closer as she fulfills one of my many fantasies and takes me in her mouth.

"Fuck… yes." I hiss out the words between gritted teeth, watching as she lowers her head, taking me deeper and deeper, until I hit the back of her throat. I'm tempted to raise my hips and see if she can take a little more, but I don't want to spoil the moment, and instead I gather up her hair, holding it behind her head while she works miracles with her tongue. "That's really fucking good, babe." She turns her head, her eyes fixing on mine as she moans and sighs, like she's getting as much from this as I am. I know she can't be… because I'm close to coming, and I'm about to warn her, when she pulls back, releasing my cock.

I'm slightly worried she'll come to her senses and realize this isn't what she wants, but my fears prove unfounded as she reaches for the hem of her top and yanks it up over her head, throwing it to the floor.

I'm faced with her firm, rounded breasts, her nipples straining against her white lace bra, but before I can do anything about removing it, she stands, unfastening her jeans. I take my chance, as it seems we're not stopping, and unbutton my shirt, discarding it over the back of the couch, before I kick off my shoes and finally remove my socks, pants and trunks, leaving them all in a pile. Robyn has already shimmied out of her jeans, her panties following close behind, and she stops, staring at my naked body, while I take in the sight of her perfectly shaved pussy. It's right in front of me, and I lean in to kiss her at the apex of her thighs… to return the favor, if you like. Her lips are swollen and glistening, and I can't wait to taste her, although Robyn clearly has other ideas, and she catches me by surprise, pushing me back into my seat, her hands on my shoulders as she straddles me.

I guess we're not bothering with foreplay, and that works just fine for me. I can't wait to be inside her, and while I'm desperate enough to forget just about everything – including my own name – I can still remember the important things in life. The most vital of which is taking care of her, and I grab my wallet from the table and pull out a condom, which I roll over my cock just as she settles herself in place and slowly lowers herself down.

She's in no hurry, and takes me an inch at a time, her body shuddering as she puts her hands behind her head, her face a picture of ecstasy already. I hold her waist, guiding her and watching the wonder in her eyes. It's a sight to behold, as is the sound of her screaming, "Yes," when she finally settles onto me, my cock buried to the hilt inside her tight, throbbing pussy.

I remove her bra, smiling as she lowers her arms to help me, and then throw it to one side, and palm her breasts, squeezing them, and then tweaking her nipples between my thumbs and forefingers.

"Don't stop," she says, placing her hands behind her head again, her hips flexing. "Don't stop."

"I won't."

Ever.

She's beside herself with need, and just as I think she's about to tip over the edge, she changes things up, raising herself almost all the way off of me before she slams back down again, lowering her hands to my shoulders and using them for leverage as she rides me harder and harder.

"Give me more," she pleads, and I grind my hips up to meet her every move. She rocks her head back, groaning out her pleasure, her nipples hardening even further between my fingers.

"Fuck me," I whisper. "Fuck me, babe."

She ups the pace, and I watch as her skin flushes, feeling the moment her orgasm builds… the tightening at her core, and as she curls in to me, her eyes lock with mine, in a moment I know will live with me forever. "Yes, Spence… yes," she screams at the top of her voice.

I've never heard anything sound so fine as my name on her lips – especially that shortened version of it – and I hold her, letting her ride out the heights of her climax while struggling to keep hold of my own. It's not easy, but I get there, and as she calms, her body slowly unbending, I sit forward on the edge of the couch, placing my arms beneath her legs, so when I stand, they're hooked over my elbows.

"Oh… dear God," she says, her voice coming out as a guttural growl. "That feels so good."

She clings to my shoulders, then leans in as I start to walk, kissing my neck, and then biting me, just gently.

She's so much more than I expected, and although I'm aiming for my bedroom, I deviate at the last minute, slamming her against the wall beside the door. She yelps in surprise, but doesn't miss a beat, leaning back as far as she can and gazing into my eyes as I pull almost all the way out of her, and then thrust back in.

"Yes," she cries. "Do that again." I hammer in to her. "And again… and again. Please, don't stop."

I hadn't realized she'd be like this, but I don't hold back, giving her everything I've got.

"You feel so fucking good on my cock," I tell her.

"That's because you have such a magnificent cock."

I never thought I'd hear Robyn say something like that, and I take her even faster… even harder. Sweat forms on my back, and although I know she needs more, I need a break… because I don't want this to end. Not yet.

I turn us, heading for the door, and although that was supposed to provide some respite, it doesn't… because Robyn shifts her hands, leaning on my shoulders, rather than just gripping them, so she can ride my cock again.

"You're gonna make me come," I say, barely in control.

"Please don't. Not yet. I need more."

"Then stop moving."

"I can't. I have to have your cock, Spence. Give it to me. I need it."

Just hearing her say that is almost enough to tip me over the edge, and I hold her up, fighting her movements as I kick open the door and carry her to the bed, lifting her off of my cock before I drop her to the mattress.

She doesn't even pause to catch her breath, but spins around, kneeling up and clasping my dick in her hands as she moves forward, pulling off the condom, which she drops to the floor before she takes me in her mouth again.

"You're driving me crazy," I say, barely keeping it together.

"No, I'm not. I'm sucking your cock," she says, pulling back just long enough to explain the obvious, before she swallows me down again. The sight of her lips stretched around me and her eyes raised to mine is almost too much, but because I'm crazy –

or being driven most of the way there – I flex my hips, and she moans around me, nodding her head.

"You want more?"

She nods again, and I give her what she's asking for, holding the back of her head while I fuck her mouth. I don't go too deep, but even so, there's no way I can keep going for long. I'm too close to coming already, but because I have control – of my movements, if nothing else – I choose my moment, and just as I feel my orgasm building, I pull out of her, smiling as she pouts up at me.

"I was enjoying that," she says.

"So was I… but now it's my turn to taste you."

She squeals as I tip her onto her back, pushing her further onto the bed so I can kneel up between her legs, parting them as I lean down and catch my first close-up of her perfect pussy. It's pink and glistening with her juices, and I dip my head, running my tongue from her entrance to her clit.

"Oh… yes."

She clamps her hand on the back of my head, raising her hips at the same time, and I take the hint, flicking my tongue over her. I've never tasted anyone so sweet, and her perfume is like something heaven-sent. I could devour her all night long, but within just a few minutes, I feel her thighs quiver, and her breathing quicken.

"I—I'm coming, Spence," she says, stuttering over her words as pleasure claims her. "How are you doing this to me? How are you…?"

With that, she's gone… lost to another climax, and I drink her down, lapping my tongue over her, until she finally relents, lowering her hips to the mattress, and releasing her hand from my head.

I lean up, looking down at her, although she's got her eyes closed, evidently still lost in ecstasy… and I want nothing more than to join her there. The sound of me opening the drawer in my nightstand seems to bring her to her senses, and she smiles up at me when she realizes what I'm doing, watching as I roll another condom over my cock.

"You want more?" she says, echoing my words, and I smile down at her.

"I'm nowhere near done with you."

"Good."

She reaches down, her fingers skimming over her skin, and then between her folds. The sight is too tempting for words, and I gaze down, studying her movements, watching as she holds her lips apart, exposing her entrance. She's doing this for me, so I nestle between her legs, my dick finding its way back to her welcoming hole, as I flex my hips, sliding all the way home.

We both sigh out our pleasure at the same time, before she moves her hands out from between us, and I take advantage of that, grabbing hold of them, one at a time, and then raising them above her head. She's pinned beneath me, and I pound into her, giving her my entire length with every stroke. I'm torn between a need to suck her hardened nipples and a desire to watch her as she writhes beneath me. Need wins in the end, and I dip my head, my tongue flickering over each pebbled bud. She gasps at the contact, then sighs as she raises her hips to mine, proving she's not done, either.

"Come for me," I say, knowing I can't hold on much longer.

"I'm not there yet. Not quite."

Seriously? "Do you need some help?"

She smiles. "That sounds good." I wonder if she's really in need of my assistance, or if she just wants to be touched… until she says, "If you prefer, you can free my hands, and I'll do it."

Fuck…

"That sounds even better."

I release her right hand, and she lowers it down between us, my eyes following as she lets her fingers delve between her swollen lips and then circle over her clit.

"Are you enjoying the view?" she asks, her voice dropping to a low rasp.

"You look fucking amazing. Is this something you do a lot?"

A blush creeps up her already flushed cheeks, and she tips her head to one side. "It might be."

"Is it something you do while thinking about your fantasy?"

"Maybe."

I wish she'd just say 'yes', but the irony isn't lost on me that while I've been hurting, and beating myself up, contemplating how to get over her, and convincing myself she didn't want me, she's been pleasuring herself, and thinking about what we're doing right now.

"You like to make yourself come while you dream about my cock deep inside you?" I say, determined to get her to admit it.

"Yes," she says, nodding her head.

That was easier than I expected, and I smile down at her.

She circles a little harder… a little faster, her eyes fixed on mine as her breathing becomes more and more labored. She's close, and because the connection between us is so intimate, I can see the moment when she finally gives in to her orgasm. I can feel it in her body, too… and it's beyond my control to hold back. As she crashes and writhes beneath me, screaming my name, and begging for more, I thrust into her one last time, losing my mind to a climax more powerful than I would have thought possible.

We come back to each other, taking our time to recover from that intense high, and I turn us onto our sides, holding her close in my arms.

"Did the reality live up to the fantasy?" I ask and she smiles at me.

"Oh, God, yes." Her voice is low and throaty, which makes me chuckle, and that movement inside her makes her shudder, as I remember my responsibilities.

"I need to go to the bathroom," I whisper, kissing her forehead. "I'll be back in a second."

She nods her head, her eyes fluttering closed, and I carefully pull out of her, taking care not to hurt her, before I roll from the bed, grab the discarded condom from the floor and dash from the room, and into the bathroom. I can't believe what just happened, but I'm not going to question it. I'm going to revel in it… because we're finally where we belong. Okay, so we haven't exchanged our first kiss yet. I'm aware of that. But we've done so much more… and we can kiss tomorrow. We can do a lot more than kissing, too, and I chuckle to myself as I wash up and return to the bedroom, where I find Robyn is fast asleep.

I'm really not surprised. After everything we've done this evening, she has every right to sleep, and I lift her, moving her up the bed, smiling to myself as she nestles against me when I lie beside her and pull the covers up. It doesn't get better than this, and I hold her body close against mine, wondering what I did to deserve this much happiness.

Chapter Nine

Robyn

I've got cold feet.

I don't know why. It's not as though we're in the depths of winter anymore, and besides, the rest of me is quite warm. In fact, I'm boiling.

There's something not right about all this… aside from the cold feet.

I can't put my finger on exactly what it is, but my bed feels different.

It's ridiculous, I know, but for some reason the bed feels smaller this morning, and I tug at the covers as I try to work out how that can be.

"You're not great at sharing the bedding, are you?"

The male voice behind me makes me jump, and I flip around, gasping when I see Spencer leaning up on one elbow, gazing down at me. He's bare-chested, and for a moment, I'm blindsided by the sight of his muscular torso, dappled with dark hairs, as he leans over slightly. The covers I've just been pulling in my direction drift further downwards as he moves, revealing his hips, and it doesn't take much imagination to work out the rest of him must be naked too.

With that thought in mind, I release the covers, only remembering at the last minute that I'm not wearing anything either, so I pull them back, clutching them just beneath my chin.

He laughs, shaking his head at me, and because I'm embarrassed, I go on the offensive.

"Do you mind telling me what you're doing in my bed?" I say.

"I'm not in your bed. You're in mine. I carried you in here last night. I don't know if you remember, but you kinda started something on the couch, and I thought it would be nice to finish it somewhere more comfortable… although we stopped off along the way, just outside the door."

Oh, shit. We did, didn't we? I remember how good that felt, and my pussy clenches at the thought, the rest of my body struggling not to respond in a similar way, as I think about what it felt like to have his cock inside me.

I cover my face with my hands to hide at least some of my embarrassment. "We had sex, didn't we?" I whisper, although that feels like the understatement of the century. We did so much more than have sex, and I lower my hands again just in time to see his smile fade.

"I thought we did a little more than that," he says, echoing my thoughts. "I thought you'd have a better memory of it. You… You said you weren't that drunk." He sounds worried, and I know I have to put his mind at rest.

"I wasn't. Honestly. And I remember what we did."

He turns slightly, and I glance down at the tented cover, recalling the size of his cock, with its veined shaft and bulbous head. It looked so good in my hands, and felt amazing in my mouth, although I don't think I'll ever forget that moment when he penetrated me for the first time. Or, to be more precise, when I took him. Because that's what happened. I was the one in charge, and the stretch was incredible. It was the best… but did we really do all that, though? Did I really do all that?

"In a good way?" he asks.

"I don't think there's a bad way to remember something like that," I say, and his lips twist up into a smile. "Except we shouldn't have done it."

He shakes his head, his frown returning.

"You didn't seem to think that last night," he says. "I recall you begging for more."

"Did I really?"

"Yes. Several times."

"Honestly?"

"I thought you said you could remember."

"Well… some of it's a little hazy."

"Then let me refresh your memory. You begged me for more when you were riding my cock on the couch, and then again, when I walked us in here. I was in danger of coming, but you said you had to have my cock. And although you couldn't speak when I was fucking your mouth, you made it very clear you wanted more. You didn't hold back, Robyn. When you didn't have my dick in your mouth, you were screaming at me not to stop, telling me how good it felt… and it did. You felt fucking amazing."

"Don't say that."

"Why not? It's true."

"But we still shouldn't have done it."

"So you're saying you regret it?" he says, and I stare at him, noticing the sadness in his eyes. It would be easy to say 'no', because the truth is, just like there's no bad way to remember what we did, it's impossible to regret it, too. Except I know it was a mistake. Deep down, I know I should never have let it happen.

"Would you mind turning away so I can get out of bed?" I say, still unable to answer his question, and he leans back slightly, shaking his head, which surprises me. "You won't turn away?"

"Why should I?"

"Because it's the gentlemanly thing to do."

"I know it is. But what have you got to hide from me? I've seen you naked, Robyn. I've watched you come."

I cover my ears with my hands. "Don't."

I remember what it felt like to come apart beneath him while he pounded in to me. There was something about that. It was more intense than when we were in the living room on the couch, or when he made me come on his tongue. He'd been holding me down, and while he'd released my hand so I could touch myself, I still enjoyed the feeling of looking up and seeing his powerful body, feeling the control he had over me, and relishing the way he looked at me as I fell into yet another orgasm. It took me to somewhere I've never been before… not with anyone else, or at my own hand, and while I'd love to go there again, I can't think like that. I have to exercise a little control of my own.

"Please turn away," I say, watching as his shoulders drop and he turns, showing me his back.

The crazy part of me wants to reach out and touch him, but the sensible part is having her say, and I sit up, realizing I need to go around the bed, and that Spencer will be able to see me when I get to the door… so having him turn away is of little use, really.

I don't have any clothes in here. They're all in the living room, where I left them last night, after I stripped out of them… although I can't think about that now, and I grab the throw from the end of the bed, wrapping it around my shoulders as I stand and run from the room.

I'm tempted to go straight up the stairs to my bedroom, but I need to shower, and besides, the bathroom door has a lock on it. I'll be much safer in there than I will with just a curtain for protection, although why do I think I need protection? It's not as though Spencer is going to do anything to me. He's not the one who started all this, is he?

Even so, I hurry into the bathroom and lock the door behind me, dropping the throw to the floor. My reflection is staring back at me in the mirror, and I take a moment to study the stranger before me.

"Who are you?" I whisper. "And what's wrong with you?"

I shake my head, confusion washing over me.

Okay, so I know it's been a while since I had sex, but I've waited longer before. Much longer… and even if Spencer is a walking fantasy, there was no need to jump the guy, was there?

Not that he objected.

Which makes little sense of why he didn't return my kiss the other week. His reaction couldn't have been more different… except I have a vague recollection that he made a point of checking how drunk I was last night.

Does that mean he'd have kissed me back if I'd been sober?

I shake my head again, trying to make sense of it all, although I don't know why.

What does it matter?

None of it should have happened, because no matter how many times I've made myself come thinking about Spencer, and no matter how much better he was in reality than even my wildest dreams, it can never be.

He's not the man for me, and I'm not the woman for him.

I want forever, and he wants for now.

I want commitment, and he wants to have fun.

I wish it could be different, but it can't.

I climb into the shower, wishing I could wash away my worries… and some of my memories. Not all of them, you understand. There's no way I want to forget the way Spencer made me come, or how it felt when he walked me from the living room to his bedroom. He certainly knew what he was doing, but I suppose he would, wouldn't he? He's a player… and that's why I shouldn't have let it happen in the first place.

"Let it happen?" I whisper as I climb out of the shower.

Who am I kidding?

I didn't let it happen. I played an active role.

Hell… I started it, for crying out loud.

I wrap a towel around me, just above my breasts, and pick up the throw, before I open the bathroom door, holding in my gasp when I see Spencer sitting on the couch. He's in almost exactly the same place as he was last night when I climbed up on his lap and straddled him, and I'm only grateful he's put on a bathrobe… even if I wish he'd stayed in his bedroom. What's he doing out here? Waiting for me, I guess, and he makes that obvious when he gets to his feet and strides over, standing in front of me.

"I think we need to talk, don't you?" he says.

"What about?"

I try to inject some innocence into my voice, although I don't know why. I'm far from innocent in all this, and he knows it. He shows it too, tipping his head to one side.

"Oh, I don't know," he says. "Maybe the weather, or the price of coffee… or the fact that we had sex last night. You choose."

He sounds so hurt, but that's the male ego for you, I guess. Even so, I feel responsible, and I reach out, placing my hand on his familiar chest, at the place where his robe gapes open, noting how his muscles flex to my touch.

"It's not personal, Spencer," I say.

He shakes his head. "Oddly enough, you called me Spence last night, every time I made you come. Every fucking time, Robyn. And yet today, I'm Spencer again." He steps back slightly as he gets to the end of his sentence, and I let my hand drop to my side, watching as he lowers his head, staring at the space between us for a moment, and then raises his head again, his eyes filled with torment. "In case you didn't notice, what we did was really fucking personal. At least, it was to me."

Hell… I think I might have really hurt him. I'm not sure how that's possible, but I step closer again, unsure how to make it right. "That's not what I meant. What I was trying to say was, you didn't do anything wrong."

He narrows his eyes. "I know," he says. "I heard it in your voice when you were screaming my name. I felt it in your fingers, too, when you gripped my cock, and in every tremble of your body. But now you're telling me it shouldn't have happened? You want me to believe you regret it?"

I can't honestly say I do. I couldn't just now in his bed, and I still can't. In fact, I can't bring myself to say anything, and instead I just stare at his chest, trying not to think about how good he looks with no clothes on, and how much I want to go back there… even though I know I can't.

Going back isn't an option, but he's not giving up either. He's waiting for my reply, and I have to think of one, even though my mind's a blank.

"I—I think it's for the best if we forget it ever happened. That's all I'm trying to say."

"All?" he says, stepping closer to me and staring down into my eyes.

"Yes."

I don't know how on earth I'm supposed to do that. It's a ridiculous idea. But it's probably for the best. Anything else would be madness.

Perfect, sublime, beautiful madness.

I clear my throat, trying not to think about that, as Spencer shakes his head. "You wanna forget about it?"

No. "Yes."

"Fine. You got it."

He turns and walks away, going back into his room and slamming the door so hard it makes me jump.

I'm still clutching the throw from the end of his bed, but I don't think it's a good idea to return it to him… not right now. Instead, I fold it up and leave it on the arm of the couch before I wander up the stairs to my room.

I can't hide from my own disappointment, or from Spencer's anger, but I know what I'm doing is for the best. He'll come to see that too, when he's thinking straight. I know he will.

He'll remember his conversation with Clark and realize we're not right for each other. He'll think it through and work out that the last thing he wants is to give up the life he's grown used to, in favor of being tied down to one woman. That's what I'm looking for. A man who'd want to share a life with me… and that's not who he is. Clark said so. He said Spencer likes to fuck and move on. I can remember his words, and even if I don't like the idea of him being like that, he's got every right to live his life however he chooses. I can't change him. What's more, I wouldn't want to. He is who he is, just like I am who I am… and we're two different people. So, no matter how good he was, walking away is definitely the right thing to do.

Well… I suppose the right thing to do would have been to show a little more self-control in the first place. But it's too late for that now, and no matter what Spencer thinks – or what I might have just led him to believe – I really don't regret it.

How can I?

The guy is just too good for regrets.

I feel like we should celebrate again.

Not because we've made it to the end of another week. We haven't come that far yet. But we survived the weekend.

Survived is the right word, too.

In fact, I was relieved to go back to work yesterday, just to escape the horrible atmosphere at the apartment. I knew it was of my making, but what could I do?

We avoided each other most of the time. On Saturday, I mostly stayed in my room, feeling I should give Spencer the run of the apartment, having caused the problem in the first place. I didn't want to make him feel uncomfortable in his own home. Except he went out… to the grocery store, as it transpired. That was another reason for me to feel guilty. It was my turn, but I'd forgotten all about it, and in my absence, he'd prepared the menu and the shopping list, and gone out to buy everything we'd need. I only found out later in the day, when I finally ventured downstairs, hunger getting the better of me at last, and discovered the refrigerator had been re-stocked.

"You went shopping?" I said, turning to face him. He was sitting on the couch, with his head buried in a book, and he didn't look up.

"Yeah."

"Sorry. That should have been me, shouldn't it?"

He didn't reply, but just shrugged his shoulders, the guilt washing over me in waves.

We didn't cook together either, although he still cooked for me, which I thought was generous of him. He didn't have to do that, but that evening, as I was wondering what to do about dinner, and how I was going to prepare it, I heard him call me down, telling me it was ready.

He'd made a simple pasta dish, and everything was laid out on the breakfast bar.

"This is kind of you," I said, sitting up in my place.

He sat beside me, picked up his fork, and shrugged his shoulders again. It seemed that was going to be our method of communication, and I decided against trying to start a conversation. It felt like it would be too one-sided to work.

Sunday wasn't much better, the only real difference being that my mom called. She was full of excitement about the work they're now having done on the house, which didn't just include a home cinema in the basement, but also a brand new kitchen. I struggled to join in, my mind occupied with other things.

"Is everything okay?" she asked, clearly noting my lack of enthusiasm. The contrast with when she'd first told me about their plans for remodeling must have been too marked for her to miss.

"Everything's fine. I'm just tired."

"Are you eating enough?"

"Of course." I cleared my throat and tried to put a smile on my face, knowing it would make a difference. "I can't wait to see all the changes."

"That's something I was gonna talk to you about," she said. "Your father and I have been discussing it, and there's no way you're gonna be able to come home while we're having this work done. The house is in chaos, and we've stored quite a lot of furniture in your bedroom. It's only temporary, but…"

"Don't worry about it, Mom," I said, interrupting her. I might have said I wanted to see what they were doing, but the reality was, the last thing I needed was to go home and face her scrutiny, knowing what I'd done. She'd see through me better than anyone, and I knew I'd never be able to explain myself.

"We miss you," she said, lamenting my absence. "But Dad thinks the work will be finished in about six weeks. Then you'll have to come back and see it."

Six weeks? That sounded like enough time to get my head around everything… maybe.

"I'm looking forward to it already."

She seemed to believe me and spent the rest of our call telling me how difficult it was having workmen in the house. I honestly didn't care and zoned out for a lot of the time, relieved when she finally had to go.

I didn't leave my room for the rest of the day, other than to use the bathroom, and to eat, and like I say, I was relieved to get back to the office yesterday. I imagine Spencer felt the same. He'd barely said more than ten words to me since he slammed his bedroom door on me on Saturday morning, but he certainly seemed to be in a slightly better mood when he got home last night. We even managed a brief conversation over dinner, although we kept it about work. It seemed safer that way.

I'd love to be able to turn back the clock and do things differently… except I know I can't. And even if I could somehow magic up a time-machine, and go back to Friday evening, I can't be entirely sure I wouldn't do exactly the same things all over again.

I shouldn't, I know, but the stupid thing is, I really miss him.

I'm not just talking about his body, or his fingers, or his tongue, or even his incredible cock, either. I'm talking about him… his laugh, his smile, his presence.

I miss all of him… so much it hurts.

And I have no-one to blame but myself.

Chapter Ten

Spencer

It transpired I didn't deserve such happiness after all.

It's been a week since I woke up with Robyn in my arms, and I still haven't come to terms with what happened.

I turn over in bed as dawn breaks, exhaustion getting the better of me, although that's hardly a surprise.

I've struggled to sleep all week, knowing she won't be beside me when I wake up, because I can remember how good it felt, to open my eyes, and find she was right here, still nestled against me, her back to my front, her breathing soft and steady.

She looked so peaceful, and I watched her for ages, recalling all the things we'd done, smiling as I remembered how wild and insatiable she was, and knowing it was Saturday morning, and we had nothing to rush up for. I contemplated what we could do with our day, wondering about maybe taking a shower together, and having brunch at the coffee shop, or going grocery shopping. Aside from the shower, none of that was desperately exciting, but the thought of doing it with Robyn made it seem so.

We could have stayed in bed, of course. It was always an option. I could easily have made us breakfast, rather than going out, and the grocery shopping could always wait. My smile widened then as I wondered about the many ways we could make love during the course of the day, my cock aching at the prospect. Except I wasn't sure Robyn would want that. Sure, she'd been hungry for me the night before, but that could have been the novelty factor. I wasn't taking anything for granted. She may have been sober enough to know what she was doing – in her words – but the cold light of day might make her react differently. She might be shy… or a little more reticent. I was prepared for that, even though I couldn't help sighing as I recalled the way she'd sucked me… twice, and ridden my cock, like we were made for each other. I could still feel her around me, her tight walls gripping my shaft.

Man, she was hot.

Hot enough to burn, it seems, because the moment she woke up, that's exactly what she did.

What we'd done may have meant everything to me, but it meant nothing to her… to the extent that she regretted it. That was what she said… or what she implied. I can't remember if she actually said the words herself, or if I did, and she just agreed with me. But I recall her saying she thought we should forget it ever happened, the idea echoing around my head.

How did she think that was possible?

I'd just spent the best night of my life with her, and she wanted me to forget it?

I couldn't.

I can't.

And I don't want to.

No matter how much this hurts.

It's strange. I've heard people talk about broken hearts before, but I never realized how much physical pain they brought with them. That was, until last Saturday morning, when she took my heart, ripped it from my chest, trampled all over it with just a few words, and left it broken… and me along with it.

I tried and tried to understand where I'd gone wrong. She may have confused the hell out of me, by asking what I was doing in her bed, and then turned everything on its head by saying we'd had sex, when what we'd done had been so much better than mere sex, but I wasn't giving up.

So, when she ran out of here, clutching my throw to her body, like I wasn't already familiar with every inch of her, I did the only thing I could.

I went after her.

Okay, so I didn't follow her into the bathroom.

That would have been weird.

But I pulled on my bathrobe and sat on the couch, waiting for her to come out.

Naturally, I realized I could have waited for her in the bedroom, but it didn't seem likely she'd return to the scene of the crime… as she no doubt saw it.

The living room was therefore my only option.

I heard her take a shower, trying not to think about one of my early morning fantasies of the two of us in there together, and I waited… and waited.

She came out eventually, a towel wrapped around her divine body, my throw still clutched in her arms, and I heard her slight gasp of surprise when she saw me. What did she expect? Did she think I'd just stay in my room and pretend nothing had happened?

It might have been what she wanted, but I couldn't do that.

Not when we so obviously needed to talk.

That was what I said to her… but it was like she wasn't listening, and I'll admit that made me mad. Not mad enough to do anything, but mad enough to resort to sarcasm. Although it didn't get me anywhere.

How could she not understand?

How could she not see?

What we'd done had meant something. No, it had meant everything… or it had to me. Except that was the moment I realized it had meant nothing to her. I'd meant nothing to her.

Even that moment when she put her hand on my chest meant nothing… not to her. It was just done to placate me. It was done to make a point… that it hadn't been personal.

I couldn't believe it when she said that.

How much more personal does it get than two people making love to each other?

Except we hadn't been making love, had we? Not in her eyes. We'd had sex.

That was what she said, and although I couldn't agree with her, for the first time in my life, I realized there was a difference.

I probably should have noticed it before. Hell… I've spent all my adult life having sex, so I should know better than anyone. Sex is a means to an end. It's a basic human need. Nothing more, nothing less.

What I discovered with Robyn is that making love is so much more. The most noticeable difference about being with her was that I craved her pleasure more than my own. I've never enjoyed a woman's orgasms as much as I did hers. Sure, I love bringing women off, but that's an ego thing. It's about proving I can when maybe other guys can't. This was different. Watching her come made me feel whole, and as I stood in the living room, gazing down into her perfect face, wishing I had the strength to pull away that flimsy towel and prove my point, I had a horrible feeling I might never feel whole again.

It wasn't a feeling I wanted to accept, but what choice did I have?

When the woman you've just spent the night with tells you she wants to forget it, you can't ask her to change her mind. It doesn't work like that, and in this case, the only unfortunate part is that I also happen to love her.

With every piece of my trampled, torn and shattered heart.

There's nothing I can do about that, although it hasn't made life easy since it happened.

Last weekend was the hardest. It was brutal. But I guess that was to be expected. After all, I'd made plans, and even if they were only in my head, the reality couldn't have been more different.

I couldn't face working out the menu and the shopping list with her, sitting at the breakfast bar over pancakes or bacon and eggs, or even just a cup of coffee, and pretending we were nothing more than roommates. That didn't seem possible to me. So, I did it by myself while she was up in her room.

Then, rather than leave her to go to the store by herself, I went.

To be honest, I wanted to escape for a while.

Everything was so different. Not just different to how it was before, but different from what I'd hoped for. The atmosphere between Robyn and me was stifling, and as I pushed the cart around the store, I couldn't help thinking that, if I'd been looking for casual sex, I'd have avoided it with a roommate, simply because it might have made things awkward afterwards. Except I wasn't looking for casual, was I? I was looking for forever. According to Clark, Robyn wanted the same thing… but evidently not with me, so what might have been merely awkward became utterly impossible.

The rejection was overwhelming, and while I've done my best to be polite, and I've cooked for her, and eaten meals with her, and even talked about our days at work together, I know I can't keep doing this.

Which is why I spent last night searching the Internet for somewhere else to live.

It was a fruitless search, as it seems there's nowhere I can afford in Hart's Creek, or Willmont Vale, or even Concord.

There's nowhere within driving distance of my job.

I was surprised by that. Surprised and disappointed. I need to get out of here, though, so I'll keep looking. It's the only way I'm going to survive.

In the meantime, though, there's nothing to be done, other than to get up and get on with things. Lying here with my own set of regrets won't achieve anything, and as it's still fairly early, I can be pretty sure Robyn won't have woken up yet.

I make my way to the bathroom, leaving my robe on the hook at the back of the door, and step into the shower, wishing Robyn could be in here with me. That's how it should be by now, because if things hadn't gone so wrong last Saturday, we'd have been together for a week by now, and showering together would have been an automatic process… like breathing.

My cock hardens at the thought of all the other things we could have spent the last seven days doing, but I ignore it, just like I have every other time this week, whenever such thoughts have crossed my mind… which is practically all the time. I know how good she is now, and thinking about her is second nature.

Like loving her.

I can't seem to stop doing either, no matter how hard I try.

I rinse off the shampoo and get out of the shower, wrapping a towel low around my hips and ignoring my hard-on as I brush my teeth, and then open the door, my breath catching in my throat when I see Robyn standing at the bottom of the stairs that lead up to her bedroom. For some reason, she's wearing nothing more than a practically see-through chemise, and my cock aches at the sight of her.

Has she done this to tempt me?

Why would she?

She's not interested in me. She made that very clear, and I shake my head, striding toward my room.

"Spencer?"

I stop in my tracks, struck by the sadness in her voice, and I turn to face her as she moves closer.

"What is it?" I ask, aware of how harsh my voice sounds.

She frowns. "I—I just wanted to say I'm sorry."

"What for?"

"The price of coffee? The weather? All of it."

She's throwing my sarcasm in my face, and while I can't blame her for that, I'm not the one who put us in this situation.

"I told you, it's okay."

"Except it's not, is it?"

I can't lie to her, and I shake my head. "No, it's not."

She sucks in a breath, then lets it out as she moves closer still, and out of self-preservation, I take a step back, hitting the wall behind me. I've got nowhere to go, and I'll admit, I feel a little exposed, standing here in nothing but a towel. She seems to appreciate that, too, and she lowers her eyes, tipping her head to one side. I can't read her... not properly, but before I can ask what she wants, she makes her intentions clear, putting her hands on my shoulders and jumping up into my arms. Catching her isn't an option. I'm never gonna let her fall, am I? But even so, I'm surprised when she wraps her legs around me, moves her hands up to cup my cheeks and kisses me. Hard.

My brain is screaming at me to pull back... to stop her. It's the logical thing to do. But logic doesn't matter. And how can I even think of stopping when she's everything I've ever wanted? Besides, this is our first kiss, and as her lips caress mine, my brain disengages. Thinking is too complicated. I settle for actions instead, and spin us around, so Robyn's back is against the wall. She squeals into my mouth, and I take advantage of the opportunity, my tongue discovering hers. I never expected her to yield, and she doesn't. She's more than my equal, our tongues colliding and clashing as she grinds and writhes against me, driving me crazy with need.

"Why?" I say, breaking the kiss. We're both breathless, but she stares into my eyes, looking confused. "Why are you doing this?"

"Because I want you."

"You do?"

"Yes." She nods her head, like she thinks she needs to confirm her spoken answer, and after what happened last weekend, she probably does.

"Are you sure?" I need to know, but rather than replying, she leans in again, and instead of the kiss I may have been expecting, she sucks on my bottom lip, and then bites it.

"What do you think?" she says, her eyes on fire.

"I think I need to hear you say the words."

She sucks in a breath. "I just did. I want you, Spence… okay?"

I'm 'Spence' again, and I nod my head. "Okay."

I turn and carry her into my room, heading straight for the bed, and once there, I lower her down my body and stare into her eyes for a moment. Is this really happening again? Should I let it? Do I even have an option? It seems not, as she reaches between us, and yanks away the towel, dropping to her knees. Her intentions are obvious, although I still let out a growl of pleasure when she takes me in her mouth, and recalling how much she liked it last time, I hold her head still and flex my hips.

She moans, looking straight up at me.

"Is that what you want?"

She nods, and I go a little deeper… a little faster. She may have made the first move – again – but I'm not being passive about this.

She wants me, and she's gonna get me.

Every fucking inch of me.

"Take my dick," I growl, wondering how much further I can go with this, although she surprises me, bringing her hands around behind me and placing them on my ass, so she can pull me in even deeper.

What the fuck? What's she doing to me?

Aside from making me lose my mind…

I pull back, releasing my cock from her mouth, and haul her to her feet. She licks her lips, biting the bottom one, and I study her beautiful face.

"Is this a tease?"

"No." She looks almost offended. "I've never been a tease."

"You want this?"

"Yes."

"You really want me?"

"I said so, didn't I?"

"I know. But I need to be sure."

"I. Want. You."

I can't mistake her meaning. No-one could.

"Then don't fuck with me, Robyn. Not this time."

She shakes her head, and I grab her chemise, pulling it off over her head before I lift her into my arms and drop her onto the bed. She gazes up at me as I lean over and place my fingers in the waistband of her tiny panties, lowering them down her thighs and discarding them over my shoulder.

She's breathing hard, her breasts heaving, and I grab a condom from the nightstand, rolling it over my cock before I crawl up over her. I could pin her to the bed, like I did the last time, but I'd rather do things differently, and I raise her legs, pulling them up toward her chest, holding them there, with my hands in the crooks of her knees as I lean over her, my cock finding her entrance, like it's the most natural thing in the world.

Why wouldn't it be? As far as I'm concerned, I'm home. I'm back where I belong.

She gasps as I enter her, and I give her a moment before I thrust all the way inside.

"Yes, Spence… Yes," she screams, slamming her clenched fists onto the mattress.

I love hearing my name on her lips like that, and I up the pace, hammering into her tight pussy, watching as she arches her back and tweaks her nipples, rubbing them between her thumbs and forefingers.

"Fuck… you're hot."

"I need you… please."

"You've got me." *I'm yours*.

I change the angle slightly, and her breath hitches, her thighs trembling, as her orgasm builds. I can feel the ebb and flow deep inside her. It would be easy to pull back… to tease her, and make her wait. But I need this as much as she does, and I don't let up… not even for a second, watching her as she stretches and curls into her climax. Her eyes don't leave mine, her voice catching in her throat, although eventually she cries out my name in a high-pitched squeal that drifts to the softest of whispers.

She takes a while to come back from that, but when she does, I pull out of her, taking care not to hurt her, and smiling at the disappointed look on her face.

"Where are you going?" she says. "We're not done yet, are we?"

"Hell, no. And I'm not going anywhere."

I release her legs, moving back slightly, and then flip her over onto her front. She yelps in surprise, and then moans her pleasure as I pull her up onto all fours, spanking her ass just a second before I slam back into her.

"Oh… I like that," she says.

"I thought you might."

She rocks back on to me, and I hold still, letting her do the work for a while. She seems to enjoy it, edging closer and closer, as she moans and sighs, her juices dripping down between us, onto the mattress.

"You like riding my cock?"

"I like doing anything with your cock," she says, looking at me over her shoulder.

"Finger your pussy. Make yourself come."

She doesn't hesitate, and balancing on one arm, she moves the other back beneath her. I can feel the movement of her fingers as she rubs her clit, and so that she can focus on what she's doing, I grab her hips, holding her still, and hammer in to her.

"More," she breathes between gritted teeth. "Give me more."

I do as she asks, and push her down, so her shoulders are touching the mattress, then move from a kneeling position to a squatting one. I part my legs, getting closer to her, my feet flat on the bed as I lean over her raised ass, giving her my entire length with every deep thrust.

"Fuck," she screams. "Fuck, Spence… you're gonna make me…"

Her words are lost as her body spasms through another shuddering orgasm, this one going on even longer than the last, and all the way through, I give her my cock, urging her on, although as she calms, I slow the pace, reining it back in before I lean right over her, drop to my knees, and carefully tip us onto our sides, her back to my front.

"That was so good," she murmurs, catching her breath.

"It's not over yet."

She twists her head, looking up at me, and I lean in, my lips hovering over hers for a second before I kiss her. As I do, I raise her leg and flex my hips, making her moan into my mouth, and while our tongues dance, our bodies sway, back and forth, both of us on the same journey. We take our time getting there, wrapped in each other, until eventually, I can't take anymore.

"I need you to come," I whisper, breaking our kiss.

"I'm not sure I can."

"You must."

I hook her leg over my hip and lower my hand, my fingers playing across her clit. She startles at my touch, but as I circle around her, rubbing harder and harder, she arches her back, writhing in to me.

"Oh, God… your touch, Spence… it's so good."

"You like that?"

"Yes. Don't stop. Please don't stop."

"I won't."

With a guttural cry, she comes apart, barely in control as she tightens around my cock, and I plunge deep inside her.

My roar fills the room as I fill her, holding her body tight against mine.

It seems impossible, but that was even better than last time, and as I slowly come down from that incredible high, I have to tell her.

"You're the best, Robyn." She doesn't move, or make a sound, other than drawing air into her lungs, and to give her a chance to recover, I pull back. "I need the bathroom," I say, and she nods her head. It seems that's all she's capable of, which makes me smile, and as I gently slide out of her, I kiss her neck, slowly working my way up to her ear, where I whisper, "I won't be long."

I get up, glancing back at her, although she doesn't move a muscle, her body prone on the bed, which feels like the best place for her to be, and rather than waste time, I hurry to the bathroom, dispose of the condom, wash up and rush back, my heart sinking when I enter the room and find she's standing by the side of the bed. Not only that, but she's pulled on her chemise.

Already?

"Why do I feel like I've been here before?" I say, taking a step forward.

She doesn't reply, but picks up her panties, holding them in her hand. I do my best not to look at her body, which is clearly visible through the sheer fabric of her chemise, and just focus on her face. She stares at a spot just above my head, which I imagine is to avoid looking at my hard-on… although I hate the fact that she can't even look me in the eye after everything we've just done.

Again.

"I'm sorry," she says. "I shouldn't have let that happen."

"Did you? Did you let it happen? Or did you instigate it?"

She blinks, lowering her eyes, looking at my chest now. "Does it matter?"

"Of course it fucking matters."

"Well… either way, we've got to stop doing it."

"I didn't."

She frowns, glancing up at my face again, just for a second. "You weren't exactly an idle participant, Spencer."

"Can you decide what you wanna call me? I'm either Spencer, your roommate, or I'm Spence, your lover. I don't think I can be both."

"No-one's asking you to be."

"And the fact that you've just called me Spencer is the big clue, is it? That's supposed to tell me where I stand?"

She lets out a long sigh. "This isn't practical."

What's that supposed to mean? Is it even an answer?

"Is sex meant to be practical?" I ask, hoping she might give me something to work with.

"Maybe not… but that's not my point."

"Then what is?" I say. "I can't even see why there's a problem."

"I can."

"Then explain it to me."

"This isn't what I want," she says, her shoulders dropping, and I feel my blood chill.

"It's not what you want?"

"No."

"But I asked you. I asked if it was what you wanted. You said yes."

"I—I know."

"I asked you several times, Robyn. You said you wanted me."

"I know I did, but…"

"But you've changed your mind again. Is that it? Or do you think it's fair to keep starting something you've got no intention of seeing through?"

"We did see it through." Her voice is so quiet, I can barely hear it, but I make out her words and shake my head.

"You think?"

She looks into my eyes at last, and although the light from the window is behind her, I wonder if hers are glistening, and if that means she might cry. I hope not, because if she does, I'll have to hold her… and then God only knows what will happen.

"I'm sorry," she says, her voice a lot stronger than I'd expected. I guess I was wrong about that glistening in her eyes, then.

"That's where I came in, isn't it?" She frowns, clearly confused. "You started this with an apology, and it looks like you're ending it with one, too."

She nods her head, and runs from the room, barely giving me time to duck out of the way.

I think about going after her, but what would be the point? She's said everything she needs to say. Regardless of what we've done – again – she doesn't want me. She doesn't want this.

She might have said she did, but she doesn't.

No matter how much I want her, it'll never be.

So, I guess all I need to do is accept that, and pick up the pieces of my broken heart… again.

Chapter Eleven

Robyn

In an ideal world, I'd spend the rest of the day hiding in my room. Unfortunately, I still have to shower, and of course, I have to eat, so hiding isn't an option.

I wait for at least thirty minutes, but my need for the bathroom soon overcomes even my embarrassment at the prospect of facing Spencer again, and grabbing my robe this time, I make my way down the stairs.

He must have had the same idea, as there's no sign of him, although whether he's hiding, or just avoiding me, I can't be sure. Either way, the place is eerily quiet, and I dart into the bathroom, relieved to lock the door behind me.

Safe in the knowledge he's already showered, I feel free to take my time, wondering what on earth possessed me to repeat my sins.

The answer to that is obvious.

I want Spencer like I want to breathe. He's like an itch I can't scratch.

But do I really need to keep acting on that?

Can't I show a little more self-control?

The sight of him wearing nothing more than a towel may have been too tempting for words, but I'm a grown woman. I should know better.

And I certainly should have thought about the consequences.

Except I didn't think, did I?

And now I'm paying the price.

So is Spencer, of course. I can't forget that.

This isn't just about me. It's about both of us.

I shake my head. That makes us sound like a couple, and we're not, although there's no denying my actions have consequences for him as well as me, which means I can't let it happen again. I really can't.

I have to find a way to stop myself, regardless of how much I want him, and how tempting he is.

I have to find a way to resist.

I step out of the shower, feeling less refreshed than I should, and dry myself off, pulling on my bathrobe before I brush my teeth.

There's no reason for me to be in here anymore, but I'm a little nervous about going outside. That may sound silly, but I'm not sure I can face Spencer right now. Even so, I can't hide forever, can I?

I open the door, my heart sinking when I see him sitting at the breakfast bar. He's got his back to me, but I notice how his muscles tense. He must be aware of me, although he doesn't say a word and simply lifts his coffee cup to his lips as I walk past.

This is horrible.

If anything, the atmosphere is even worse than it was before, although I don't know why that surprises me.

I've made things more complicated. And I've hurt him… or at least his ego. Again.

I hurry to my room, pulling the curtain closed, and although I'd usually dry my hair first, I quickly pull on some underwear, jeans and a top. I don't know why, but I feel safer being dressed.

Safer?

What am I saying?

Spencer's done nothing to make me feel uneasy, has he?

If anything, it's the other way around.

But I suppose I'm aware there's nothing more than a curtain between us, and that if I'm going to resist, I need something stronger than that… because I have no such strength myself.

Once I've dried my hair and made my bed, I reason it must be safe to go back downstairs. Spencer can't still be sitting there, can he?

Surely not.

I open the curtain and make my way down, sighing out my disappointment when I see he hasn't moved a muscle. Except rather than sipping his coffee, he's scribbling on a notepad.

I guess he must be working out the menu for the coming week, which is fair enough, and although it would be easier to go back upstairs, I need coffee… and food, so I wander over.

There's an empty plate beside him, which I guess means he's already eaten, and unwilling to spend too long in the kitchen, I simply pour myself a coffee and grab a blueberry muffin from the cabinet. It's not the ideal breakfast, but it's late, and I'm hungry.

"I'll work out the list and go shopping," he says, his voice taking me by surprise, and I spin around, almost spilling my coffee.

"I should go. You've been for the last two weeks."

He looks up, his eyes filled with something that looks like sorrow… sorrow that's entirely my responsibility, and I step closer, although he leans back in his seat, which I guess is his way of letting me know he's not comfortable with me getting into his space. I heed that and step away again.

"I don't mind," he says.

"No. Honestly. I'll…"

"Fine," he says, raising his voice just slightly and halting our conversation as he tears off the top sheet from the notepad to write the list on the one beneath.

I take the chance and glance down at what he's got planned, and can't help noticing a change from our usual meals.

"This is all casseroles and curries, and…"

"And things I can prepare, but that we don't have to eat together," he says, explaining himself. "You can't cook well enough yet to survive by yourself, but I can leave yours in the pan and you can help yourself whenever you like."

"We're eating separately, are we?"

"I think it's for the best." He stops writing and looks up at me, that sadness even deeper than it was before. "I'll be honest, I think it would be better still if I moved out."

"M—Moved out?" I put down my cup before I drop it.

"Yes. I'd already started looking for somewhere else to live, but after what just happened between us, I think it's even more important, don't you?"

I want to say 'no', but I keep quiet, stepping closer, and although he doesn't lean back this time, I can sense he's not comfortable. "You're already looking?"

"Yes."

"Is that because of what happened last Saturday?"

"You know it is."

"Then it should be me who leaves, not you. I'm the one who caused the problem." There's no point in trying to pretend otherwise, although he shakes his head, surprising me.

"I can't afford this place on my own," he says, making his meaning clear. He's not absolving me of responsibility. He's just explaining. "Even with my promotion, I don't make enough for somewhere like this. Unfortunately, there isn't anything smaller available at the moment, but I'll keep looking, and in the meantime, I guess we'll just have to get by."

He sounds so resigned. "I'm sorry," I whisper.

"You've apologized enough already," he says as he gets down from his chair, grabbing the pad. "I'll finish this in my room."

Before I can say a word to stop him, he's gone, darting into his bedroom and pulling the door closed behind him.

I feel overwhelmed with guilt… not just that he's thinking of leaving, but that he wants nothing to do with me. That's how it feels… and I guess I can't blame him for that. Not after everything I've done.

The grocery store was horribly busy, but at least that meant I didn't have much time to think. I was too busy trying to grab everything on the list and dodge other people. And that was probably a good thing. I knew if I thought too hard about what I'd done, I'd probably break… and I didn't want to do that in public.

By the time I got back, I was exhausted, but determined to carry everything up to the apartment by myself, even though Spencer offered. He accepted my refusal without an argument, and left me to unpack, obviously wanting to be anywhere but with me, given the choice.

I had to allow him that. Our situation was entirely my fault, after all, and once I was finished, I called out to him that I'd be upstairs, and went up to my room, where I spent the rest of the afternoon.

I didn't wallow too much, but read a book instead, unable to really think straight.

I knew he'd be making a chicken curry, the smells wafting up to my room late in the afternoon, reminding me how hungry I was. I could hear him moving around, and the clatter of silverware and china. Was he eating by himself? I couldn't be sure, and I wasn't brave enough to go down and find out. So I waited… and eventually, he called out that my dinner was there for me, whenever I was ready.

It seemed a little petty to me that he wouldn't let us eat together, but I could hardly argue, and I went downstairs where, sure enough, my delicious curry awaited. There was no sign of Spencer, though. His bowl, glass and silverware had all been cleared into the dishwasher, and the man himself was nowhere to be seen.

I'd made things so much worse by my actions, but I couldn't think what to do. He didn't want my apologies, and by the time I climbed into bed last night, I was surprised by how upset I was about that. Like anyone in the wrong, I wanted forgiveness… and yet Spencer wasn't even giving me the chance.

It shouldn't have mattered, should it? His forgiveness shouldn't have meant a thing to me.

And yet it did.

It still matters today, and after a morning spent in my room avoiding him, my loneliness only interrupted by a brief call from my mother, I can't face any more. I have to get out of here.

I pull on a sweater and some sneakers, checking out the window to make sure it's not going to rain. It doesn't look like it will, so hopefully I'll be okay, and I head down the stairs, surprised to find Spencer in the kitchen. He's putting a cup in the dishwasher and doesn't notice me until I tell him I'm going out.

He spins around, confusion etched on his face.

"Out?"

"Yes. You've made it clear you think we should put some distance between us, and we can't stay cooped up in our rooms all day… or I can't. So I'm going out."

"Would you rather I went instead?" he says.

"No. It's fine."

I turn, leaving the apartment before he can say anything else. There's no point in debating this… or anything else, and once

I'm outside, I suck in a lungful of fresh air before I head along the track, noticing there's a break in the trees. I have no idea what's on the other side, but I make my way over, and step through onto a rough pathway that leads down to a fast-flowing stream.

I guess this must be the creek from which the town gets its name, and I turn to the left, unsure where the path will take me, and whether I even care.

It's peaceful here, and just what I need to clear my head.

Except I can't.

Because my thoughts and feelings keep getting in the way.

I can't seem to turn them off, no matter how hard I try, and after a little while, I stop trying, and give in to them, letting them wash over me.

I've never felt like this before, and I honestly don't know what I'm doing.

I think that much is obvious.

My experience with men may be limited, but no-one I've ever been with has made me feel like Spencer does. When I'm with him, I feel alive, happy, needed, wanted, desired… and in any other circumstances, my reactions to him would be so different.

They'd certainly be a lot more reasonable… and a lot more rational.

He may give me all those things, and we may be good together, but we're too different to make it work. I know we are, even if he won't admit it. Which I guess makes my behavior even worse.

How can I justify the fact that I keep instigating sex with him?

At least when I did it the first time, I had the excuse of being a little lightheaded… and, of course, he'd come back early from his date, looking sexy as hell, fueling my fantasies as only he can.

Like I said to him at the time, though, I wasn't so drunk I didn't know what I was doing, but there was at least alcohol involved… unlike yesterday.

That was entirely me.

It was entirely my fault, too.

I saw him standing there, wearing nothing but a towel, and for some reason, my brain disengaged. All the reasons to stay away from him just evaporated, and I couldn't think about anything other than reliving that fantasy.

Except it wasn't a fantasy, was it?

It was a reality… one I'd created.

It was like being possessed.

There was nothing I could do about it, and although he gave me enough chances to back out, I didn't take any of them. Not one.

Because I wanted him. Again.

And who can blame me?

Wanting Spencer is completely understandable, as any woman he's been with would probably testify.

But that's part of the problem, I guess.

He's the kind of man who'll always want to find out what the next woman has to offer.

And while there's nothing wrong with that, it's not what I'm looking for.

Which means he was right. I should never have started something with him in the first place.

It was wrong of me. But now it's happened, I feel so… so cheap.

Tears fill my eyes, and I sit down beside a large boulder, leaning back against it, as I let them fall. I wish now that I'd brought some tissues with me, as I can't seem to stop crying. The guilt and sorrow are overwhelming, and even as I cover my face with my hands, I know there's no hiding from what I've done. I have to make it right… and if Spencer doesn't want to hear my apologies, then the only option I have is to move out.

Spencer may have said he can't afford to keep the apartment by himself, but I could wait until he finds someone to take my place, and then leave, couldn't I? It seems only fair. After all, why should he have to go because of something I've done?

I've got no idea where I'd move to, but there must be somewhere… not that it matters right now. The priority is to find someone who can move in with Spencer. I can worry about everything else later.

My tears dry themselves, and before they start up again, I head for home. It's getting cooler out here, and I need to talk to Spencer, even if he doesn't want to talk to me.

When I get back, he's in the kitchen, slicing an onion, and I go straight over to him, waiting until he turns to face me, which takes a lot longer than it would have done a couple of weeks ago. Back then, he'd have greeted me the moment I walked in the door. We'd have been doing this together, too… or to be more precise, he'd have been showing me what to do, and we'd have been enjoying ourselves a lot more than either of us is right now.

As it is, he puts down his knife and looks at me, his brow furrowing as he tips his head to one side.

"Have you been crying?" he asks.

I hadn't expected that, but there's no point in lying. I imagine my eyes are puffy, and my nose is probably swollen and red, too. "Yes."

He turns, moving closer. "Is that my fault?"

How can he think that? "No. It's mine. What I did yesterday was wrong."

He sighs, stepping back again. "I think you already said that… more than once."

"I know, but I just wanted to assure you, it won't happen again. I was out of line, and I'm… well, I'm sorry." He doesn't say a word in response, but just continues to stare at me. "I—I also wanted to say, I've decided I should be the one to move out."

"You can't," he says, folding his arms across his chest. "I've already explained…"

"I know, but I thought that if we advertised for someone to take my room, then I could look for somewhere of my own."

He takes a moment, clearly thinking about my suggestion, and then pushes his fingers back through his hair. "If that's what you want," he says, and turns away, picking up the knife again, so he can continue chopping the onion.

I feel dismissed, and although I don't think we've achieved anything, I can't make him talk.

I can't stay around here all evening, either, so once I get up to my room, I pull out my phone and connect a call to Jodie.

We've never spoken on the phone before, and she seems surprised to hear from me.

"Is everything okay?" she asks.

"Not really. I wondered if you felt like going out for dinner with me tonight."

"Um… sure. Why not? We can go to the French restaurant on Main Street, if you like?"

"Would you mind if we went to the hotel instead?" I can't bear the thought of sitting in the same place I sat with Spencer, knowing how I've ruined everything between us.

"Not at all," she says. "I'll meet you there at six-thirty?"

"Perfect."

We end our call and I check the time, realizing I've only got just over an hour to get ready. I'm unsure what to wear, not knowing if the hotel is formal, and take a while before deciding on black pants and a cream-colored sweater. That should work either way, and once I'm dressed, I fix my makeup and put my hair up into a loose bun behind my head. I wouldn't normally worry about it, but I feel a little windswept after my walk this afternoon, and putting it up is easier than washing and drying it again.

I've allowed myself a few minutes to walk to the hotel, and once I'm ready, I pull on my coat and make my way down the stairs. There's no sign of Spencer, but I don't feel as though I can just leave, so I call out to him, and he pulls open his bedroom door, standing on the threshold as he leans against the doorframe, staring at me.

"I'm going out," I say, even though that must be obvious.

"At this time of night?"

"Yes. I'm meeting someone for dinner."

He takes a deep breath, his eyes wandering over me for a moment before he nods his head.

"Fine," he says, and then he steps back inside his room, closing the door.

I can't think what to say, but as he's not here, I don't need to worry, and rather than make myself late, I go down the stairs and let myself out.

The walk to the hotel takes no time at all, although Jodie's here before me and is waiting outside.

"We didn't say where we'd meet," she says. "So it seemed best to stay out here."

I nod my head and lead the way inside, although I let her guide us to the restaurant, as I don't know where I'm going.

As we pass through the doors, we come face-to-face with a man in a black suit and bow tie, his attire making me wonder if I should have made more of an effort with my outfit. Still, he doesn't seem worried, and smiles and nods his head at us.

"Good evening, ladies. Can I help?"

"Um… I hope so. We haven't made a reservation," I say, realizing the error of my ways.

"You need a table for two?"

"If you have one."

"I'm sure we can do something." He glances around the room, which is large, with dim lighting, and an annoyingly romantic atmosphere. It's also alarmingly busy, and he takes a moment before he glances back in our direction. "Would you like to follow me?"

I nod my head and smile at Jodie, who seems just as relieved as I am as we let the man guide us toward the back of the room, where he stops by a table near the window. It overlooks a terrace, and beyond that there's a view of some hills in the distance.

We both remove our coats and take our seats, the man waiting until we're settled before he leans in and says, "Flynn will be your waiter for this evening."

"Okay. Thanks." I look up at him, nodding my head, and he scurries away again.

"We should have made a reservation," Jodie says.

"That's my fault, not yours. I invited you."

"Well… we won't worry about it. We're here now."

We both open our menus, studying them for a moment. "I don't feel like having an appetizer," she says. "Not now I've seen the stuffed baked haddock."

I glance down, discovering that it comes with a lemon herb butter, although immediately below it on the list is something that really catches my eye.

"Oh… I don't know. I like the sound of the ginger and sesame crusted salmon."

"No, I'm sticking with the haddock."

We both close our menus at the same time, just as a young man appears beside us. He glances at me, but then turns his attention to Jodie, his eyes widening slightly. She has the same reaction, twisting in her seat, and staring up at him. I can't say I blame her. He's certainly handsome, in a blond-haired, blue-eyed kind of way, which has never appealed to me, although Jodie doesn't seem to mind one bit. In fact, it seems the two of them are impressed with what they see, and it takes a full minute before the man remembers why he's here.

"C—Can I take your order?" he says.

"Sure," Jodie says before I can. "I'd like the haddock, please, and my friend wants the salmon."

He nods his head, tapping on the screen of the tablet he's holding.

"You don't want appetizers?"

"No, thanks."

"And to drink?"

We didn't think about that, and I'm about to open the menu again, when Jodie leans even closer to the man, who I remember is called Flynn.

"What would you recommend?"

"With fish? We've got a nice Pinot Grigio. It's pretty good value for money, and most people seem to like it."

"You've never tried it yourself?" Jodie asks.

"I haven't been working here long enough to have tried all the wines," he says, giving her a smile, which she returns, the two of them staring at each other again, until he remembers to take our menus, and gives me a very brief nod of his head before departing.

Jodie gazes after him for a moment, and then turns to me. "Man… things are definitely looking up around here."

I chuckle. "You're pleased I called, are you?"

"You could say that. I was starting to despair of this place."

"What about the guy you went home with from the bar the other night?" I ask, doing my best to forget how that evening ended for me.

"Neil, you mean?"

"Was that his name?"

"Yeah… and let's just say he didn't live up to expectations."

"Oh."

She shakes her head. "I've yet to meet a man who does."

"But you think Flynn might?"

"I hope so… although you didn't invite me here to discuss my sex life, did you? I got the feeling you needed to talk."

"I might have done."

"Do you want to elaborate? Or do you need a drink first?"

"I think I'd better at least start my story while I'm sober. Drinking too much doesn't seem to work very well for me."

She tilts her head to one side. "Okay… now I really need to know what's been going on."

I fill her in on the events of the last week or so, from that drunken 'thank you' kiss after our evening at the bar, to yesterday's mind-blowing sex, grateful that Flynn is taking his time with the wine, although he returns just as I finish telling her what happened yesterday morning… without going into too much detail, of course.

He gives Jodie the chance to taste the wine, and as she seems happy with it, he tops up both of our glasses, leaving the bottle in a wine cooler at the side of our table.

She sighs, watching him leave again, and then returns her attention to me.

"You say you rejected Spencer after the first time?"

"I didn't reject him… not as such. I just told him it shouldn't have happened, and it wouldn't be happening again."

"Which sounds like rejection to me… but then you threw yourself at the guy a week later?"

"I know," I say, shaking my head.

"Why?" she asks. "If you didn't enjoy it the first time, why do it again?"

"Who says I didn't enjoy it?"

She frowns. "Are you saying you did?"

"Oh God, yes."

"In that case, you've got me confused. Why did you tell him it couldn't happen again? Or shouldn't happen again, or whatever it was?"

"Because he's not right for me, and I'm not right for him. I heard him talking to Clark, and they made it clear Spencer's not the kind of man who's looking to settle down."

"And that's what you want, is it?" she asks.

"Yes."

She sucks in a breath, staring at me for a moment, although it's not a judgmental stare. She's not about to tell me I'm crazy. I can tell that just from the look in her eyes. "Okay," she says eventually. "But if you knew all that, why did you repeat the same mistake?"

"Because it was hard to regard it as a mistake when he was standing in front of me wearing nothing more than a towel."

She takes a sip of wine, gazing across the table at me. "Are you sure you regret it?"

"No. I may have told Spencer I did, but I didn't… and now I'm not sure about anything. Except that I'm confused about how I feel, and I'm ashamed of what I've done, and I'm sorry I've hurt him."

"You've hurt him?"

"Yes."

"How do you know?"

"I don't for certain, but he's said some things that have made me wonder."

"Well, don't beat yourself up. It's probably just a male pride thing."

"No, I think it's more than that. Why else would he say he was gonna move out of the apartment?"

"He's gonna move? Because you slept with him? Twice?"

"Because I rejected him twice. He asked me not to fuck with him the second time. I could hear the emotion in his voice, and I said I wouldn't… and then promptly did."

"I see."

"So, I've told him I should be the one to go, not him. It's only fair when he was there before me, and when this was all my fault, but…"

"You don't wanna go?"

"Not really."

"Because you like the apartment, or because you like Spencer?"

I think about that for a moment. "There's nothing special about the apartment."

"Then it's him you want to stay for?"

"How can it be? We don't want the same things."

"Are you sure about that? It seems to me you might want exactly the same things."

"No, we don't. Even back home, when I trying to find my prince and was into kissing a few more frogs than I am now, I was never into guys who play the field like Spencer."

"That's not what I meant."

"But you just said…"

"I know what I said, but you misunderstood what I meant."

"Did I?"

"Yes. Has it occurred to you that he might be the prince in all this? Have you thought that he might care about you?"

"Don't be ridiculous."

"What's so ridiculous about it? You said yourself how hurt he was. I don't think it's possible to hurt someone who doesn't care."

She has a point, but I shake my head. "No. It's not like that. It's male pride… just like you said."

"You don't believe that, so stop kidding yourself. No matter what Spencer said to Clark, or Clark said to Spencer, I think you're wrong about him. I wouldn't be at all surprised if it turns out he wants exactly the same things as you do."

Chapter Twelve

>>><<<

Spencer

I thought it was bad enough the first time, but now it's so much worse. Seeing Robyn every day hurts me to my bones, because I know I'll never watch her come again. Hearing her voice breaks my heart, because I know I've heard her scream my name for the last time.

And yet, being without her is so much harder.

I miss her every time we're apart, and since last weekend, that's been practically all the time.

Why?

Because every time I'm near her I'm reminded of what I've lost, and whenever we try to talk, it goes wrong.

That's my fault, not hers.

My reactions to her aren't what they should be.

I'm putting that down to self-preservation… a fear of letting her get close enough to do any more damage, because the truth is, this woman could break me.

She'd already come close enough on Saturday, but on Sunday, when she returned from her walk, I honestly thought there was no way back.

She'd so clearly been crying, and I couldn't think how to react. My head, my heart and every fiber of my being were screaming out at me to hold her, to clasp her to my body and tell her, whatever was wrong, we could work it out. But she didn't want me, did she? What she wanted was to tell me she'd decided to move out.

I didn't know why that had made her cry, but in the end it didn't matter.

It was just another thing to add to the list of many things I don't understand.

We're not meant to be together… not in her eyes, and now she can't wait to leave.

That said, neither of us has done anything about it since the weekend. But we've hardly spoken since then, either. We've gone out of our way to avoid each other. In my case, it's for the reasons already given; self preservation and a desire not to break in front of her. For Robyn? Who knows? I guess she doesn't want to be reminded of what we've done. Or the mistakes she's made.

It wasn't a mistake as far as I'm concerned. By which I mean, the act itself wasn't a mistake. I loved every second of what we did together, even if the aftermath wasn't what I'd hoped for.

Would I do it again?

I don't think I could… not without knowing what the outcome would be.

Because I know I wouldn't survive a third rejection.

Not like this.

Still, it doesn't look like I'll get the chance.

Despite her tears, she went out on Sunday night. She let me know she was going, and when I came out from my bedroom, I'll admit I was surprised. I hadn't expected to find her at the bottom of the stairs, looking so lovely.

Don't get me wrong, she looks lovely all the time, but she looked especially lovely on Sunday, in black pants and a tight-fitting cream-colored sweater. She'd put her hair up, too, leaving just a few loose strands framing her perfectly made-up face, and it took all my strength to keep my distance.

Which I had to, of course… because the fact that she'd arranged to go out made her feelings clear enough. It's not me she wants. I didn't need to be told.

She wants whoever she was going to dinner with.

She didn't tell me the guy's name, and I didn't ask.

It was bad enough to know she was going, but there was always a chance he might have been someone I'm familiar with. He could have been a colleague from work, or someone I know from around the town, and the last thing I needed was to spend my evening picturing the two of them together. To be fair, it could have been worse. At least she didn't bring him home afterwards, and she was back by about nine-thirty. I heard her come in, and went out into the living room just in time to see her go up the stairs to her room… all by herself.

I was grateful for that.

I couldn't have coped with having to picture the two of them together, writhing on her bed… Robyn begging him for more, and giving herself to him.

It would have been too much for me to bear.

But I was spared that agony, and we spent the rest of the evening alone, in our rooms.

We've done everything alone ever since, too… dodging each other in the mornings, one of us having breakfast while the other takes a shower, and we've eaten separately every night. I know that was my idea, but it felt like a good one at the time. I couldn't expect her to fend for herself when she can barely boil water, but I also wasn't sure how I felt about sitting right beside her, pretending everything's okay, when it's not.

The problem is, eating alone, and knowing she's just upstairs, has been just as bad.

I even called her down on Wednesday evening, just after I'd sat down to eat, rather than waiting until I'd finished, in the hope she'd stay there with me, and maybe we could talk. Not about us, obviously. That would never have worked. But it would have been good to clear the air.

Except she took her food up to her room.

For me, that was the final straw. Short of putting it in writing that she wanted nothing more to do with me, I couldn't think how she could have made it more obvious.

Whatever we had – if we had anything at all – it's over.

Which I suppose must be why I've arranged to go out tonight.

I don't really want to. What I want is to spend some time with Robyn. Despite all our problems and misunderstandings, I can't help wanting her. I can't help loving her. It's not something I can just unlearn… and I have no idea how I'm supposed to put these thoughts and feelings behind me. But I have to try, because there's no point in pretending things are going to work out between us.

Besides, it's Friday night. Work has been a little crazy this week, and I feel like getting out of the apartment. Obviously, I'd rather do that with Robyn. I'd rather gaze across a table at her than at anyone else, but as that's not going to happen, I'd prefer not to be here.

I'll be better if I don't have to look at her. At least I think I will. I don't see how I can feel any worse.

And I'd rather not know if she's going out with someone else. It's possible. She could be seeing the guy she saw on Sunday night… and if that's the case, ignorance is bliss as far as I'm concerned.

Because knowing would kill me.

I get home a little early, simply because it's Friday, I'm in charge of the department, and we've had a rough week. Telling everyone to go home thirty minutes ahead of schedule is one of the perks of being the boss. There's nothing that can't wait until Monday, and we've all earned a break.

Everyone seemed grateful for my decision, and as they packed away their things and ran out the door, they were all keen to wish me a good weekend. I returned the favor, unsure how I felt about the prospect of spending the next couple of days in the apartment, but knowing that at least for tonight, I'd made plans to escape.

Getting back early has given me a chance to shower before Robyn comes home. Was that my motive in letting everyone leave early? I don't think so… although I guess it could have been at the back of my mind. She told me what she'd done on Saturday morning was out of line, and it wouldn't happen again, but I still think it's for the best if we steer clear of each other… especially when one of us might not be wearing too much.

I'm not saying she wouldn't be able to resist. I'm not that bigheaded.

But things are difficult enough between us already. I'm not looking to make them any harder.

As it is, I'm already dressed and am just putting my phone and wallet into my jacket pocket when she comes up the stairs.

She stops at the top, pulling off her coat, and looks across the room at me, her eyes wandering lazily up and down my body. There's a certain hunger in her eyes, but I ignore that, knowing better than to react, and grab my keys from the coffee table.

"Are you going out?" she asks.

"Yes."

She nods her head. "Anywhere nice?"

"Just the French restaurant."

She frowns, her eyes betraying something that looks a little like remorse, and for a moment, I wonder if she's recalling the night we went there together. That feels like a lifetime ago, but I guess a lot has happened since then.

A lot has changed, too.

I had hope back then.

Hope that something might happen between me and Robyn, and while it has, none of it has panned out how I'd have liked.

"Are you going with anyone in particular?" she asks.

Part of me wants to tell her it's none of her business. I didn't ask who she was seeing on Sunday night, did I? Except that was because I knew there was every chance I wouldn't like her answer, or the way it would make me feel. She doesn't have the same emotional attachment. And besides, I can't be rude to her.

"I'm taking Ruth."

"Who's Ruth?"

"She's the receptionist at one of the companies in the industrial area."

"Is she a friend of yours?" she asks.

"No. I've seen her around, and thought I'd ask her to have dinner with me." *Because you're not interested*.

She nods her head, turning away and heading for the stairs up to her room, but then she stops and looks back. "You seemed confused about why we couldn't be together… about why I said we weren't right for each other."

"Yes." I can't deny that, although I don't appreciate her reminding me.

"Well… this is why."

What the fuck?

I move closer, and as she puts her foot on the bottom step, I grab her arm. "That doesn't make the slightest bit of sense, Robyn."

"Why not?"

"Because it doesn't." She pulls free of me, but I'm not giving up, and I join her on the bottom step, looking down at her upturned face. God... I love her. At times like this I wish I didn't, but I do. I can't help myself.

"You're gonna need to give me more than that," she says, and I remember why we're here. It's not so we can stand, staring at each other, while I wish there could be more to us than there is. It's because she's expecting an explanation... of sorts.

"Why is it okay for you to date and not me?" I say, stating the obvious, although she seems confused by my reply.

"Date?" she says, her brow furrowing. That look is really cute on her, and it makes me want to kiss her more than ever.

"Yes," I say, stepping back slightly, for my own benefit. "You went out on Sunday night."

"I know I did... with Jodie from work. We had dinner at the hotel."

"Jodie?"

"Yes. I called and asked if she'd meet me. I needed some time away from here... and from you."

I move down off of the step, clenching my fists to disguise the pain in my chest, or to distract myself from it, anyway. "Away from me?"

"Yes. Why? Did you think I was with another man?" I'm still recovering... still trying to breathe, so I'm not thinking straight when I nod my head, and she steps down to my level, her hands on her hips as she glares up at me. "Thanks. For your information, I haven't dated anyone since I moved here."

"No, but you've slept with me... twice. Or to be more accurate, you've fucked me... twice. And you regretted it."

I shouldn't have said that. I'm only hitting out at her because I'm hurt, and because I misjudged her. My assumptions about last Sunday were misplaced, and I feel guilty about that.

"That doesn't mean I slept with someone else – or fucked anyone else – within a few hours... or even a few days," she says, her voice dropping to a whisper. "It doesn't mean I've dated anyone else, either."

"Maybe not, but you weren't the one being told everything we'd done was a mistake. You don't want me, Robyn. I've got that message loud and clear. Hell, you've practically shouted your regrets from the rooftops… and yet it seems you're criticizing me for going on a date with another woman. Why the fuck shouldn't I?"

"No reason," she says, shaking her head and squaring her shoulders. "And I'm not saying you shouldn't go. I'm just telling you it's the reason we're incompatible."

"Oh… is that what we are?"

"Yes."

I move closer to her… close enough that I can see when her breath hitches in her throat, watch her pulse flicker in her neck, and feel the heat from her body seeping into mine. My lips are only a couple of inches from hers, and she lowers her gaze, staring at them for a moment before she looks up into my eyes again.

"You really think we're incompatible?" I say.

"Yes, I do."

"Then you're wrong. I've never met anyone with whom I'm more compatible." I step closer still, so my body's pressed against hers, and although she gasps, she doesn't step away. "I want you, Robyn, more than I've ever wanted anyone in my life… but that's a one-way street, isn't it? You may have seduced me on both occasions that we've been together, but I'm not the man for you. That's what you keep telling me… when you're not grinding on my cock, that is. Or screaming my name while you come on my tongue, or lying beneath me writhing in ecstasy." She bites her bottom lip, although I ignore her reaction, and the effect it has on me. "The thing is, you've got me so I don't know which was is up anymore, and I'm done being played by you. So, if you don't mind, I'm gonna spend a little time with someone who doesn't mess with my head quite so much."

I step around her and run down the stairs, regardless of how tempted I am to stay. Because staying would be a mistake… for both of us. She had that look in her eyes. It's the same look she had right before she jumped up into my arms the other morning. I know what that means, and I know what happens afterwards, and no matter how tempted I am, I can't go there again.

I wasn't lying when I said I want her. I can't imagine a moment in my life when I won't want her.

But what does that even mean?

Nothing, evidently… because we both want different things.

That's what she said. And maybe she's right.

I want a lifetime of happiness… of comfort and laughter, and love, all of which I know I can find with Robyn.

The problem is, even though I think she wants the same things, she doesn't want them with me.

Chapter Thirteen

Robyn

Even before I hear the door slam shut, I'm overwhelmed with guilt… again.

Why did I say all that? I shouldn't have interfered. I had no right.

He can see whoever he wants. He's a free agent, and what he does on a Friday night – or any other night, for that matter – has nothing to do with me.

So why did I ask? Why did I make that stupid remark about him dating someone else being the reason we couldn't be together?

I'm the reason we can't be together… not him, or any part of him, or the way he lives his life.

This is all my fault, and no-one else's.

I've thought that since the beginning, but I know it for sure now. If it wasn't for me, he'd still be here.

I can't help the fact that I pushed him away. That's in the past. But if I hadn't ignored him and his feelings, we'd have been able to talk about what happened, and work out what we can do about it… because that's what we need to do.

In reality, it's what we should have done from the start.

And the fact that we didn't is my fault, not his.

I've been trying to decide how to start a conversation with him all week. After I came home from seeing Jodie on Sunday, I realized that talking was the way to go… not with her, but with him. I couldn't be sure she was right about everything else, but some of what she said made sense. Actually, a lot of it made sense when I got back here and thought about it. And that was when I realized the only way to find out the truth was to ask him.

I knew it wouldn't be easy, but the reality is, it's been even harder than I thought. Not because I feel so guilty all the time, or even because I can't think how to start a conversation like that, but because Spencer has been working late almost every night. We've passed in the kitchen, or at the top of the stairs, and from time to time, I've wondered if he's been avoiding me, although I heard on the grapevine on Wednesday that the finance department has been slammed with work, so I knew I was being unfair… which wasn't at all unusual. Even so, when we've briefly seen each other in the apartment, the time hasn't been right to ask if we can sit down and clear the air, and the only advantage to that is that it's given me plenty of time to work out what to say, even if I'm still not sure how to say it.

First, I suppose I need to know how he feels about me. The thing I keep asking myself is, how to say that without sounding arrogant. Coming straight out and asking, 'Do you care about me?' isn't an option. But there has to be a way to find out… to discover whether Jodie was right, or if she'd read the situation completely wrong.

The thing is, though, even if asking the question isn't straightforward, why on earth did I just tell him we're incompatible?

It's not the first time I've said that, but why do it now, when I'm trying to work out whether there might be a chance for us?

Not that there is now, of course… because he's going out with Ruth.

So none of this matters, does it?

Except it matters to me, and as I sit down on the bottom step, I have to face the fact that I've blown it.

I've really blown it.

He may have said he wants me, and even put that in the present tense, but he's not here, is he? He ran out of here at the first chance he got. And I mean 'ran'. Did he think I was going to seduce him again? Those were his words, not mine, but it was like he was scared I was going to start something… and I'll admit, I was tempted.

I think it was his words this time. It wasn't about how handsome he looked in his suit… although he did. No, it was what he said.

Hearing him talking about me grinding on his cock, coming on his tongue, and writhing beneath him… it did something to me. Obviously, it reminded me of how magnificent he was. But it was more than that. It was the way he said it.

He wasn't holding anything back. He meant every word, and I think that's what made me think about how good we were together.

Because we didn't hold back. I certainly didn't, and I don't think he did either.

We gave each other everything… until there was nothing left to give. The first time it happened, I gave so much I was too tired to move. I fell asleep before he even returned from the bathroom.

The second time?

Well, I'd rather not think about that.

I don't want to recall how I let that end, but I guess I can't blame him for being confused. I know I am.

He must be wondering how I could have done all those things with him… how I could have lost myself with him so wildly, given myself to him, and taken everything he had to offer, fallen asleep in his arms, and then turned my back on him the very next morning. I can't imagine how that must have felt, although I got a glimpse of it in his eyes, and I should have paid more attention to that. If I had, I might not have done it all again.

Except I did. I threw myself at him in every sense of the word, and he caught me. I didn't deserve that, and I wouldn't have blamed him if he'd let me fall in a heap at his feet.

It was what I deserved.

And yet, he gave me a chance... and I took it with both hands, while he took me to places I'd never dreamed of. The pleasure he's given me is beyond anything I've ever experienced, and yet I still couldn't give myself to him. Not completely. Not emotionally.

I still couldn't take the chance. I still wouldn't take the risk of showing him how I really feel.

How could I when I don't understand it myself?

There's no logic to my behavior. All I know is, I've never felt more ashamed in my life.

Because it has to be said, if the shoe were on the other foot, there's no way I'd have allowed a man to do those things to me. Not without calling the cops, anyway.

I mean... did I ask him?

No.

If anything, it was the other way around... certainly the second time. He asked if I was sure, even though I was the one making the moves.

He was more responsible and more considerate toward me than I've ever been toward him. But has he said anything about that?

No.

And that just makes me feel worse.

God… I wish he could stand in front of me right now. Not so I could rip his clothes off again, but so I could apologize, and do it properly this time.

Because it needs to be said. Not only was I out of line, I crossed a line.

And I'm more sorry than he'll ever know. In ways I don't think I'll ever be able to explain.

Although I'd like the chance to try.

I get up, and while I know I should go upstairs to change, I really can't face it. Just the thought of climbing the stairs is too much for me, so I wander into the kitchen instead.

Without Spencer, I can't even think what to have for dinner. There are no pizzas in the deep freeze, and while I know I could drive to the grocery store and get one, that's even more of an effort than climbing the stairs.

I check the menu. It seems he'd planned to make that tomato pasta dish tonight… the one with the garlic and herb cheese. I guess I could try to do it by myself, but how would I make it for one person? The thought alone is too depressing for words.

He and I had so much fun cooking together… before I screwed up and brought sex into our relationship.

Except it didn't feel like I was screwing up at the time. That's one of the most confusing things about all this. When we were together, it felt right. Despite my fears about crossing the line, I got the feeling he agreed. I felt like he wanted me as much as I wanted him. Hell, he confirmed that himself, just before he left. So, something about it must have been right… even if it all went wrong afterwards.

Thanks to me.

I shake my head and go into the living area, flopping down on the couch. The room feels too quiet, and although I know I could turn on the TV, that's not what I want. I want Spencer.

I want him in so many ways… but mostly because if he were here, he wouldn't be with Ruth.

I hate the thought of him sitting at a table, like we did, staring at another woman in the candlelight. What's she like, I wonder? Is she similar to me, or the exact opposite? The idea of him being with someone who looks like me feels a little weird, and highly improbable. I imagine he wants to put all thoughts of me behind him. In which case, I imagine she's tall, slim, and probably blonde.

She'll laugh easily, too… and she won't have any hang-ups.

And as for looking for Mr. Right? That'll be the last thing on her mind.

She'll be easygoing, and just what Spencer needs.

Damn her.

I wonder if maybe she's holding out a morsel of food for him to taste, or if they're deep in conversation, discussing all the things they like and dislike… forming a bond that'll last.

"Don't be ridiculous."

Spencer doesn't do lasting bonds, does he? He's a player. Which means he's more likely to be thinking about how he can get into Ruth's panties than anything else.

"No," I say out loud and get to my feet.

I've already started down the stairs before I stop myself, and I turn and slowly climb back up again.

Was I seriously thinking of going down to the restaurant?

I must have been.

Where else would I have been going?

But how could I?

Even if it was just to spy on them and see what Ruth looks like, it's a ludicrous idea. What would happen if he saw me? It would put all my other humiliations in the shade.

No. I have to stay here.

I wish I didn't, but I do, and I stagger to the couch, sitting down again.

Staying here might drive me crazy, but the thought of them together is so much worse. They'll be holding hands across the table by now, I'm sure. That would probably be Spencer's first move. Will he be staring into her eyes? I hope not. It seems a little too intimate for a player, although I remember him gazing deeply at me while we ate our meal in the French restaurant. That didn't mean anything though, did it? Okay, so it's one of the reasons I couldn't bear to go there with Jodie, but he wouldn't do something like that with Ruth, would he?

Possibly…

It might be one of the things he does with women… to put them at ease. Not that he needed to worry about that with me. I proved I was easy enough when the time came.

Would Ruth be like that, too? It's hard to say, having never met her, but I guess if Spencer's looking for a night of mindless sex to take his mind off the mindless sex he had with me, he may have gone for someone who wouldn't make him work too hard.

Although I hope that's not the case.

Not that it's any business of mine.

I'd like it to be, but it's not.

He can do what he wants.

So… will he put his arm around her when it's time for them to leave? He didn't do that with me, but it wasn't that kind of night. We barely knew each other back then. We were celebrating his promotion and my having survived my first week here. He and Ruth probably have a very different agenda. They'll have other things in mind, and I imagine he'll use the excuse that the weather is cool in the evenings to take her in his arms. Either that, or he'll come straight out and tell her he just wants to hold her. I imagine she'll like that idea. Why wouldn't she? She'll smile up at him, and invite him back to her place, and he'll accept… because he can hardly bring her back here, can he?

My imagination is running away with me now, and in my mind, I've decided she lives somewhere close. Close enough that they can walk, and they do so, gazing into each other's eyes in the moonlight… although once she lets them through the front door, they won't be able to contain their need for each other any longer. They'll tear at each other's clothes, and the moment he's peeled her out of her tight dress – the one she's wearing in my mind's eye – he'll push her back against the wall, free his cock, and enter her.

She'll cling to him, because with the way Spencer fucks, clinging isn't an option, and she'll smile when he tells her she's the best… because I have no doubt he says that to every woman.

"No," I say again, shaking my head to banish the thoughts and the images. He wouldn't do that.

Okay… he might go home with her. He might even fuck her.

But he wouldn't say that to her, would he? Not when he only said it to me a few days ago.

He couldn't.

Or what I really mean is, I couldn't bear it if he did.

I suck in a breath, surprised by the sudden pain in my chest. I'm not having a heart attack, or anything like that. It's not that kind of pain. This goes a lot deeper. In fact, it fills my entire body, amplifying over and over, until I can barely breathe.

Why is this happening?

Why does the thought of Spencer being with another woman hurt so much?

I've pushed him away. I've told him we're not right for each other. And we're not.

Are we?

Can Jodie really be right?

Should I call her and talk it through again?

Maybe she can help me make sense of it all in Spencer's absence.

I reach forward and grab my purse from the coffee table, pulling out my phone and flipping it over before I connect the call.

Jodie takes a while to answer, and I'm just thinking she won't and I'll have to leave a complicated message, when she finally picks up.

"You've just caught me," she says, sounding a little out of breath.

"I have?"

"Yeah. I'm on my way out the door."

"Going somewhere nice?"

"I hope so. I'm meeting Flynn."

"Flynn from the hotel?" I say, sitting up slightly.

"Yeah."

"I didn't realize you were seeing each other."

"We weren't. This is our first date. I… well, I gave him my number the other night, when you went to the bathroom, and he called me the next day. We spoke for a while, and then he asked if I'd go out for a drink with him tonight. He's been working every night since, so…"

"I should let you go," I say, realizing she's got a life that doesn't revolve around my problems.

"No, it's fine. I'm only meeting him outside MD's. I can walk and talk at the same time."

"You're sure?"

"Positive. What's happened?"

I let out a sigh. "It's Spencer."

"I thought so. You haven't jumped into bed with him again, have you?"

"No." I'm aware we're short of time, and I have to get to the point. "I wanted to talk to him about the horrible atmosphere between us."

"But he didn't wanna know?"

"Oh, it's worse than that. He's gone out with someone else. He's in the French restaurant as we speak, gazing into her eyes."

"You've checked?"

"No, but that's what he did when he took me there, so…"

"He gazed into your eyes?" she says, sounding surprised.

"Yeah."

"And you still maintain this guy isn't interested in you?"

"He's having dinner with another woman, Jodie."

"Yeah, because you keep pushing him away."

"I know," I say, rocking my head back. "And I think I made it worse tonight."

"How?"

"I told him we're incompatible."

"Was that your way of trying to make things better?"

"No. It just… I don't know, it just came out. He told me he was seeing this woman, and I told him that was why we were incompatible."

"I'd like to say that makes sense, but it doesn't."

"Oddly enough, he said that, but it makes perfect sense in the context of him being a player and me wanting to settle down. He's proving he's exactly what I think he is."

"Is he?"

"Yes… and no. He told me, he's never known anyone with whom he's more compatible."

"Right. And you still maintain this guy doesn't care?"

"How can he? He ran out the door just a couple of minutes later, saying he needed to be with someone who didn't mess with his head."

"Those aren't the words of a player, Robyn. They're the words of a guy who feels like he's being played."

"But I'm not playing him. Honestly."

"I didn't say you were. I said that's how he feels. And you're talking to the wrong person."

"I know… but he's not here."

"No. He's at the French restaurant. Speaking of which, I've just walked by there. Do you want me to go back? I can take a look inside and see what he's doing, if you want?"

I think about that for a moment, unwilling to admit I came within seconds of going down to spy on Spencer myself.

"No. I think I'd rather live in ignorance. And besides, you don't wanna be late for your date."

"No, I don't, but it won't take a moment. If you wanna know…"

"I don't think I do."

"What do you want?" she asks, and I take a moment, knowing the answer before I even open my mouth.

"I want him to come home."

"He will," she says.

"Yeah… eventually."

"Well… when he does, you guys need to talk. You need to tell him how you feel."

"You make it sound so easy."

"It's not, but no matter how hard it is, talking and working things out has gotta be better than where you are now. Right?"

I nod my head. "Yeah. You're right."

"Okay. Then make sure you do it."

"I will."

"I've just arrived at the bar," she says.

"Is Flynn there?"

"He is." I hear her suck in a breath. "God, he's gorgeous."

"Be good," I whisper.

"No way."

She chuckles and hangs up the call, making me laugh, although it quickly fades as I put my phone down on the coffee table.

Can I really talk to Spencer?

I have to if I want to resolve this, and I want that more than anything… but first he needs to come home.

And I've got no way of knowing when he'll do that.

It could be later tonight.

But more likely, it'll be sometime tomorrow.

God. I hate that thought. I hate the idea of him spending the night with Ruth.

Would he do that? Would he sleep with her?

Of course he would. He's a player.

I heard what he said to Clark, and what Clark said to him. It's how he lives his life… flitting from one woman to the next.

He may have told me he wanted me, but that's a physical thing. It's got nothing to do with emotions, or with wanting to stick around, and with that thought in my mind, I struggle not to cry.

What's wrong with me?

Why am I being like this?

Why am I acting like a lovesick…

"Oh, shit…"

I shake my head. It can't be love. That's not possible. He's all wrong for me. And yet… and yet he feels so right. Not just as a lover, but in every way.

So, why did I let him go? Why did I let him leave, knowing he'd spend the evening – and probably the night – with another woman?

I curse out loud and get to my feet, going straight over to the refrigerator. There's a bottle of wine in here, which I think we were saving to have with dinner tonight, and even though I still haven't eaten, I pull it out. Drinking won't help, but I can't see it'll hurt, either, and I grab a glass, opening the bottle before I return to the couch to drown my sorrows.

Chapter Fourteen

Spencer

What on earth made me think I could do this?

Coming out with Ruth was supposed to help me get my head straight. That was the plan. I can remember thinking that being with Robyn was getting me too muddled, and I needed to be somewhere else. I can't remember thinking I wanted to sleep with anyone else, though… just that I wanted to be away from the apartment, so I didn't have to feel second-best.

Except being here is just making things worse, not better.

Ruth is sitting across the table, talking, but I'm only hearing about one word in three, because my mind is filled with images of Robyn. I'm not thinking about her grinding on my cock, or screaming my name while she comes on my tongue, or writhing beneath me while I hold her down and take her… or anything like that. The only thing on my mind is her face, and the look in her eyes when I ran out on her.

That's guilt, I imagine. My guilt, not hers. Although I don't know why I should be the one to feel guilty.

I'm not the one who's been playing games.

Is that what Robyn's been doing, though? It's hard to say. It sure feels that way, but I guess that's part of the confusion.

Seducing me twice, telling me it was a mistake, and I'm not the man for her… that felt like she was playing with me. Or fucking with me, to be more precise. Even though I'd asked her not to.

What made it more puzzling still was her reaction just now.

She seemed upset, or at least put out, that I'd arranged to have dinner with someone else… and I genuinely don't understand why.

I don't think I ever will, either.

I suck in a breath and do my best to focus on Ruth. It's the least I can do, having invited her to dine with me, and as she dips her dark head, studying the menu for a moment, I'm reminded of how much I regretted that decision… the moment I called at her house.

That was partly because I was still harboring regrets about Robyn, and the way we'd parted. But it was also because of how Ruth looked.

There was nothing wrong with her as such, and in a past life, I don't think I'd have wasted any time in suggesting that we should abandon dinner and spend our time more fruitfully at her place… in her bed. But that was a past life, and as I watched her lock her front door, it was all I could do not to suggest she might want to put on a coat. Not because of the chill in the air, but to cover herself.

I felt like someone's dad, but her dress left absolutely nothing to the imagination.

Black, short, and low-cut, it was every man's dream… and my worst nightmare.

Because I wasn't in the mood.

And I'm still not.

"I've never been too sure about ordering steak in a restaurant," she says, looking up at me again, her dark amber eyes sparkling in a way that does absolutely nothing for me. "If they don't cook it right, it can be disastrous… and a waste of money."

"I'm pretty sure they know what they're doing here."

"You think?"

"Yeah. I was gonna have the ribeye."

She nods her head. "In that case, I might have the chicken."

I frown, unable to help myself. "I thought you wanted steak."

"I do, but I can always have some of yours, rather than ordering one of my own and taking the risk that I won't like it. If I do, I'll know for the next time we come here, won't I?"

There won't be a next time, but to avoid telling her that, I bury my head in the menu again, trying not to think about Robyn, and how much easier it was to bring her here. It was certainly less tense, even though I'd already worked out I was in love with her, and I knew she didn't feel the same. I still enjoyed every moment of our time together. She chose her salmon dish within about ten seconds of opening the menu, without fussing about how it was cooked, while I spent most of the evening admiring her. She wore that sexy black dress, which I haven't seen since, and while Ruth's outfit is similar, it doesn't have the same effect. Neither does she. Sure, she's pretty, but to be honest, I couldn't be less interested. I'm not quite counting the minutes until I can take her home, but I couldn't honestly say I'm enjoying myself… whereas with Robyn, I remember thinking I'd never forget a moment of our time together. And I haven't. It's still there… etched in my head. Every look, every sound, laugh, and word… spoken and unspoken.

Robyn and I talked about a next time too, and while we've had numerous dinners together at the apartment, we haven't done anything as romantic as that first night out.

We never will now.

A woman approaches the table to take our order, and I let Ruth go first, before I ask for my ribeye.

"How would you like that cooked?" she asks.

"Rare, please."

"Wait a second." Ruth reaches out, placing her hand on the table between us. "Would you mind getting it medium-rare? I really don't like rare steak."

The waitress looks a little confused, and I can't say I blame her. It's my meal we're talking about. Part of me wants to argue that point with Ruth, but I'm more interested in getting out of here, so I nod my head.

"Fine. Make it medium-rare."

The waitress tips her head, raising her eyebrows at the same time. I guess she thinks I'm a pushover, and that's fine with me. I'm not interested in what she thinks.

As I'm driving, Ruth orders a glass of Chardonnay, and I stick with mineral water… which is annoying. I had a really lovely red when I was here with Robyn. It went well with my lamb, and I know it would complement the steak. But I have to drive Ruth home… so water it is.

The waitress takes our menus and leaves, and I regret her departure. At least studying the menu and talking about food gave us something to do. Now I have to face the fact that I don't belong here… not without Robyn.

"How long have you lived here?" Ruth asks.

"Just over a year."

She nods. "It's about the same for me. I moved to Willmont Vale last February. I wanted to move here, to Hart's Creek, to be closer to work, but I couldn't find anything suitable at the time. And in any case, I quite like Willmont Vale. It's livelier than Hart's Creek, and I prefer that. I don't…"

Her voice fades as I zone her out, which I know is unfair, but I really don't care how she feels about Hart's Creek, or Willmont Vale, or anywhere else for that matter.

The only thing I care about is Robyn... and that's what makes this so damn hard.

Because she doesn't care about me.

"Hey, is that you, Spencer?" I glance up at the male voice saying my name, grateful for the interruption... not just to my thoughts, but to Ruth's monologue, too, and realize the man standing beside me is no stranger. It's Gabe Sullivan and I stand up, nodding my head.

"Yes, it is."

He smiles, turning to the beautiful woman who's holding his hand. She's dark-haired, and a lot shorter than Gabe, with a slim figure... allowing for the slight bump she's just placed her hand over. "This is my wife, Remi," he says, glancing back at me. "Spencer's the head of our finance department."

I smile inwardly. No-one's ever said that out loud before, and I like the way it sounds. The title has a ring of permanence about it, which I never thought I'd appreciate... although I do now. Heaven knows why, but I do.

"Oh, I see." Remi nods her head. "It's nice to meet you."

I realize I ought to introduce Ruth, who's still sitting at the table. "Ruth works for Jacobson Electronics," I say, unwilling to give her any other title, like 'girlfriend', or even 'date', and they all nod at each other.

"We thought we'd come out to celebrate," Gabe says, putting his arm around his wife.

"Oh?"

"Hmm... Remi's birthday was last month, but she was still suffering from morning sickness, so going out for dinner was out of the question."

I do my best to get my head around that, and fail dismally, shaking my head at him.

"I'm sorry, but why would morning sickness have any effect on going out for dinner in the evening?"

"Because it didn't restrict itself to the morning," Remi says with a smile. "And I was never actually sick, to be fair. I just felt sick... the entire time."

"That sounds horrendous."

"It wasn't great, but Peony tells me waking up and throwing up every morning is a lot worse, so I'm not complaining."

"Ryan... Ryan told me you were going for an ultrasound the other week. I hope you don't mind my asking, but is everything okay?"

Gabe smiles. "Everything is just fine, thanks. And at least we know what color to paint the nursery."

"Oh?"

He nods his head. "Yeah... pink."

"You're having a girl?"

"We sure are."

I've never seen a man look more pleased with himself, and although it's not something I've ever thought about before, there's a part of me that can understand how he feels. Or I could if my life wasn't such a mess.

Because a life, and a family and forever – even if they come with pink walls – are exactly what I want with Robyn.

Except she doesn't feel the same.

I swallow my disappointment and nod my head. "That's great," I say.

"We'll need to sit down in the next couple of weeks," Gabe says.

"We will?"

"Yeah. I've already had to take a few days out of the office, and as you know I've been busy with meetings lately, but we need to catch up, just to make sure we're on the same page with everything at work."

"Is there anything wrong?" I ask and he smiles.

"No. On the contrary. I've been hearing good things about you."

I don't know who from, but I can't help smiling. "That's nice to know."

"Well… it's a relief that I can leave the department in your hands, while I get on with my other work, and with looking after Remi."

"Not necessarily in that order," I say, and he smiles.

"No. Remi's my priority."

She shakes her head, nudging in to him as a slight blush touches her cheeks.

"If there's anything you need me to do, just let me know."

"Thanks," he says. "Like I say, it's good to know I've got someone I can count on, but if you need anything and I'm not around, just talk to Ryan."

"When you're not talking to him, you mean?" Remi says, and I glance down at her, surprised when Gabe bursts out laughing. I wait for him to calm, and then he turns to me.

"You'll have to excuse us. It's a private joke… although it's not that private. It's just that Ryan and I go back a long way, and as he's been down the fatherhood road already, I've been turning to him for advice over the last few months."

"I see," I say, looking down at Remi. "What about you? Who do you turn to?"

"Oh, believe me, there's no shortage of people offering advice."

"Is that a good thing?"

"Mostly."

"They all mean well, don't they, babe?" Gabe says, and she nods her head. "And there are so many pregnant women in the town, at least their advice is relevant."

"Even if I don't always want to know the details," Remi says, pulling a face. "Although to be fair, some of the women who were pregnant when I first started on this journey have already given birth."

"They have?" I say, frowning. "Oh… I guess you're talking about Macy from the bar. She had her little girl not that long ago, didn't she?"

"Yes." Gabe nods his head. "But there's also Imogen."

"Who's Imogen?" I ask, racking my brain, but failing to place the name.

"She's married to Walker Holt," Remi says.

"The novelist?" I'm unable to hide my surprise. "The guy who writes that TV show? What's it called?"

"McKenna's Mill," Gabe says.

"That's the one. You mean he lives here, in Hart's Creek?"

"Yeah. Didn't you know?"

I shake my head. "I had no idea."

"Well, he does," Gabe says. "And Imogen had their second daughter last month. They've called her… Ingrid, isn't it?" He turns to Remi, who nods her head.

"That's right." She looks up at me. "Their first daughter is called Ava."

"So, Walker's surrounded by women?"

"Absolutely… not that he minds."

I don't think I would either. Like I say, I'd take it if Robyn was offering, pink walls and all.

"Apart from Peony, Eloise has probably been the most helpful, in terms of offering me advice," Remi says, giving the matter some thought.

"Who's Eloise?" I ask. "I feel like I don't know anyone."

Gabe laughs. "She's married to the guy who owns this place. His name's Archer Steele, and Eloise used to be the chef here before she stopped work."

"I see."

"Her baby was due ten days ago," Remi says. "She's had enough of waiting now."

I can't say I blame her.

"Surely they won't let it go on much longer, will they?" Gabe says, turning to face his wife.

"No. I think Eloise said they're giving her the weekend, and then they'll induce the labor. She doesn't want that to happen, but obviously, she might not have a choice."

I have no idea what they're talking about, so I stick to things I understand.

"And what are they having?" I ask. "A boy or a girl?"

"They decided they didn't want to know, so it's gonna be a surprise."

The waitress returns, dodging around us to bring Ruth's wine, and top up my water, and I realize we've been ignoring Ruth, and talking among ourselves. That ought to make me feel guilty, but it doesn't. I'd rather stand and talk to Gabe and Remi than sit back down with Ruth, and for a moment, I wonder about asking them to join us… except I recall they're here to celebrate, and Gabe clearly remembers Ruth's presence at the same time as I do, and smiles down at her.

"I'm sorry. We've been monopolizing your date."

"Don't worry," she says. "We've got all night."

Like hell we have.

Gabe turns to me with a kind of sparkle in his eyes, which suggests he's misinterpreted Ruth's comment. I've got no intention of spending the night with her. In fact, as far as I'm concerned, the sooner I can call a halt to this farce, the better.

"I'll see you Monday," he says to me, and they depart… more's the pity.

I have no choice other than to resume my seat, and the moment I do, Ruth leans in a little closer.

"Who was that guy?" she says. "I caught his name, but I didn't really understand who he was."

I feel like telling her it doesn't matter. We won't be seeing each other again, so it's irrelevant. Except I can't be that rude.

"Gabe is my boss." That's all she needs to know… although it seems that's not enough, and rather than just accepting my answer, she leans closer still.

"But I thought you worked for Ryan Andrews."

"I do, but I report directly to Gabe, not Ryan."

She nods her head, licking her lips. "Now… there's a handsome guy," she says, her voice a little dreamy.

"Who? Ryan?"

"Yeah. I've seen him around, and he's my idea of the perfect man."

I ought to be insulted, but I'm not. I honestly couldn't care less.

"He's a happily married man," I point out, nonetheless.

"I know. Doesn't stop a girl from dreaming, though."

Dreaming is all she'll get. There's no way Ryan would risk what he's got with Peony. Not for anyone.

At that moment, the waitress arrives, bringing our meals, and I'm grateful for the interruption, and while I half expect Ruth to demand half my steak the moment the waitress has gone, she doesn't do any such thing. Instead, she leans in again and says, "Is there something about this place?"

"In what way?"

"Well… the town seems to be full of handsome men, doesn't it? There's Ryan Andrews, and that guy you were just talking to… and you, of course."

I'm added as an afterthought, and once again, I really don't care.

"The town has more than its fair share of beautiful women, I can assure you."

I should know. I live with one of them… just not in the way I want.

"Oh? Do you know many of them?"

"A few."

She frowns. "A few? That doesn't sound good. Should I be worried?"

"Not at all."

She smiles, misunderstanding my reply, and I realize that, for the second time running, I'm going to have to modify my date's expectations… and cut short our evening into the bargain.

I'm not sure how I'll do that, but I can't go on like this. Not when my mind is elsewhere, along with my heart.

Obviously, there's no point in following my heart. Robyn has no interest in it, or in me. But dating other people isn't the answer to my problems. I've realized that now. I'm not ready, and the sooner I can get out of here, the better.

Chapter Fifteen

Robyn

Oh, my word.

Have I really drunk nearly three-quarters of the bottle?

How can that be?

I haven't changed out of my work clothes, or switched on the television to drown out the silence… which I guess explains why there's so little wine left in the bottle.

Because that's all I've done since I finished my call with Jodie… drink.

Well… drink and let my imagination run wild.

I may have agreed with Jodie that Spencer and I need to talk, but we can't if he's having a blast with someone else… and maybe deciding his future lies with her, and not me.

I hope he's not, but I have to face reality.

I also have the face the fact that I haven't eaten anything… and I really should. It might stop the room from spinning, although I doubt it.

And if I'm being honest, I think it would be really foolish of me to cook anything in my current condition. I'm pretty dangerous when I'm sober, but I dread to think what I could do to the kitchen when I've had several glasses of wine.

The results would be lethal, I imagine, and I don't think anyone would thank me if I burned down the building.

Least of all Spencer.

It might be a way of getting him to come home, though. If the place was in flames, he'd have to, wouldn't he? Not to rescue me, obviously. I'd be the last thing on his mind. But he must have things he values… things he'd want to save.

Other than me.

The issue is, I don't want it to be like that. I want him to come back for me… me and no-one else.

I know that now. Even though the room is spinning and I'm struggling to focus, I can still think clearly enough to know I want him here. Now.

Except he's not, is he?

He's with Ruth. For all I know, they could be at her place by now. They probably decided to forgo dessert in favor of something sweeter. So, even if I burned the building down, he'd be none the wiser.

Because he's elsewhere, lighting other people's fires.

I close my eyes, just to stop the spinning, and imagine her apartment. I don't know where it is, but as she's blonde, tall and sexy, the decor would have to suit her, wouldn't it?

Does a blonde woman's apartment look any different from a brunette's?

I've never thought of it before, but for some reason, I imagine something girly… not childish, but feminine. She'll have a vase of peonies on the coffee table, and a dusky pink throw over the back of her pale cream couch.

That's probably where they're sitting – or lying – right now, and although I'd prefer to strike that thought, I can't. It's in my head. I may be drunk, but I'm not so drunk I can't picture the two of them… her taking Spencer's cock in her mouth, swallowing him down. She'll be wearing lipstick, and he'll like that. He'll like the way it makes her lips shimmer as they stretch around him, and he'll flex his hips, like he did with me, holding her blonde hair behind her head, while he tells her how good she is. Then she'll ride his cock… not in the abandoned, uncontrolled way I did, but in a sexy, sensual way, taking it slow, her body rocking against his, giving him everything he needs, with more sophistication than I could ever hope to muster. He'll appreciate it, too, raising his hips to hers, taking her really hard, and a sob leaves my lips, a tear striking my cheek as I cover my face with my hands.

"No, Spence… please, don't."

I can't bear the thought of losing him… even though he's not mine to lose.

And I know that probably makes me the most contrary woman in the world, given everything I've said and done, and the way I let him walk away earlier this evening… but I can't help that. I can't help what's gone before, or how I feel about him now.

All I can hope is that he'll come home, and that he'll be able to forgive me, and maybe give me a second chance.

Because that's all I'm asking.

Just one more chance.

I check the time, squinting at the microwave and letting my eyes focus on the display, realizing it's just after eight. It's not even late… which not only means I consumed that wine in no time at all, but I guess means they might still be at the restaurant.

Should I run downstairs and talk to him?

I may have dismissed the idea earlier, but I could ask him to step outside, couldn't I?

I get to my feet, the room swaying. Okay, so running anywhere is out of the question, but I refuse to be beaten, and I make my way slowly to the top of the stairs.

"I can do this," I mutter under my breath, going down five steps before I realize I don't have my keys. I'll need to get back in, so I turn around, almost toppling backwards down the stairs, and actually drop to my knees and crawl back up. It seems safest.

Is this such a good idea?

Probably not, but I have to do something, so I grab my keys from my purse and make a second attempt, holding the handrail with both hands, and going down sideways. It takes a lot longer than it should, but there's less chance of me falling and breaking my neck, and I feel stupidly pleased with myself when I reach the bottom step. The next thing is to get out through the back door, which is fairly easy… other than the blast of fresh air, which almost knocks me off of my feet.

I hadn't been expecting that. The wind has picked up since I got home, and rather than think about Spencer putting his arm around Ruth to keep her warm, I take a moment to get my bearings before I step outside.

I don't feel too bad… although the wind tugging at my hair makes my head feel strange, and I wish I'd tied it up. I rarely do, though, and obviously, I hadn't realized I'd be coming out in a drunken state, so I'll just have to cope, won't I?

I make my way around the side of the bar, taking care over each step, and then go along Main Street. I'm getting used to walking now, and speed up just a little, impatience getting the better of me.

I still haven't decided what to say, but I guess the priority is to find out if Spencer's still there. If he isn't, then I guess it'll be too late to say anything, and while that thought makes my heart hurt, there's no point in worrying about it yet. Not until I know the worst.

I approach the restaurant, slowing my pace, and then stop, peering through the window. There's no sign of him, and my heart sinks. They've gone already… except. Wait a minute. There he is, with his back to me, sitting by the wall on the left-hand side. It's quite dark back there, and I'm desperate to see Ruth, so I move a little further to my right, and tip my head, realizing my mistake as I nearly fall over.

"Damn," I mutter, hoping no-one saw me, as I glance up and see her.

She's beautiful.

There's no getting away from it.

Although she's not the blonde I imagined.

Instead, she's a brunette with slightly olive-colored skin and dark, mysterious-looking eyes. Her hair falls in loose curls over her bare shoulders and across the tops of her partially exposed breasts. I can't see her dress, but there doesn't appear to be very much of it.

Still, maybe that's what Spencer likes.

My heart sinks at that thought… because I've never been someone who can flaunt themselves like that. Okay, so a couple of my blouses might gape a little, but that's only because of the way I'm built. It's not intentional.

Still, if it's the kind of thing that turns Spencer on, I guess there's nothing I can do, and I wonder if that's another thing that makes us incompatible.

Or whether I'm overthinking.

To be honest, I'm not sure I'm thinking at all.

I mean, what on earth made me choose to come down here in the first place?

A need to talk to Spencer?

Why? He's already moved on… if there was ever anything to move on from.

So why would he want to talk to me?

It's a ludicrous idea.

I can't do it, and before he sees me, I dart out of sight, regretting my decisions… not just to spy on him, but to drink so much that I'd even considered this to be a good idea in the first place.

I roll my eyes, regretting that too, as it makes my head spin, and I make my way back to the apartment.

I can't decide how I feel, other than miserable.

After all, I'd expected a blonde, and I found a brunette… a brunette who's the polar opposite of me. What does that say?

I don't know, and I don't think I'll be able to work it out until my head stops spinning.

Letting myself back into the apartment takes a few minutes. The key won't go into the lock, and I'm reminded of that night when Zane followed me back from the bar, and Spencer came to my rescue. I was drunk then, too, and I remember how I kissed him and he didn't react. That confused me. It embarrassed me, too… but so much has happened since then, it doesn't seem important. Not as important as getting the damn door open, anyway, and I take several attempts before the key finally turns. Once I'm inside, I let out a sigh of relief that at least Spencer didn't see me.

That's something.

Although it's not much, and as I slowly climb the stairs, I realize it's a poor solace when I'm here on my own, and he's there, with her.

There's no way he'll be able to resist her. Not when she looks like that. No man could.

Which means I'm too late.

Except I'm not, am I? They're still at the restaurant. They haven't left yet…

And I love him.

I love him too much to give up so easily.

I get to the top of the stairs, wishing I'd taken my phone with me, because then I wouldn't have to struggle over to the couch. As it is, I get there eventually, and flop down onto the seat, grabbing my phone from the table, and flipping it around in my hand so it's facing the right way.

I can't call him. I don't know what I'd say, and as he's busy with Ruth, I can't be sure he'd even pick up, which would leave me pouring my heart out to his voicemail.

I shake my head, wishing I hadn't, as the room shakes with it. There's no way I'd talk to a machine. It's Spencer or nothing… in every sense.

Which means I have to text him.

Or try to.

I take a moment to focus on my phone and look up Spencer's details, relieved we swapped numbers now, even if I was reluctant at the time. That was only because he was going on a date with someone else, and I was jealous. I can't remember her name, but that was the evening he came home early, and… and… well, the least said about that the better.

Although I loved every second of what we did, no matter what Spencer thinks.

Still, I need to concentrate, and I take a deep breath, slowly typing out…

—*I know you're mad at me. I get that. You have every right to be. I've hurt you. At least I think I have. It's hard to tell. But the thing is, I don't want you to go back to Ruth's place. I don't have the right to ask this, but please, Spence… please don't sleep with her.*

That's exactly what I'd say to him if he were standing in front of me… if I'd had the courage to go inside the restaurant and ask him to step outside. So I press send rather than dwelling on whether I should say more, or less, and then I reach for my wineglass, swallowing down the last of its contents.

I probably shouldn't have done that, and I'm certainly not going to drink any more.

In fact, I think I'll fix myself a coffee.

Before I do, I glance down at my phone, surprised to see my message is showing as 'read'. It was read two minutes ago, which means he picked it up within seconds of me sending it.

I don't know how to react to that.

Especially as there's no sign of a reply.

Does that mean I'm too late?

Have they left for Ruth's place already?

Is he too mad at me to want to reply?

Or is it just that he's done with me?

That was what he said. He said he was done, right before he said he was going to spend time with someone who didn't mess with his head so much, and I guess I should have believed him. He clearly meant it.

If he didn't, he'd come back… he'd forgive me.

And he'd give me a second chance.

But I guess I've blown any hope of a second chance now.

Or is it a third chance?

I can't think straight.

Either way, it's too late.

Chapter Sixteen

Spencer

Ruth finishes the last of her chicken, puts down her silverware and takes a sip of her wine.

"That was amazing," she says, leaning back in her seat.

I finished my meal a while ago, but she's taken longer… mostly because she also ate about a third of my steak, and most of my fries.

"They look so good," she said, reaching over to help herself.

Not that I cared. She could have taken the entire plate if it meant getting out of here.

"Are you okay?" she asks, surprising me.

She's hardly been the most attentive of dates. In fact, she's spent most of the evening eating my food and talking about herself, and while I wouldn't usually object to that, I think the fact that I don't want to be here hasn't helped.

"I'm fine," I say, although even I'm struggling to believe myself, and she tips her head to one side.

"Have you had enough of this place?" she says.

"Something like that."

Her eyes light up. "Me too." She leans forward. "I just need to visit the ladies' room, and then we can go."

We? Shit, that's not what I had in mind. I open my mouth to say so, but she gets to her feet and is gone before I can utter a sound.

Well… I guess I'll just have to give her the bad news when she gets back, and I glance around, searching for our waitress, who's nowhere to be seen, just as my phone vibrates. It's in my jacket pocket, and I pull it out, flipping it around, and sitting up straight when I see Robyn's name on the screen.

Oh, my God… what's happened?

Is she okay?

Where is she? Is she hurt?

The panic rolling through me is astounding as I picture her in all kinds of trouble, either at the apartment, or – worse still – somewhere else, and my fingers shake as I tap on the message, waiting for it to appear on the screen.

When it does, I feel even worse… my head filled with confusion as I read…

—I know you're mad at me. I get that. You have every right to be. I've hurt you. At least I think I have. It's hard to tell. But the thing is, I don't want you to go back to Ruth's place. I don't have the right to ask this, but please, Spence… please don't sleep with her.

What the fuck?

I'm Spence again?

I don't understand what that means. It can't mean what I want it to mean… and yet…

I've made a point of explaining the difference between her calling me Spence and Spencer. Why would she use that name now if she wasn't trying to tell me something?

And why would she think I'd sleep with Ruth?

More to the point, why would she care?

I rack my brain, recalling our conversation before I walked out of the apartment, and the look on her face, remembering what

I said. I wanted to spend some time with someone who didn't mess with my head. Those were my words. That was what I meant… not that I wanted to fuck Robyn out of my system.

I could never do that.

It's not possible.

She obviously thinks it is, though. She clearly believes I've come out tonight with every intention of going back to Ruth's place and spending the night there.

The reality is, I've spent the last hour wishing I could have been sitting opposite Robyn. Even with the atmosphere between us being as bad as it is, I'd still rather spend time with her than anyone else… no matter what I said to her.

As I watched Ruth demolish my steak, I was wondering if Robyn and I might be able to sit down tomorrow morning and talk, because I'd already reached the conclusion that we can't go on like this.

I know she said we should advertise for someone to take her room, but I don't want her to go. I want us to work this out… somehow.

And if we can't?

Then I guess one of us will have to leave.

Although I still think it should be me.

Because if we can't be together, I don't think I want to live here anymore. I'm not sure I can even stay in Hart's Creek.

That was the decision I'd reached while Ruth was eating her meal, and part of mine.

And now Robyn sends me this?

I read it again just to make sure I've understood.

She's right. I am mad at her… but only because she keeps messing with me. Even she seems to think I'm entitled to be angry about that, which I guess means we agree on something for once.

She knows she's hurt me. Or she thinks she has. She says it's hard to tell.

Why?

It's not as though I've hidden my feelings that well. The fact that I've talked about moving out should have given her a fairly big clue.

But I didn't think feelings mattered to her. At least not my feelings, anyway.

Does this mean they do?

Does this mean I matter to her?

No.

That's too much to hope for.

But if I don't matter, why is she so worried about me going back to Ruth's place? Why is she asking me not to sleep with her?

It doesn't add up.

And that means I need to see her.

Of course, the infuriating part about that is she's just along the street. She's upstairs in our apartment. Only I can't go to her, because I have to take Ruth home first.

I could reply to her, though.

Except I'm not sure what I'd say.

I have a hundred questions, but none of them can be asked in a text message.

I want to know why? Why now? What's changed? What does she want from me?

I need to know what this means, and whether it means anything, and for that reason alone, I have to wait. Because any response she sends will probably be just as opaque as this one.

It feels like she's put herself out there by sending this, though. So, should I take hope from that?

Not really.

She's put herself out there before. She's given herself to me… twice. And then she's crushed me.

Which means I have to stand before her. I have to look into her eyes, and I have to know – once and for all – what's going on. Her message has to mean something, but to find out what, I need to see her… and now, more than ever, I really, desperately need to get out of here.

"Are you ready?" Ruth's voice startles me, and I put away my phone.

"Ready?"

"Yes. To go back to my place."

She stands beside me, looking expectant, and I shrug my shoulders. "I haven't paid yet."

"What have you been doing all this time?"

Trying to understand the woman I'm in love with… and whether the text message she just sent me means what I hope it means.

"Trying to find the waitress," I say.

Ruth sits back down again, glancing around. "There she is." She waves her hand in a very obvious and quite obnoxious way, and the waitress comes over.

"Sorry," she says, picking up our plates. "Archer's not here tonight, and the new manager's off sick, so…"

"We just need the check," Ruth says, cutting across her words.

I can't believe she did that, and I give the waitress a sympathetic smile before she hurries away.

"Did you have to be so rude?" I say to Ruth once we're alone again.

"I wasn't rude. It's not our fault if they're understaffed, is it?"

"No, but it's not hers either. She said the manager's off sick, and I think we can be pretty sure where Archer is."

"I don't even know who Archer is," she says, shrugging her shoulders.

"He owns this place. Didn't you hear Gabe explaining earlier? His wife's about to have their baby. It's overdue. I imagine he must be beside himself with worry." I know I would be.

"Oh… was that who they were talking about?"

"Yes."

"Even so. It's still not our problem."

The waitress returns, depositing the check. "I'm sorry about that," I say, and she smiles down at me.

"It's okay."

I hand her my credit card, and she makes quick work of taking the payment, to which I add a significant tip to make up for Ruth's behavior. She smiles her thanks, and without even a glance in Ruth's direction, she leaves us.

"Did you just apologize for me?" Ruth says, narrowing her eyes at me.

"Yes. It needed to be said."

"No, it didn't."

She gets to her feet, glaring down at me, and I wonder if that brief episode has done me a favor. I was trying to work out how to explain that I didn't want to go back to her place… and now I probably won't have to.

Ruth's already halfway to the door, and knowing I have to take her home, I catch up with her in time to open it and let her pass through ahead of me.

She sighs and shivers slightly as we get out onto the sidewalk, and I wonder if she regrets not bringing a coat. I'm about to ask if she wants my jacket for the ride home when she turns and looks up at me, that sparkle back in her eyes again.

Oh, hell.

"Shall we put that behind us?" she says, resting her hand on my chest.

I step back, so she's forced to release me. "We can, but it won't change anything."

She frowns. "What does that mean?"

"It means I'll take you home, but I won't be staying."

"You won't? But I thought…"

"Then you thought wrong." I say, using her tactic of interrupting to get my point across.

"Why?" she says, moving closer again and looking up into my eyes. "I know it's our first date and everything, but I've never let things like that worry me. I like you, Spencer… and I don't see why we can't make the most of that."

"I do."

She steps back again. "What do you mean?"

"Just what I say. I won't be staying."

She sighs, shaking her head. "Okay, if you insist. But maybe next time we can…"

"There won't be a next time."

Her shoulders drop. "Why not?"

I could tell her that I haven't enjoyed myself less for ages, and how truly annoying she can be. But I don't want to prolong this conversation any longer than I have to. And in reality, it's not her fault. It's mine.

"There's someone else," I murmur.

"Excuse me?"

"There's someone else."

"You mean you're seeing another woman?"

"No."

"Then I don't understand."

"I'm in love with another woman… only she's not in love with me."

"And what? You thought you'd use me to get over her, did you?"

"I didn't use you, Ruth."

"Really? You think?" She raises her voice, her eyes alive with anger.

"Yes," I say, keeping calm. One of us needs to. "Using you would have meant coming back to your place, fucking you senseless, and *then* telling you there's someone else. All we did was have dinner."

"Except I wanted more than that."

"Hmm… it's a trait with you, isn't it?"

She tips her head, looking confused. "What do you mean?"

"Wanting more. You ordered your dinner and ate half of mine." I know I'm exaggerating, but I don't care. She's not the only one who's getting mad.

"You said you didn't mind."

"I didn't say anything of the sort. You just assumed… a bit like you are now."

"Most guys think themselves lucky when I invite them back to my place."

"I'm sure they do. But I'm not most guys."

She narrows her eyes again. "No… it seems not."

"I'll take you home," I say, heading for the parking lot, although after just a few paces, I sense she's not with me, and turn around to find she's exactly where I left her. "Are you coming?"

"No. I'll call a cab." She pulls her phone from her purse as she's speaking.

"Don't be childish, Ruth. I brought you here. I'll take you home."

"You don't need to."

"I know, but you don't need to call a cab, either."

As I'm talking, she's already stabbing her finger at her phone, and rather than fight about it any further, I admit defeat, dawdling back to her as she connects the call. She tells them where we are and gives them her address in Willmont Vale, asking for a cab as soon as possible. Just like she was with the waitress, she's abrupt, and I know if I were on the receiving end, I'd make her wait… although I hope they don't.

"What did they say?" I ask as she ends the call and puts her phone away.

"They'll be here in ten minutes."

I nod my head. "I'll wait with you."

"That's not necessary. I'll be fine by myself."

"I'm sure you will, but I'll wait, anyway. We don't have to talk."

"Good," she says, turning her back on me. "I've got no intention of talking to you."

Man… I thought Robyn could be contrary, but she's a breeze compared to Ruth, and I step away, giving her space. She wraps her arms around herself, moving to the edge of the sidewalk, and while I still think she's being petulant, I can't help feeling a little sorry for her. Especially as she's obviously freezing… and regardless of what she thinks, I'm not a total asshole.

I pull my phone from my jacket pocket and slip it off before I walk up behind her, placing it over her shoulders, and while I half expect her to turn around and throw it in my face, she doesn't. Instead, she murmurs a curt, "Thank you."

"You're welcome, and I'm sorry I wasn't straight with you from the start."

She doesn't reply, and rather than going over old ground, I step away again, checking my phone to see if Robyn's sent another message. She hasn't, but why would she? I didn't reply to her, so she probably thinks I don't care.

Either that, or she's assumed I'm already at Ruth's place, doing God knows what.

That thought makes me shudder, and I glance along the street, hoping her cab won't be much longer.

I need to get back to Robyn… not just to put her mind at rest, but also so we can talk.

Heaven knows how we'll start the conversation.

I feel like this text message has changed everything.

Even if I can't work out how. Or why.

We need to talk that through… among other things.

But first I need Ruth to leave.

She steps forward slightly, just as a silver sedan pulls up, and I recognize the name of the local cab company on the side of the door.

"Thanks for your jacket," she says, holding it out to me as she opens the passenger door behind the driver.

I nod my head, watching as she climbs in, and I tap on the driver's window.

"How much to take her to Willmont Vale?" I say.

"Twenty bucks." I pull out my wallet and give him thirty in cash. "Thanks, man," he says, and they set off, much to my relief.

I don't even wait for the cab to disappear before I turn and run around the back of the building, impatient to know what's going on.

I'm so impatient, I can barely function, and I fumble with my keys, nerves getting the better of me… although why I'm nervous, I don't know.

I mean… this could be my entire future at stake. What's there to be nervous about?

I get the door open eventually, and hurry up the stairs, taking them two at a time. I may be unsure how we're going to start this conversation, but we need to start it, and the sooner the better.

"Robyn?" I call as I get to the top.

She's sitting on the couch, still wearing her work clothes, clutching a cup of coffee, and she spins around, taking a moment before she focuses on me.

"Oh… it's you," she says, her voice a little slurred, and my heart sinks… especially when I notice the bottle of wine on the table in front of her. It's almost empty, and although it takes me a moment, I realize what that means.

She must have been drunk when she sent that text.

I feel like we've been here before… only without the sex this time.

She didn't mean it, and probably regrets it, just like she regretted sleeping with me, and although I don't mind cutting my date short, I wish things could have been different.

I wish I didn't feel like I'd come back here for no reason… other than to humiliate myself, all over again.

Chapter Seventeen

Robyn

His eyes linger on the bottle, and I feel a wave of shame creep over me.

Why does he have this effect on me?

It's so unfair… and yet it's all of my own making.

There's no-one to blame but myself.

Which isn't anything new, really.

And I suppose that's what I need to tell him. That's how to start this conversation… by explaining how wrong I've been.

I'm pretty sure I've said that before, but this time I need him to understand, and I get to my feet, turning to face him, and almost fall over.

"Jesus, Robyn," he says, hurrying forward, although I right myself before he actually reaches me.

"What?" I look up into his eyes, trying not to think about the disappointment that stares back at me. What right has he to be disappointed in me?

"Don't you think it's time you stopped drinking so much?"

Is he serious? Judging by the look on his face, it seems so, and I step closer, shaking my head at him. "Who do you think you are?" I say, aware that my words sound nothing like the apology I'd intended. I was going to explain how wrong I'd been, and yet here I am, accusing him instead. "You have no right to tell me how to live."

That didn't help my cause, but honestly… from the way he's speaking, anyone would think I spent my entire life drinking.

And he knows better than that.

"I'm not trying to do anything of the sort," he says, sounding a little huffy. "I'm just trying to save us both the humiliation of any more drunken episodes."

"Drunken ep—episodes?" I say, struggling over my words and proving his point.

"Yes. More text messages you don't mean… more sex you'll regret when you're sober."

"Who says I didn't mean the text message? And do I need to remind you, I was sober the last time we had sex?"

"No, you don't, but you still regretted it, and reminding me of what happened just makes it worse."

"Are you saying you regret it now, too?"

I hope not… although at least I haven't admitted anything. I haven't told him how I feel. All I've done is send him a text message he clearly doesn't believe. Otherwise, why would he think I didn't mean it?

"No, I don't regret what we did. I made that pretty clear before I went out… or I thought I did."

It's a struggle to remember what he said before he went out. There was something about compatibility… or incompatibility, I think. But I'm not about to admit how much of a blur it all is and give him even more ammunition.

"You did," I say, trying to sound more certain about that than I feel.

"In which case, I think the best thing we can do is get you up the stairs to bed."

"I'm sure I'll manage."

I'm not sure about that at all, but given how badly our conversation has gone so far, it seems wise for us to part company… at least for now.

Everything I planned to say has come out wrong, and although I'd hoped he might want to talk, it seems he just wants to get rid of me.

I feel even more of a fool for hoping he might want me. He said he did, but I guess he's changed his mind. He's still mad at me, and it probably doesn't help that I've interrupted his evening with Ruth… because I think I have. I must have done. Why else is he here, frowning at me and talking about text messages?

I take a deep breath, doing my best to focus on the stairs, but because he's in the way, I have to dodge around him, and in doing so, I trip again. This time, he's close enough to catch me, and rather than just holding me up, he lifts me into his arms.

"I'll take you," he says.

"You don't have to."

He looks down at me, tipping his head to one side. "You sound just like Ruth."

"Is that an insult, or a compliment?"

"It's an observation."

"Where is she, by the way?" I ask as he puts his foot on the bottom step.

"She's not waiting downstairs, if that's what you're thinking." I hadn't been, but I'm relieved to hear it.

"She's gone home?"

"Yes."

"You left her to walk by herself?"

"Walk? She lives in Willmont Vale."

"Oh." I feel foolish now for imposing my daydreams onto his reality.

"I drove over there and picked her up earlier."

"And you didn't take her back?"

"I offered… okay?" he says, rolling his eyes. "I didn't abandon her on the street, and I paid her cab fare."

"Sorry. I didn't mean to imply…"

"Yes, you did," he says, climbing up the rest of the stairs. "I know your opinion of me is pretty low, but I also know the difference between right and wrong."

"Did I say you didn't?"

"You didn't need to," he says, lowering me to the floor.

I'm beside my bed, and as my legs don't feel too strong, it seems best to sit. Spencer watches me, like he feels to need to make sure I'm not going to slide to the floor. It's a possibility, but fortunately, it doesn't happen, and once he's sure I'm safe, he steps away.

Everything has gone so wrong, and having had the evening from hell, I don't feel I can let it end like this, so I grab his hand, surprised by his gasp, when he stops and looks down at me.

"What is it?" he says, sounding a little gruff.

"I was gonna ask you to stay for a while."

He shakes his head, pulling his hand from mine. "Are you kidding?"

"No." I was thinking we could talk, but I guess he doesn't want to. "I—I've ruined everything, haven't I?"

He lets out a long sigh and crouches in front of me, looking up into my face. "It's not that simple, Robyn."

"Yes, it is. I should never have started this."

He stands, surprising me, and I lie back, resting on my elbows as I watch him push his fingers back through his hair. "There you go again, voicing your regrets over what we've done."

"I'm not."

"Yes, you are."

"No. That's not what I meant."

"It sounded that way… although what I really don't get is why?"

"Why I regretted it?" I say, confused by his reaction as I sit up again. "Jeez… Can you hear yourself? Do you think you're so good in bed that every woman you sleep with is gonna think you're the best thing ever?"

He moves closer, his eyes darkening as he places on knee up on the mattress, and I lean back again… further and further away as he bends over, his hands either side of me, his lips almost touching mine.

"You screamed my fucking name, Robyn," he growls. "I felt you come on my cock, and on my tongue. I watched your body writhe in pleasure… pleasure you found with me. Not some other guy. Me. So don't tell me you didn't enjoy it. Don't pretend it wasn't just as good for you as it was for me."

"I—I didn't mean that."

"Then what did you mean?"

"I don't know."

He's got me too confused to think… but that's hardly a surprise. Not when he says things like that. My brain feels like cotton candy, swirling around my head. Clear thoughts are beyond me.

"You don't know?" he says, standing up again. "Because you're drunk?"

"No. I'm never so drunk I don't know what I'm saying, or what I'm doing."

That might be a white lie, considering how tough I found it to get up and down the stairs earlier, but he doesn't need to know about that. It won't help my cause.

"Maybe not," he says. "But you still haven't answered my question."

"Which one?"

"Why? I asked you why? Why are we here?"

Oh... that's what he meant. It seems I jumped to conclusions... and not for the first time, although understanding him doesn't help very much.

"I don't really know."

"Why not? You're the one who put us here, Robyn."

"Did I?"

"You know you did." He huffs out a sigh and turns away, although he spins right back again. "Don't you get it? You instigated sex with me on two separate occasions, then said it was a mistake. The regrets were all yours, not mine. You made it clear I wasn't the man for you, regardless of everything you'd done, and I thought I could come to terms with that... or try to. God knows how, but I knew I couldn't go on as we were. But then you sent that text message. You got me to come back here tonight... and now you're telling me you don't know why?"

"It's a muddle," I say, tapping the side of my head. "I don't understand most of it myself, so explaining it to you is kinda tricky."

"Obviously."

"Why do I keep doing this?" I say, and he frowns.

"That was my question. Repeating it back at me isn't gonna get us any answers."

He paces up and down beside my bed, and I watch him for a minute, trying to resist the temptation to reach out and pull him onto the mattress with me... not because he's making me dizzy, but because I want him. I want him so much, I think I have to tell him.

"I don't have the answers," I say. "All I know is, I can't resist you."

He stops and slowly turns, looking down at me. "Sorry?" he whispers.

"I can't resist you." I enunciate each word as carefully as I can, and he steps closer, looking down at me.

"You mean that?"

"Yes. I know I should try harder… not because you're not right for me, or any of that bullshit, but because what I've been doing is wrong. I was thinking about this earlier, after you went out…"

"Before or after you started drinking?" he asks.

"Before," I say with a touch of sarcasm, which he acknowledges with a nod of his head.

"Okay. What were you thinking?"

"That what I've been doing is wrong."

"You've said that already. What you haven't explained is what you mean."

"No… because it's not that easy."

He hesitates for a moment, and then takes a step forward, pausing before he moves even closer and eventually sits beside me. It's like he's scared… or at least wary, and I guess I can't blame him for that.

"What's wrong?" he asks, his voice a lot softer than I have any right to expect. "What's troubling you?"

"The things I've done… seducing you, as you put it…"

"What about it?"

"If a man had done that to me, without at least asking first…" My voice fades, shame overwhelming me, and I lower my head, unable to say another word.

"You'd have called the cops?" he says, and I nod my head.

"Probably. Well… almost certainly."

"You'd have felt violated? Is that what you're saying?"

"Yes. I think I would."

"I see, and have you been beating yourself up over this?" he asks.

"A little."

"Then don't." He reaches out, cupping my chin with his hand, the contact making me gasp as he turns my head so we're facing each other. "You didn't do anything wrong. Not in that way."

"I should have asked… not taken."

"Did I seem unwilling?"

"No, but…"

"There are no buts, Robyn. We already established I wasn't an idle participant." I shudder at the recollection of the last time we said those words… or rather when I said them to him, and he moves a little closer, his eyes locked on mine, and I struggle to breathe. "You didn't force yourself on me. I wanted you," he says.

"Past tense?" I say without thinking, recalling what he said earlier.

"It happened in the past, so yes. And I didn't feel like you were taking advantage of me. If I'd wanted to stop you, I could have done. But stopping was the last thing on my mind."

"Are you sure?"

"I'm positive." He stands up again, as though he doesn't feel the need to be beside me… to offer comfort anymore. "I may not have liked what happened afterwards, but I didn't object to anything you did. In fact, I loved every second. I—I told you, you're the best."

"Yeah… but that's just something people say in the heat of the moment."

"I don't. I've never said that before… to anyone. And in any case, it wasn't in the heat of the moment, was it? It was right before I went to the bathroom, after the heat had died down. I was about as cool as I could be, considering what we'd done… at least, until I came back to find you getting dressed and telling me it shouldn't have happened."

I remember now, and I nod my head, although I think the less said about that the better.

"So, you didn't feel I'd overstepped the mark?"

"No. I'm not gonna say I understand why you did it… especially not the second time. Like you said, you were sober, and you'd already expressed your regrets after our first encounter."

"I know, but the thing is, you're like… you're like really good chocolate, or great ice cream."

He shakes his head. "Are you saying I'm edible?"

Very.

"Not necessarily," I say out loud, unwilling to admit how much I need him. "What I guess I'm trying to say is you're impossible to say 'no' to."

"That would make a lot more sense if I'd been the one asking. But I wasn't, was I?"

"No, you weren't."

"It makes more sense of your regrets, though."

"Does it?"

"Yes. You know just as well as I do that there's always an element of regret when you over-indulge. That's probably why you keep reacting the way you do. It's guilt."

I stare up at him, wondering how he can make it sound so straightforward when my head is still spinning. That's got nothing to do with the wine, either. It's because he's here in my room, tempting me to make those same mistakes again.

Except I know they wouldn't be mistakes.

Not this time.

And besides, even if he is more tempting than the best ice cream in the world, I don't just want to rip his clothes off. I want him to hold me. And more than that, I want him to keep holding me and never let go.

While he's doing that, I want him to whisper that he's forgiven me, that we can put the past behind us and move forward. I want him to lean back, look into my eyes and tell me he loves me, and that he'll make it okay. And finally, I want him to kiss me… not with a view to taking it further, but just because he wants to.

We've never kissed like that before, but I know if we did, it would be magical.

Just like everything we do together.

Except fight.

I'm done fighting, and I look up into his eyes as he gazes down at me, holding my breath until he tips his head to one side, and rather than whispering his forgiveness, or his love, he just says, "Goodnight," and leaves the room.

What?

Goodnight?

That wasn't supposed to happen, and as I listen to his footsteps on the stairs, I wonder about calling out to him… to tell him I love him.

Except he'd probably assume I was playing games.

I'm not, but I wouldn't blame him for thinking it.

Not after everything I've done.

I can't leave it like this, though, and although I've got no idea what I'm going to say, I leap to my feet and rush to the top of the stairs, calling out his name.

Chapter Eighteen

Spencer

I'm almost at the bottom of the stairs when I hear Robyn call out to me, and I turn around, looking up at her.

"I came to the restaurant this evening," she says, blurting out her words. She's clinging to the curtain, like her life depends on it, which it probably does, because she's swaying so much, she looks like she could fall at any moment. I'd catch her if she did – obviously – but the sight of her like this only reminds me of the fact that, no matter how tempting she is, I can't act. I can't do anything, other than ask the natural question.

"Why?"

"To see you." She shakes her head, then frowns. "No. Not to see you. To talk to you… which would obviously have involved seeing you, too." She's not making much sense, but I guess that's the wine talking. She lowers her gaze, biting her bottom lip. I'm more than a little distracted, but before I can do anything, or even talk myself out of doing anything, she adds, "And maybe to see Ruth, too."

That's a surprise. "You wanted to see her? What for?"

"I was curious."

"About what?"

"What she looked like," she says, her voice a barely audible whisper.

"And?" I ask, intrigue getting the better of me.

"She's very beautiful," she says, tipping her head slightly. "And not at all like me."

Is she saying she thinks Ruth is more beautiful than she is? Surely not. There's no comparison. While I'm not denying Ruth is a beautiful woman, there's no-one in the world who compares to Robyn.

"No, she's not like you at all," I say, aware that my response is a little cryptic, although it seems to fly over Robyn's head.

"She's so much more soph—sophisticated." She struggles over her words, reminding me that the wine is responsible for at least some of what she's saying, and I shouldn't get carried away.

"She really isn't." The dress she had on was nowhere near as elegant as the one Robyn wore when we went to the restaurant, and Ruth was so obvious in her intentions. I let out a sigh, recalling the way Robyn seduced me… which I guess was pretty damn obvious. Except that was different. I wanted Robyn. I welcomed her seduction, and I craved her attention, in a way I've never craved anyone before.

Certainly not Ruth.

"Was she mad at you?" she asks.

"Yes."

"Was that why she insisted on getting a cab home?"

"It was."

"This is all my fault, isn't it?"

I'm not sure which part of 'all' she's referring to, but I remember the last time she apologized like this, and where it led us… and while I'm not saying I'm too weak to say 'no' to her, I'm also not sure I want to.

Regardless of the wine, things have changed tonight. I don't know exactly how, but they're different. She's different, and it would be really easy to go back up the stairs and join her.

Except I know I can't.

Why?

Because I need her to be sober. I need to be sure that whatever happens next happens for the right reason.

And that means I have to walk away while I still can.

"I think we should leave this for tonight," I say.

"Oh." I can hear her disappointment, but I daren't take the risk. What if I go back up to her, we make love, and she says she regrets it… again?

Just the thought of that is enough to break me, and I shake my head, taking a step back. "You need to get some sleep."

"I guess," she says, although I can hear the reluctance in her voice.

She gazes down at me for a moment longer, and as though she's suddenly decided to do as I suggest, she slowly pulls the curtain.

There's something final about that. It's like she's blocking me out… although I have no right to complain. She's only doing what I asked.

Except I know, deep down, I'd much rather be up there with her, holding her in my arms.

I don't want to be down here by myself.

So, should I ignore my instincts and go back up?

We don't have to make love. I could explain that I'd rather wait and just hold her while she sleeps. It wouldn't be the first time.

I remember what that felt like… her soft body curled into mine, and I smile at the thought. It soon fades, though, when I recall what happened the next morning. I can't face that again, or anything like it, and I trudge down the stairs, wondering if we'll ever work this out.

I'd hoped we might this evening. That was the thought in my head when I left the restaurant. Why else would she have sent that text message? That was what I was thinking when I came back here… little realizing she was drunk when she sent it.

And because of that, nothing else has gone as I'd expected… or hoped.

It started badly and got worse.

I shake my head, wandering to the couch and flopping down onto it.

Why is it that Robyn has a way of misinterpreting everything I say? When I said we should leave this for tonight, I meant for tonight. Just like I said. I didn't mean forever. And yet she looked so defeated when she closed the curtain and shut me out. Even now, I'm tempted to go and explain… except my explanations don't seem to work, do they? It's like when I suggested she should curb her drinking habits. All I meant was that I wanted us to be able to talk properly and coherently. I didn't mean that I wanted to rule her life. I'd never dream of doing that. Why would I? Her carefree spirit is one of the things I find most appealing about her. I especially love the fact that she initiates sex between us.

It's the aftermath I can't handle.

I think she understands that now, though.

She must do.

I just explained it to her.

And she just explained that she finds me irresistible… evidently.

I chuckle to myself. I'm like chocolate or ice cream, it seems. And not just any old ice cream, but 'great' ice cream. I know enough about women to get what that means.

It means she can't get enough of me.

I feel the same about her. Or I would, if I didn't appreciate the regret that always follows such overindulgence.

It exactly mirrors Robyn's reactions to me when we've made love together.

It's like she feels the need to indulge, and then feels bad about it afterwards, and in beating herself up about it, she takes me down with her.

What I still don't really understand, though, is why she feels so bad.

We're not doing anything wrong. In fact, when we're together, we're about as right as it gets.

So, feeling bad about it makes no sense. It's the last thing I want for her. She should feel happy, and wanted, and loved.

I sit up straight, realization dawning.

Does that mean I'm failing her?

I guess I must be.

I guess she's not the only one with a communication problem, because, let's face it, I haven't told her how I really feel.

I had the perfect opportunity just now, when we were up in her room, sitting on her bed, and I didn't take it. I could have done when I clasped my hand around her chin, and gazed into her eyes. It was the ideal moment to tell her I'm in love with her. And yet, I didn't.

Admittedly, I was more concerned with convincing her she hadn't done anything wrong… because I felt that needed to be said. That was the priority. She'd obviously been giving herself a hard time over the way she'd gone about things, even though she had no cause. I mean, how on earth could she have thought I was unwilling?

Was that another failure on my part?

Didn't she realize how much I wanted her?

Evidently not.

Was that why I told her she was the best… again?

I can't be sure.

It felt like an instinct at the time. Something I needed to say, and something she needed to hear. But maybe words aren't enough.

Actions sometimes speak louder, and I get to my feet, heading for the bottom of the stairs, although I stop, my foot poised to climb.

Should I do this?

If I go up there, it won't just be about holding her in my arms, or even making love… if we get that far.

We need to talk first.

I need to tell her how I feel… of course I do. But I also need to explain what the last few weeks have meant to me. She has to understand that being with her was – and still is – the most incredible experience of my life. I need to get her to see that, however we are together, it's not about asking, or even taking, but about offering ourselves to each other… because love is about giving, and not holding back.

I don't know exactly when I worked that out. It was probably when I was inside Robyn, knowing I was hers, and always would be. I think that was when I realized she owned me… and how much I liked it.

But knowing that won't achieve a thing unless I tell her.

I have to say the words out loud for her to understand, and I take a step up, leaving my doubts on the floor below as I climb up to her room.

I still don't know exactly what I'm going to say, but as I get closer to the curtain, I realize there's no turning back, regretting that there's nowhere to knock.

"Robyn?" I whisper.

She doesn't respond, and I call her name again, just a little louder.

There's still no reply, and although I know I probably shouldn't, I take a chance and nudge the curtain open, poking my head through the gap. I half expect to be greeted with a yelp of surprise, or even indignation, but the room's in silence… and there's a reason for that.

Robyn is already in bed, and from the looks of things, she's fast asleep.

I wonder if I should check, but she'd have said something if she'd heard me, and I really shouldn't go into her room unasked… not when she's unaware of my presence. If she woke and found me there, I dread to think what she'd say.

Or what I'd do in response.

"No," I whisper under my breath as I pull the curtain closed again.

This is definitely best left… for tonight.

We can talk tomorrow. It'll be better then, in the cold light of day. I know it will, and I slowly make my way down the stairs again, pausing at the bottom and recalling that drunken kiss she gave me on this very spot.

That was where this all started, I guess… and I shake my head remembering her apology. It wasn't what I wanted to hear, but there's no denying, she's even more drunk tonight than she was then.

My heart sinks at the thought. Because I know what that means…

It means she could wake up tomorrow, and amid her hungover embarrassment, realize this all meant nothing. Hell… she might not even remember what happened tonight. Not properly.

There may be evidence, in the form of the message she sent me earlier, but she can easily delete that from her phone and pretend it never happened. She can put it down to drinking too much wine and maybe vow never to do it again… for the time being.

I can't delete it. Not yet. Aside from seducing me, it's the first thing that's given me any hope… and so far, she hasn't said she regrets sending it. In fact, I seem to remember her saying she meant it. So, even though I know she was drunk when she typed it out, I'm gonna hold on to it for now.

Because hope is all I've got… until we can talk.

I go back to the couch and sit down again, spying her phone beside me. I could move it, but I won't. She'll be expecting to find it here in the morning, so I just nudge it aside, glancing at the wine bottle that's still on the table in front of me, and smiling to myself when I realize the text message she sent me earlier isn't the only sign of hope.

She came down to the restaurant.

I wish I'd seen her now, but how could I? I had my back to the window… and in any case, I'm not sure what I'd have done.

I'd have questioned why she was there… naturally. That's what I'm doing now, even though she gave me an explanation of sorts.

She wanted to see Ruth. That was part of it, although she didn't really explain why. Was it more than curiosity? I can't be sure, and even if it wasn't, what did she have to be curious about? Right before I left, Robyn made a point of telling me how incompatible we were, and why. In which case, would she care who I spent my evening with?

It seems unlikely.

There has to be more to it than curiosity.

But what? Jealousy?

That makes even less sense. And besides, she doesn't seem the jealous type.

Although is she? Why else would she have wanted to make sure Ruth and I hadn't gone back to her place? Why else would she have asked me not to sleep with her?

Does jealousy make it add up, or am I reading too much into a drunk text?

I probably am. Except I'd like to know whether she sent the message before or after she came down to the restaurant.

After seems more logical.

If she was contemplating sending the message, she'd have wanted to ensure she wasn't too late. I know I would.

So would most people. Although I can't imagine many people would get themselves into a situation like that.

But if they did, they'd want to avoid the embarrassment of sending their message when it was already too late.

Which brings me back to the message again. I'd never have expected Robyn to send something like that. She's far too independent to plead for anything… and yet she did.

It has to mean something… even if I don't fully understand what.

It seems Robyn doesn't either.

But maybe she will if I ask her tomorrow.

I get up and go to the kitchen, bringing the wine bottle with me. There isn't much of it left, but I put it back in the refrigerator anyway, and close the door before I make my way to my bedroom.

The last time I was in here, I was mad at Robyn, desperate to escape the horrible atmosphere between us, and looking for a way out.

Now, I'm just confused.

I can't deny the atmosphere has improved, and I don't feel like I need a way out anymore.

As for being mad at Robyn? Nothing could be further from the truth.

I just need some answers.

But I guess I'll have to wait a little longer for those.

Chapter Nineteen

Robyn

I crack my eyes open, hoping for the best.

I've been dozing for a while, plucking up the courage to do this, and now it's done, I have to admit, I feel better than I expected… and better than I deserve.

I've definitely had worse hangovers in my life, even if my head feels a little fragile.

Whether I've felt worse about myself is debatable.

I can't recall a time when I've felt more guilty… more ashamed… more embarrassed.

What was I thinking last night?

Sending that text message was a mistake. It's like I said to Spencer, I didn't have the right, and as for our conversation when he got back here…? I don't think that could have gone much worse if we'd both tried really hard to screw up.

Because it was both of us who got things wrong this time. It wasn't just me.

We misunderstood. We jumped to conclusions.

Although I can't blame Spencer for any of it. Not really. He's not the one who started it… just like he hasn't been the one to start anything between us.

That's been down to me. Every single time.

And while I can't honestly say I regret seducing him – twice – there are elements of last night that I definitely wish hadn't happened.

Obviously, there's the message, but there's also my drunken stumble down to the restaurant. I remember feeling relieved he didn't see me… but, in that case, why did I think it was a good idea to tell him?

I'd deliberately hidden myself from him… and yet I blurted out my presence.

Why did I do that? Why did I explain how jealous I was?

I did that, didn't I? I told him I wanted to see Ruth… to know what she was like.

I think I even told him I thought she was beautiful… more beautiful than me. Or did I say I thought she was more sophisticated than me? I can't remember. I recall struggling to say the word, and feeling embarrassed about that.

But why did I say it all in the first place?

In the hope he'd stay?

Probably.

Although he didn't, did he?

He told me I needed some sleep, and although he was right about that, I wish he'd been willing to come back up here and sleep with me.

I wouldn't have ripped his clothes off. Not this time. But I'd have sold my soul to spend the night with him… to lie in his arms and drift off to sleep.

And to wake up beside him.

As it is, I'm alone.

There's nothing new there. Except this morning, I feel lonelier than ever.

Which doesn't make any more sense than the rest of this sorry tale.

I've woken up alone practically every day of my life. So why should I feel lonely today?

Because I miss him?

I nod my head, surprised that it doesn't hurt, and turn over to face the window.

It's true. I miss him so much it's like a physical ache, deep inside me, and I guess I'm a little scared that he might not miss me. Even though he said he wanted me, I'm aware of how much I've hurt him, and that you can't keep hurting someone and expect them to come back for more.

At some point, they're going to walk away.

And I'm worried I might have reached that point with Spencer.

I guess there's only one way to find out… and that's to get up. I'll have to take it slowly, though. My head may be less fragile than I'd expected, but I'm not pushing my luck. There's a world of difference between lying in bed and feeling okay, and actually coping with life.

Or even standing up.

I sit up first, letting myself get accustomed to the change of position, and then swing my legs over the side of the bed, recalling what it felt like last night when Spencer came and sat beside me. He held my chin and looked into my eyes. I remember that. I also remember feeling like he cared… until he let me go again.

Still, that was yesterday, and I have to hope that today can be different.

I have to hope he won't let me go again.

Otherwise, what's the point?

I stand up, swaying slightly, although the room remains still, which is an improvement on last night, and once I'm sure I feel steady enough to walk, I make my way to the curtain, pulling it back. There's no sound of movement coming from downstairs, but Spencer can be very quiet when he wants to be, and although I'm only wearing a thin chemise, I head down to the floor below.

I was wearing something similar to this when I last ripped Spencer's clothes off and I'm aware I should probably have put something else on. Except he's seen it all before, and I'm through playing games… which means there's no point in hiding from him.

Or there wouldn't be, if he were here.

"Spencer?" I call, raising my voice, relieved that my head doesn't hurt when I do. What hurts is the silence that greets me.

Where can he be?

I turn around, checking the time on the microwave, which is easier than it was last night. I don't have to squint to see it's just after nine-thirty. That's later than I thought, so I guess Spencer was right; I needed to sleep.

I also need to know why he's not here.

Maybe he's avoiding me. I wouldn't blame him.

Although I guess he could have gone to the grocery store. It's possible he got bored waiting for me to wake up, and decided to do something useful instead.

The notepad is on the coffee table, with the first page flipped over. There's a pen beside it, and now I'm awake enough to notice, there's also a cup by the sink. That explains it. He's written a list and gone to buy food, and although it would have been nice to do that together, I guess he couldn't wait around all morning… and I should make the most of his absence and get dressed.

Although first, I need a coffee, and I fix one, taking it into the bathroom with me.

I take my time over showering, mostly because I can't do anything quickly today, and once I've brushed my teeth, I come out, wrapped in a towel. I half expect to see Spencer unloading the groceries, but there's still no sign of him, so I climb the stairs to my room, leave my coffee on the dresser and sort out some clothes.

It looks like a sunny day, so I pull out some jeans and a t-shirt, leaving them on the bed, alongside my underwear, before I dry my hair.

I even put on a little makeup, telling myself it can't hurt to make the effort, and once I'm sure I look okay, I finish my coffee and get dressed.

My bed looks like someone had a fight in it, so I take a while to make it, but when I'm done, I grab my cup and go back down the stairs, stopping in surprise at the bottom when I realize Spencer still isn't back. The apartment is exactly as it was earlier, and an icy shiver runs through my body.

Have I misunderstood?

More to the point, has my behavior driven him away?

"Oh, God…" I clamp my hand over my mouth as a horrible thought occurs.

Has he gone to Ruth's place?

My text message obviously interrupted their evening. It made Ruth mad… mad enough that she went home in a cab, rather than letting Spencer take her. But has he gone over there to make amends? Or worse still, did he go there last night, once we'd finished talking?

He didn't say that was their arrangement, but that doesn't mean he didn't feel the need to explain or apologize. If he did though, I wonder what he said.

Did he tell her he'd come home to find me drunk?

Did he tell her I'd said he was like chocolate, or ice cream… or both?

I can't remember exactly what I said now, but I know it was something to do with him being irresistible. Because he is.

Although the thought of him telling Ruth any of that is beyond humiliating.

Is it worse than the thought of them being together?

Of course not, but as I think about that, and put the picture in my head, like I did last night, I know I can't stand here and do nothing.

Even if he's not with Ruth – and I really hope he's not – I need to know where he is, and noticing my phone lying on the couch, I realize what I have to do. Obviously, I'm aware I might regret this, but not knowing is killing me, so I lean over and grab hold of it, taking a deep breath before I type…

— ***Sorry to text again. I promise I'm sober. I'm also worried about you. Can you call or text me back, just so I know you're okay? And if possible, can you come home so we can talk? I'm sorry, Spence. For everything.***

I pause, my finger poised over the 'x' as I try to decide whether I should add a kiss.

It seems like a friendly thing to do, but would he misunderstand? Would he think I'm trying to pressure him into something?

"It's a kiss," I mutter to myself. And it's not even a real one.

I press the 'x', nodding my head, just as I hear a key in the lock downstairs.

I turn around, facing the stairs, holding my breath. It's Saturday, after all. That means whoever just came in might not be Spencer. They could be someone connected with the bookstore.

I wait… my heart racing, until I hear footsteps coming up to the apartment.

It's him, and I drop my phone onto the couch, my relief almost overwhelming.

I don't know why I'm so relieved. After all, I still don't have a clue where he's been.

He could have been out all night for all I know.

Except for the coffee cup. The voice in my head tries to make sense of the evidence… if I can call it that.

And I'd like to believe it. I really would.

But I know the cup means nothing. He could have made a coffee last night, and drunk it before going back to Ruth's place. There's no proof he drank it this morning, is there?

I wish there were, but…

I suck in a breath as he reaches the top of the stairs and glances over, his eyes widening when he sees me.

"Good morning," he says, and I let my eyes wander, taking in his jeans and tight-fitting t-shirt.

"Hi."

He takes a step closer, holding up a bag I hadn't noticed. It's in his right hand and has the coffee shop's logo on the side.

"I thought I'd get us some breakfast."

"On your way back from somewhere?" I ask as he puts the bag on the coffee table and turns to face me.

"Like where?"

"I don't know… Ruth's place, maybe?"

I can hear the fear and uncertainty in my voice, and it looks like Spencer can, too, as he steps closer to me and gazes down into my eyes.

"Ruth's place? Why would I wanna go there? You sent me a text message, asking me not to."

"I know, but that was last night, and after you got it, you came back here, realized I was drunk when I sent it, and said you didn't think I meant it."

"Yes… and then you said you did." His lips twitch upwards slightly. "That's what I'd hoped you'd say, by the way."

"You did?" I can't hide my surprise, and he nods his head.

"Yes, although while we're on the subject of your message, can you put me out of my misery? Can you tell me, did you send it before or after you came down to the restaurant?"

"After," I say, feeling myself blush.

It's the first time we've discussed this while I've been sober, and I can't help feeling the full depths of my embarrassment. I even lower my head, gasping when he reaches out and places his finger beneath my chin, so he can raise it again.

"I thought so," he says. "It made more sense to do things that way.

"Have you been trying to figure it out?"

He smiles, nodding his head. "That's what I was doing last night after I left you upstairs."

"But you didn't leave me upstairs, did you? I remember us talking. You were down here and I was up there," I say, pointing to my room. "I closed the curtain and…"

"And went to sleep," he says, licking his bottom lip.

"How do you know that?"

"Because I came up to see you."

"You did?"

"Yes."

"Why?"

"There were things that needed to be said."

"But I thought you said you wanted to leave it."

"I did… and then I changed my mind," he says.

"So y—you came up to my room?"

"Yes. But you'd already gone to sleep. So, I left you there, like I said I did." He steps closer. "I wasn't with Ruth, Robyn. I didn't go to her place. The thought didn't even cross my mind. I was here on the couch, going over what had happened, trying to work out what it all meant."

"Did you reach any conclusions?" I ask.

"No. So, I went to bed. My bed. No-one else's."

I feel bad for having doubted him, although my uncertainty doesn't feel completely unfounded.

"It's just that you've been gone for such a long time."

"I know," he says. "Sorry about that. I got talking to the woman who owns the coffee shop."

"Oh?"

"Yeah." He smiles down at me. "But of course, you weren't there last night, were you, so it won't make sense to you."

"What won't?"

"Eloise having her baby."

"No… you're right. That makes no sense at all."

He chuckles. "Well… she had it last night."

"And you were there? You were with her?"

"No. I was here. I just told you that. But yesterday evening, when I was at the restaurant with Ruth, Gabe Sullivan came and talked to me. He was there with his wife, Remi, and…"

"Wait a minute. Is this Gabe Sullivan from work?"

"Yes. He's my boss… which is to say, I guess Ryan's my boss, like he's yours, and everyone else's, but Gabe's the one I report to."

"I see. And you met him last night?"

"Yeah, he came over to our table with his wife, and we got talking."

"What about?"

"Mostly about the fact that his wife is pregnant. Ryan had already told me, but I don't think Gabe was aware of that."

"Oh… okay. Although I still don't see what this has to do with this other woman… Eloise, was it?"

"It didn't. Not directly. It was just that we got around to talking about how many women there are in the town who are pregnant, or who have just given birth, and one of them was Eloise. Remi was explaining her baby was ten days late or something. She said they were gonna give her the weekend and then do something about it, although I can't remember what."

"Induce the labor?" I suggest.

"That was it."

"But I guess that's no longer required."

"No."

"I'm sure that's lovely, but who exactly is Eloise?"

"She's the wife of the guy who owns the restaurant."

"I can see how that made it a little more relevant… although I can't believe you sat there with Ruth, and your boss and his wife and talked about pregnant women."

"We didn't sit; we stood, and Ruth didn't join in."

"Why not?"

"She didn't seem interested."

"And yet you carried on talking, anyway?"

He blushes, just slightly, and I have to smile. It's a look he wears well, and while I wouldn't have thought you could improve on perfection, it seems I was wrong. He looks even better than ever, and my body heats, although I do my best to ignore the feelings building inside me and focus on our conversation.

"Yes," he says. "To be honest, I'd already worked out that I didn't want to be with her. I worked that out before I even got to her place, so I welcomed Gabe and Remi interrupting us, and I didn't want them to leave. I'd have been happy to carry on talking to them for as long as I could."

"Then why didn't you invite them to join you?"

"Because they were celebrating."

"Remi's pregnancy?"

"No. Her birthday… although I'm not sure that's what's important here. What matters is that I got delayed this morning because I was talking to the woman in the coffee shop about Eloise."

"I understand that now… and what did she have? Eloise, I mean. Was it a boy, or a girl?"

"A boy. He was born just after midnight, and was enormous, evidently. I can't remember the size now, but they're calling him Rowan."

"You got all this from the lady in the coffee shop?"

He nods his head. "It's the place to go if you wanna know what's happening in Hart's Creek."

"Clearly."

He smiles. "To be fair, the woman who owns the coffee shop wasn't the one spreading the word. It was a customer of hers. They were having a conversation about it when I went in. I overheard what they were saying as I was standing in line, and because of what I'd been told last night, I joined in."

"And that took an hour?"

He frowns. "God… was it really an hour?"

"Nearly. I've been awake since nine-thirty, and it's…" I turn and look at the clock. "It's just after ten-twenty."

"Well… that's a good way to waste a morning," he says. "Which reminds me, we should eat these cinnamon rolls. I imagine they're already cold, but hopefully the coffee will still be warm."

He grabs the bag, and we sit together, side by side on the couch. I watch as he opens it, handing me a cup of coffee, and then a cinnamon roll, wrapped in a paper napkin.

It smells delicious, and I take a bite, recalling that I didn't get around to eating anything last night, although I don't think I'll mention that. He'll only tell me off for drinking on an empty stomach, and instead, I look over at him, and whisper, "You were right."

He's just taken a bite of his cinnamon roll and he frowns, chewing his mouthful before he says, "What about?"

"Everything, I think." I sip my coffee. It's warmer than Spencer thought, and I appreciate it almost as much as the one I made earlier. I need it too. "Definitely the drinking less part," I say.

He shakes his head, putting down his cinnamon roll. "I'm sorry I said that. I didn't mean it the way you thought."

"I know. That's what I meant when I said you were right. We need to talk, and I need to make sense of everything when we do. There have been too many misunderstandings… and you have a right to know where you stand."

He sucks in a breath. "Is that what you wanna tell me? Where I stand?"

"I'd like to try. Like I said last night, I don't fully understand it myself, but I've realized if we don't talk it through, we're never gonna get anywhere. We certainly won't get out of this spiral of hurt, and I think we both need to."

"We do," he says, sounding a little downhearted. "Although before we start, can you tell me… is this something I'm gonna want to hear?"

"I can't tell you that."

"Why not?"

"Because it depends on what you want to hear."

"The truth," he says. "All I want is the truth."

"I've never lied to you, Spencer."

"Really? Even when I asked you not to fuck with me? You said you wouldn't… and then you did just that."

"Maybe. But I didn't mean to." He frowns, and I realize I have to explain. "I didn't mean to hurt you. To be honest, I didn't think I could."

"Because you don't think guys have feelings?"

"No. I know they do."

"Oh… so it was because you thought I was a player, and feelings didn't come into it? Is that what you're saying?"

"Yes. I think so."

"Then you were wrong."

My heart stops, skips a beat and then starts again. It's a strange feeling, but in a way, I like it. "I think I kinda worked that out."

"Good… because I'm done playing games, Robyn. I want something real."

"Then it has to start with me saying sorry."

"Okay, but you've said that before… more than once. The last time you seduced me started with an apology. It ended with one too, if I recall correctly. Is this about the same thing? Or are you apologizing for something else this time? Is this about the drunk text message? Or telling me you didn't enjoy what we did together? Is it something I haven't even thought of? I know I've failed you, but…"

"You've done what?" I say, interrupting him, my apology forgotten for a moment. "You think you've failed me? How?"

"I haven't communicated with you. That was one of the things I came to your room to talk to you about last night. I haven't told you how I feel. If I had, you'd have realized the consequences of your actions… or I hope you would."

"Probably," I say. "But this isn't your fault, Spencer. It's mine… and just to get one thing clear, I may be sorry for a lot of things, but I'm not sorry for seducing you."

"Seriously?" He sits forward, resting his elbows on his knees. "You apologized both times. You said it shouldn't have happened."

I can't deny that. "I know, but that doesn't mean I didn't want you."

"You just regretted putting your desires into action? You regretted making the fantasy a reality?"

"Something like that. But I was wrong," I say, reaching out and placing my hand on the couch between us. He looks down at it, but doesn't move. He just lets out a sigh and eventually sits back, turning to face me, and the look of disappointment on his face takes my breath away. "Don't tell me you've never made a mistake before… or hurt someone?" I say, going on the defensive. That's probably the wrong way to tackle this, but I can't seem to help it.

"Of course I've made mistakes," he says. "More than I care to remember. I'm pretty sure I've hurt people, too. The difference is, I've never done it intentionally. I've never gone out of my way to cause pain to anyone."

"You… You think I'd…?" I can't believe he thinks so badly of me, and I get to my feet, ready to run. I'm not sure where I'll go, but before I can decide, he grabs my hand.

"Where are you going?"

"Anywhere but here."

He stands, looking down at me, although he doesn't let go of me. "You think that's the answer? You think running away is how we get out of this spiral, as you called it?"

"No, but I'm not sure we can. I'm not sure you want to."

"Of course I do. I have to."

"Why?"

I stare up at him, and he pulls me into his arms, crushing my body to his. "Because I'm in love with you," he says, his voice a low growl.

"L—Love?"

"Yes. Bone-numbing, mind-blowing, head-spinning, life-affirming love."

"With me?"

He smiles. "Yes. With you."

"After everything I've done? Everything I've said?"

"It happened before most of the things you said and did, if I'm being honest."

"And that hasn't changed your mind?"

"If last night taught me one thing, it's that nothing – and no-one – ever could."

"What does that mean?"

"It means that spending an evening with Ruth made me realize I don't wanna be with anyone but you… ever again."

"So you want to work this out?"

He shakes his head, surprising me. "Like I said, I have to work this out. I can't go on like this… and I sure as hell can't live without you, so if you're thinking about running away, forget it."

"I'm not… not anymore."

He smiles and pulls me back down onto the couch, holding me in his arms. "Glad to hear it, although I could use a little reassurance."

"What about?" Is he going to ask whether I love him back? And if he does, what will I say?

You'll tell him the truth. You'll tell him that, even though it's taken you a while, you're so in love with him, you can't even think straight.

"About something you said last night."

"Which something would that be?"

"The part where you accused me of being arrogant."

"I know I was drunk, but I don't remember saying that."

"You didn't. Not in so many words, but you implied it."

I lower my head as I realize what he's talking about. "Was this the part where I suggested you thought you were so good in bed that no woman could ever think otherwise?"

"Something like that." I think I'd prefer him to have asked if I loved him. The answer would have been easier than the one I think he's looking for now, and I wait a moment, wondering how to answer, until he dips his head and he says, "Did you mean it?"

"You know I didn't. I said so at the time."

"But then you didn't qualify that, did you? You didn't explain."

"No. I'm not great at explaining, in case you hadn't noticed."

He smiles. "It had come to my attention, and I'm not asking for details. All I need to know is, did I get something wrong? Were you happy with what we did?"

"I seduced you twice," I say. "The second time should have been enough of a hint. But you took me to places I've never been before, and as you pointed out, I screamed your name, Spence."

He leans in and kisses the tip of my nose.

"I'm Spence again, am I?"

"You were Spence last night, weren't you? Or have I misremembered that?"

"No. I was Spence last night, but it means so much more this morning."

"Because I'm sober?"

"Partly… but mostly because I need to hear you say my name like that in the cold light of day. Not in a text message, or when you're coming on my tongue, or when I'm buried deep inside you, but just like this, when you're sitting here beside me. Can you understand that?" I nod my head, letting out a sigh. "What's wrong?" he asks.

"When you say things like that… about me coming on your tongue, or you being buried deep inside me… it does strange things to my head, and that's not very helpful when I'm still trying to work out how to explain."

"Explain what?"

"My remarks about your supposed arrogance."

"It's okay. You don't need to tell me what you meant… not now."

"I don't?"

"No. I'm Spence again… and that's all I need to know. We'll put everything else down to a misunderstanding."

"Another one?"

"Probably."

He smiles, and looking up into his eyes, I see something I've never seen before. It's like a warm glow, and it heats me from within. I'd like to do something about that, but before I can, he reaches out, caressing my cheek with his fingertips. I lean into his touch, and he pulls back slightly, studying my face.

"Can I ask another question?" he says.

"Sure."

"Can you tell me why you sent that drunk text message? I understand more about when you sent it but what I still don't really get is why."

"The clue was in the message."

He tips his head to one side. "You didn't want me to sleep with Ruth?"

"No, I didn't. I may not have had the right to send it, or to ask anything of you, but…"

"You did have the right," he says. "But what you haven't explained is why you thought I'd sleep with her in the first place."

"You'd said you wanted to be with someone who didn't mess with your head. I assumed…"

He shakes his head. "I guess I can't blame you for thinking the worst of me. You didn't know how I felt about you, so how were you to know that the thought of sleeping with anyone other than you wouldn't even enter my head."

"I still shouldn't have sent it."

"I shouldn't have made you feel so insecure that you had to."

"Will you stop taking the blame for things that are my fault?" I say, leaning away from him.

He pulls me back and says, "No," and I have to laugh. "God, you're beautiful," he says, cupping my face with his hands.

My breath hitches in my throat, and I wonder if he's going to kiss me. I wish he would, but he leans away a little, biting on his bottom lip and looking doubtful.

"What's wrong?" I ask.

"There's something else I need to know. Only I'm a little scared of asking."

"There's nothing to be scared of. Just ask."

"Okay." He pauses for a moment and then says, "If we've established you enjoyed what we did together, and you didn't want me to sleep with anyone else, can you explain why you told me you regretted sleeping with me? Twice? I understand that you felt guilty for indulging yourself, but why? What was there to feel guilty about?"

"It's complicated."

"Nothing about this is simple, Robyn, but I need to understand."

I guess he has every right, and I let out a sigh, looking up into his perfect face. "It's to do with my mother."

He frowns. "Okay. I wasn't expecting that."

"No? Even though Clark told you about her?"

"When?"

"During that phone call you had with him on the day I moved in here."

"Shit… you mean you overheard us?"

"Yes."

"Our entire conversation?"

"Yes."

"Fuck… I'm sorry. I wondered at the time, but you didn't say anything, so I hoped it had gone unnoticed."

"No, I'm afraid not. Don't get me wrong, everything Clark said was true. It was just I'd rather he'd kept most of it to himself."

"So you didn't want me to know you were looking to settle down?"

"Not especially. Although I was more concerned with him telling you I'd been 'saving myself', as he put it."

"I think it was me who said that first," he admits.

"Was it? That was an old-fashioned way of phrasing it."

"I hoped I was being respectful," he says, trying not to smile.

"Maybe. And I'm sure there are other, far less respectful ways you could have said that, but it was still really humiliating."

"I know, and I'm sorry. We shouldn't have talked about you like that."

"It wasn't you as much as Clark. He had no right to tell you that much detail about me… although, even then, he didn't tell you everything."

"You mean there's more?"

"In a way."

"Is this where your mom comes in?" he asks, and I nod my head.

"Yeah. I heard Clark say she can be a little stifling, but the truth is, she's so much worse than that. She means well, and I love her dearly, but I think I'm only just starting to realize she lives in a goddamn fantasy."

"A different one from yours, I presume?" he says, giving in to that smile.

"Oh, God… yes."

"Would this be the Prince Charming part?"

"It would. She's spent almost my entire life convincing me he's out there somewhere, waiting for me. I'll admit, I kinda liked the fairytale, but that's all it is. She filled my head with so much nonsense, I didn't know which way to turn."

"But you stuck by it?"

"Of course. I didn't know any better… and like I say, the fairytale sounded pretty appealing. It's just that every man I've met until now has been a frog."

He chuckles. "I'm gonna guess you thought I was exactly the same?"

"According to the conversation I heard you having with Clark, I assumed you were the king of the frogs."

"And you didn't wanna go there again?"

"No. I was done with men like that."

"Okay, but if that's how you felt, why did you come on to me?"

"I did a lot more than come on to you, and I explained this already… you're like the best ice cream in the world."

"Impossible to resist?" he says.

"Yes. Just not part of the plan."

"You realize plans can be broken, don't you? They're like diets."

"I get that. But you're not supposed to break them permanently."

"Why the hell not? I've always thought diets were overrated. You're better off having what you like."

"In moderation?" I ask, wondering where he's going with this.

"Not necessarily," he says. "It depends on what you like. If it's not gonna do you any harm, then you should feel free to have it as often as you like. And as I can guarantee you will never come to any harm while you're with me, then breaking your plan for me can't be a problem, can it?"

"Can't it?"

"No. I broke my plan for you."

"You had a plan?"

He chuckles. "Don't sound so shocked. My life isn't completely disorganized. Although to be fair, I never thought of it as a plan, as such. It was more of a way of life."

"What did it involve?"

"Doing exactly what I pleased," he says and I have to laugh.

"That's not really a plan, Spence."

"I know, but I was having a blast doing it."

"Until I came along and spoiled everything?"

He shakes his head. "You didn't spoil anything. You made me realize what I really wanted."

"Which was?"

"You."

"Just me?"

"Yes. I know you had me down as a player, and until a few weeks ago, you'd have been right. I'd always lived my life by my own set of rules, until I opened the door, and saw you standing there… and I knew I'd break every rule in the book for you."

"Just like that?"

"Well… it may have taken me a few days to work it out properly, but it was no longer than that."

"Really?"

"Yes."

"I feel so bad now," I say and he frowns.

"Why?"

"Because it took me a lot longer than that."

"To do what?"

I can't believe he's being so dense, and I smile, shaking my head at him. "To work it out. Obviously, when you opened the door, I was attracted to you. Who wouldn't be? As for everything else… well, with all the complications, it's been difficult to pin down how I feel."

He leans back, staring into my eyes. "What are you saying, Robyn?"

"That I love you just as much as you love me."

"That's not possible."

"Yes, it is. You don't have a monopoly on love, you know?"

"No… I know. But how can you love me? I'm not the man for you. That's what you've been telling me. Even last night you said how incompatible we were."

"I know, and I was wrong."

"But… I thought I'd have to convince you to love me. I expected it to take me weeks and months to wear you down and persuade you to give me a chance."

"Then I'm sorry to disappoint you."

He laughs, throwing his head back as he lifts me onto his lap and shifts back on the couch.

"You haven't. Oh… what's that?" he says, leaning forward again and reaching beneath him. He pulls out my phone, handing it over to me. "I found this last night, but I'd forgotten it was here."

"So had I… although I shouldn't have done. I was only using it this morning, just before you came in."

"Oh?"

He sits back, pulling me with him, and although I'd rather forget about the phone and make something of our position, I know he's intrigued, and it's not fair to keep him waiting for explanations… even if I'm not very good at them.

"I was gonna send you a text message," I say.

"Another one?"

"Yes. But a sober one this time."

"Why did you need to?" he asks.

"Because you weren't here."

"Oh. I see. What was it about?"

"You can read it for yourself, if you like?" He nods his head and I unlock the phone, handing it over to him. The message is still on the screen, and I watch as he looks down, taking a moment to read.

When he looks up again, he smiles. "I like that you added a kiss," he says. "Although you had nothing to worry about, you know that, don't you?"

I shrug my shoulders. "That's easy for you to say, but I couldn't find you, and after everything that had happened, and everything we'd said…"

He shakes his head and I stop talking. "That's not what I mean. I get that… well, things weren't right between us. That was why I went to get us some breakfast. And it's why I left you a note."

"You did?"

"Yes." He leans forward, my breasts pressing against his chest just briefly as he reaches around behind me, grabs the notepad and sits back again, flipping the page and turning it around so I can see what he's written…

'Gone to get some breakfast. Back soon xx'

It's concise, but I can't help smiling. "You added two kisses."

"I know, but it's not a competition. The point is, I wanted you to know where I was… because you have a right to know things like that."

"Do I?"

"Yes. I couldn't send you a text message because your phone was down here, and I couldn't be sure you'd look at it, but I didn't want to just go out without telling you. It looks like the page must have flipped over somehow, probably when I closed the door downstairs, but…"

"I wish I'd seen it, and I imagine I would have done if I hadn't been so focused on coffee."

"I can't blame you for that, and it doesn't matter. I'm home now, and I don't know about you, but I feel like we've resolved our differences, don't you?"

"Yes, I do."

"So, is there anything else I can do for you?"

There's a glint in his eye, and I flex my hips, reaching between us, my fingers dusting over the button on his jeans, just as he grabs me, his hands placed firmly on my ass.

"Uh-uh. We're gonna do things my way this time," he says, sitting forward and standing up without making it look difficult at all.

I wrap my legs around him as he turns and carries me toward the stairs.

"Where are we going?"

"Your room. Your bed's bigger than mine."

"Oh? We're gonna need a bigger bed, are we?"

"You bet we are."

Chapter Twenty

Spencer

I love watching Robyn sleep.

I've spent the last week doing it, in between everything else we've done together, and I have to say, it's been a magnificent week. The best of my life… so far.

I was right when I said we'd resolved our differences, and we proved it in her room… which is where we've spent every night since then. But on that particular Saturday morning, I felt I had a point to prove. We were doing things my way, after all, so once I'd brought her up here, I lowered her down my body, and without taking my eyes from hers, I stripped her out of her jeans and t-shirt. Her underwear followed, and as she was already breathing hard, clearly anticipating whatever I had in mind, I wasted no time in lowering her to the mattress.

I could have gone down on her there and then, but I wanted the contact of skin on skin, so I pulled off my clothes, leaving them in a pile on the floor, alongside hers.

She stared up at me the entire time, and as I lifted her a little further onto the bed, and then lowered my head to taste her, she let out a long, slow sigh.

What followed was a frenzy of pleasure. It started with Robyn coming on my tongue, and when she did, she went wild. I could feel her clit pulsing… her screams so loud, I think everyone on Main Street must have heard my name, and I didn't care one bit.

I didn't give her time to calm either. The moment I felt her breathing change, I licked up the last of her juices and crawled up over her. I'm pretty sure she thought I was going to enter her, but I had other things in mind, and I smiled at her wide-eyed expression as I kept going, until my cock was right above her face.

"Oh," she said. "Is that what you want?"

"Yes."

She giggled and opened her mouth.

I took her, holding nothing back, hitting the back of her throat with every stroke.

"Take me. Take my fucking cock," I said, kneeling up and gazing down at her. She nodded her head, and the eagerness in her eyes was nearly my undoing. I'd never come across anyone so willing… or so able, and it wasn't long before she had me on the verge of coming.

I don't think she'd have minded if I had, but I wanted to save that pleasure for another time. I had other things in mind, so I pulled my cock from her perfect lips and shimmied downward again.

"That felt good," she said.

"Sure did. But I think this will feel better."

She smiled, nodding her head, and I settled between her legs. I was about to enter her when I remembered… I needed a condom. I didn't relish the prospect of running downstairs to my room, but fortunately, I had some in my wallet, which was in my jeans, and I didn't take more than a few seconds to retrieve one and roll it over my straining dick. She watched me, her eyes betraying her need, and I soon resumed my position, raising her legs and holding them by the ankles as I lifted her ass off of the mattress and plunged my cock deep inside her. She arched her back, writhing beneath me as I upped the pace, hammering into her.

"Oh, God…" She spoke between gritted teeth. "That's so deep."

"It's meant to be. Being deep inside you is where I belong. But tell me you like it."

"I love it."

I smiled down at her. "Then come for me." I parted her legs even wider, exposing her clit, and she reached down with her right hand, letting her fingers circle over it. "I love watching you play with yourself."

"I love everything about you," she said, breathing hard.

I knew she was close, and I slammed into her, even deeper, pushing her over the edge. As she came, she squealed, and then yelled, and then screamed, her climax taking her even harder than all the rest.

How I held on, I'll never know, but I did, and once again, I barely gave her time to recover before I pulled out of her and flipped her over onto her front. She went to kneel up, but I pushed her back down, moving my legs so I was straddling her.

"What are you doing?" she said, twisting her head and doing her best to look over her shoulder at me.

"I'm doing things my way… remember?"

"Okay."

It felt good that she trusted me, and rather than make her wait, I lifted her ass off of the bed, just slightly. She seemed to know what I needed, and held it there while I moved into position, plunging my dick deep inside her. She felt so damn tight like that, it was all I could do not to come, but I held it together, leaning over her and taking her as hard as I could, my hands on her waist, holding her down.

"You're gonna make me... You're gonna make me..." Her voice was a little indistinct, but I knew what she meant, and as she clamped around me, I also knew I couldn't wait another moment.

"Take my come. Take my..." My words were lost in a sea of ecstasy, and I threw back my head, roaring her name as I gave her everything I had.

And more.

I wanted to believe everything would be different that time, but as I came down from that soaring high, I couldn't help feeling a little wary. We'd been here before, after all, and it hadn't ended well. Not for me.

I rolled us onto our sides, her back to my front, my cock still deep inside her. She wasn't fully recovered from her orgasm and was breathing hard.

"Are you okay?" I whispered in her ear. She nodded her head and snuggled back in to me, which felt promising, although I remembered her doing something like this the first time we made love... right before we spent the night together. The next morning, of course, she ran out on me, so I refused to be swayed by that particular memory, and held her a little tighter against me, kissing her exposed neck. "Will you be okay while I go to the bathroom?" I asked.

"Of course. I don't think I'm capable of moving."

"Are you sure? If you're having any doubts about us, then I think you should come with me."

She twisted her head, looking up into my eyes, and then pulled her arm from beneath mine, caressing my cheek with her hand.

"I'm not having any doubts, Spence."

"So you'll be here when I come back?"

She frowned, an echo of sadness crossing her eyes. "What did I do to you?"

I didn't want to tell her how much she'd hurt me, but I wasn't going to lie to her, either. "I think we both know the answer to that question," I said. It was the best compromise I could think of, and she nodded her head, leaning up to kiss me.

"I'm sorry."

"Enough apologies. Just tell me you'll be here when I get back."

"I'll be here."

I kissed her… a lot harder than she'd kissed me, and as I broke the kiss, I pulled out of her, surprised by her sigh of disappointment.

"You won't be long, will you?" she said.

"No."

"Good."

She rolled over to face me as I climbed out of bed, and I walked backwards to the top of the stairs, my eyes never leaving hers.

"Don't go anywhere."

"I won't."

I blew her a kiss, which she returned, and then I ran down the stairs, going straight to the bathroom, where I disposed of the condom and washed up as quickly as I could, running straight back to Robyn's bedroom.

She'd promised to be where I left her, but as I got to the top of the stairs, I glanced at the bed, my heart sinking when I saw it was empty. Robyn wasn't there. She was standing over by the window, the throw from the end of the bed wrapped around her shoulders.

"Please don't," I said, unable to hide the despair in my voice.

"Don't what?" She turned back, looking across the room at me.

"Don't do this to me again. Don't tell me it was all a mistake. You can't say you regret it… not this time."

She shook her head. "I wasn't going to," she said, pulling the throw around her as she walked across the room toward me. "I was just wondering what we've got to eat." She glanced down at my cock as she finished speaking, and I had to chuckle.

"It's yours if you want it."

"I do," she said. "I'd love to feel you come in my mouth, but right at this moment, I'm desperate for food… the kind of food I can actually chew on."

I leaned away from her. "You're not chewing on this," I said, gripping my shaft.

"I had a feeling you'd say that." She lowered her eyes to my cock again, licking her lips, and then biting the bottom one. I ached at the thought of what I could do with her, but before I could move an inch, she looked back up at my face and smiled. "So… what do we have to eat?"

"Are you that hungry?"

"Yes. I didn't eat last night, and I only had a bite of cinnamon roll before we came up here."

"Why didn't you eat last night?"

"Because I can't fend for myself yet, Spence. I thought you realized that."

I nodded my head, lowering my hand and moving closer to the bed. "Sorry. I should have thought."

"It's not your fault, and I don't wanna talk about what happened last night. We've put all that behind us now… haven't we?"

I hated the slight doubt in her voice, and I reached out, pulling her close to me and wrapping her in my arms.

"We have."

"In which case, what can you feed me? Apart from the obvious…" She pulled back and lowered her gaze to my cock once more, but didn't let it linger, her need for food clearly greater than her need for anything else.

"Not very much," I said. "That's why I bought breakfast. But why don't I take you for brunch at the coffee shop?"

"I think you mean lunch, don't you? It's gone noon," she said.

"Okay. We'll call it lunch if you like. And while we're there, we can work out next week's menu, then we can go to the grocery store together this afternoon, if you like?"

"That all sounds very organized."

"Well... we have to keep you fed, don't we?"

"Do we?"

"Yes. Because when we've finished all that, I'm gonna bring you back here and make you scream my name until you're too tired to think."

"Hmm... I like the sound of that."

"I thought you might."

She smiled up at me, and then let her eyes wander slowly down my body.

"Will you come in my mouth?" she whispered, reaching between us and holding my cock in her hand, her grip firm but soothing.

"I'll come anywhere you like."

She moaned, gazing into my eyes, and despite her hunger, she dropped to her knees.

"Fuck, yes," I murmured as she took me in her mouth and I gathered her hair behind her head, flexing my hips, my cock hitting the back of her throat. "Play with your clit... make yourself come." She changed position slightly, her eyes closing in delight as I upped the pace just slightly. "You look so beautiful with my dick in your mouth." She groaned, nodding her head, and I was aware of a change in her breathing. She was close, but so was I, and I held back until I knew she was right on the edge, waiting... waiting, and then finally letting go down her throat at the same time as she squealed, her lips clamping around me, and her tongue working its special magic.

It was all I could do to stand, but as we both came down to earth again, I pulled her up into my arms, and held her close to me.

"Satisfied now?"

"Yes, thank you."

I shook my head. "You don't have to thank me. If anything, it's the other way around. But I'm sure I can find a way to pay you back."

"Later," she said. "I'm hungry."

I had to laugh, and once we were dressed, we spent the rest of our day doing exactly as we'd said, and although it wasn't our first meal in public, or even our first visit to the grocery store together, there was something different about doing those things as a couple.

We laughed over lunch, holding each other's hands while we planned our meals for the week ahead… and when we got to the grocery store, I pushed the cart while Robyn darted off, gathering up all the things we needed. Every time she came back, she'd look up into my eyes, or I'd dip my head and kiss her.

It was wondrous.

And I never thought I'd say that about grocery shopping.

But that's the thing, I guess.

Life has become wondrous since then.

We do everything together, from taking a shower in the morning to meeting up for lunch. We even drive to work together, and I'm teaching her to cook again, too… although we don't always get much cooking done. How can we when there are so many other temptations on offer?

"Good morning."

I glance down, smiling at Robyn's sleepy face.

"You're awake at last."

She shakes her head. "You can't blame me for sleeping in."

"Because it's Saturday?"

"No. Because you kept me awake really late last night."

She's not lying, and I lean over, kissing her gently. "I'm sorry. I'll try to be more considerate."

"Don't you dare," she says, pushing me onto my back and straddling me. "I don't want considerate."

"What do you want?"

"You. Now."

"Will you settle for me in the shower?"

She nods her head. "You know I will."

"Good."

I grab her ass, shifting to the side of the bed and then swing my legs over the edge, getting to my feet and bringing her with me. We've done this enough now that she knows the drill, and wraps her legs around me, gripping my shoulders as I carry her down the stairs to the bathroom and straight into the shower.

Robyn turns on the water as I lower her down my body and grab a condom from the shelf. We brought a supply in here last weekend, realizing there would be a need for them. Although looking at the dwindling pile, I'll have to get some more, I think. We've almost exhausted them. That's not a problem for today, though, and I spin her around, so she's facing the tiled wall as I roll the condom over my cock.

"I need to be inside you," I growl, burying my cock to the hilt in her wet pussy.

"Yes! Yes!" Her voice fills the room, and she slaps her hands against the wall, edging her ass back toward me.

"You want my cock?"

"Yes. Give it to me."

This is what we're like. This is who we are, and I pound in to her, holding her hips, taking her so hard, I lift her feet off of the floor with every stroke.

"More," she yells. "Give me more."

I don't know how much more I've got to give, but I do my best, feeling that familiar quivering at her core, right before she ignites around me. The sound of my name on her lips, and the sight of her taking me, are too much. I tip over, losing myself to her… yet again.

I'm still regaining my breath when I pull out of her and spin her around. She's sucking in lungfuls of air, but she throws her arms around me.

"God… that was good," she says, and I stare down into her upturned face.

"When was the last time I told you I love you?"

She thinks for a moment. "Last night, just before we went to sleep."

"That long ago? I'm slipping." She giggles, and I pull her closer still, her body hard against mine as I crush my lips to hers. Having not kissed very much at the start, we've discovered we like it, just for the sake of it, and we do it a lot now. As ever, she responds to my touch, our tongues dancing for a while, until I pull back, cupping her face with my hands. "I love you, Robyn," I say, her eyes sparkling into mine.

"I love you," she says.

And all's right with the world.

I've already finished my scrambled eggs and toast, but Robyn is still getting through hers, when she turns to me and says, "Am I right that it's Easter this weekend??"

"Yes. Why?"

"Did I see there's gonna be some kind of Easter egg hunt on the green today?"

"I think so. Did you wanna go?"

She takes a sip of coffee. "It's for kids, isn't it?"

"I have no idea."

"You mean you didn't go last year? You and Clark were living here, weren't you?"

"Yes, but I imagine we were otherwise occupied."

She raises her eyebrows at me. "I don't think we need to talk about that."

I lean over and kiss her cheek. "No, we don't… and if you wanna go to the Easter egg hunt, I don't see why we can't. We live here, and even if we don't have kids, we can still join in."

She lowers her gaze, staring down at her plate. I think I may have just hit a raw nerve, but before I can say anything, she looks up, a smile adorning her perfect lips, the moment having passed.

"I think we should," she says. "It'll be fun."

Part of me wants to ask what just happened, but she seems keen to go out, and finishes her breakfast, jumping down from her seat.

"Are we going now?" I ask.

"I think the poster I saw said it was due to start at ten."

I check the time on the microwave. It's already ten thirty, and I grab her plate, putting it in the dishwasher. "In that case, you'd better put some shoes on."

"So had you."

"I will… but I'll be quicker than you."

"You will?"

"Yeah. It won't take me ten minutes to decide which pair to wear."

She shoots me a glare, which I know she doesn't mean. Her smile gives her away, and she runs up the stairs.

My shoes are still in my bedroom because we haven't gotten around to moving all my clothes upstairs yet. We will though. We talked it through last weekend, while we were lying in bed, agreeing that it made more sense for us to use the bigger bedroom.

"You don't mind giving up your space for me?" I said.

She looked up at me. "Have you got that many clothes?"

"No, but I don't wanna crowd you."

She smiled. "Oh… I don't mind."

I remember she rolled me onto my back at that point, and we forgot all about clothes, and bedrooms, although I suppose we should try to get it done. It's a pain in the ass having to come down here whenever I need something… like my shoes, which I slip on, grabbing a sweater, and pulling it on over my head before I wander back out into the living room.

"I was just thinking we should get on with moving your clothes up here," Robyn says as she comes down the stairs, and I laugh.

"I was thinking exactly the same thing."

"We could do it tomorrow, if you like?"

"We'll need to go grocery shopping first, but I guess we could find time in the afternoon."

"Okay."

She comes over, pulling on her cardigan. It's long and gray, and suits her… just like everything she wears, and I pull her into my arms.

"You're adorable. Did you know that?"

"No."

"Well, you are. Now… let's get going, or we'll miss the Easter Bunny."

"That would never do," she says, chuckling, and I take her hand, leading her down the stairs.

Main Street is really busy, full of people flocking to Hart's Green, and we join them, hand-in-hand.

"I didn't realize it would be like this," Robyn says, looking up at me.

"Neither did I. The Fourth of July picnic was pretty busy, but…"

"There's a Fourth of July picnic?"

"Yeah. They hold one every year, evidently."

"We'll have to go to that," she says, and I nod my head, leaning in to her as we get to the green.

This is much more of an event than I'd expected… and between the band playing live music, the stalls selling food, and the Easter Bunny hopping around, it's hard to know where to look.

There are children running around all over the place, and it's impossible not to be swept up in their enjoyment.

We recognize a few people… Gabe and Remi are here, with Ryan and Peony, and their son, who seems enthralled by everything that's going on. Tanner makes a point of coming over to see us, and bringing Zara with him.

"You don't have Nash with you?" I say, and he shakes his head.

"No. He's with my ex-wife this weekend."

"That's a shame. He would have enjoyed this."

Tanner nods. "He would. He always does… but Sabrina never cared too much about other people enjoying themselves."

I can hear the bitterness in his voice, and wonder how hard they must have fought over who was gonna have Nash this weekend. It seems really sad that they can't co-parent more harmoniously, and even though Tanner's clearly happy with Zara, and they have so much to look forward to, I can't help leaning in to Robyn as we step away.

"Tell me we won't ever get like that?" I say.

"Never."

She leans up and kisses me, letting her lips linger, which feels good.

"I love you," I whisper.

"And I love you, too."

I'm about to kiss her back when Robyn waves to someone. It's a blonde woman who's standing by the edge of the green, holding hands with a tall man. He's even blonder than she is, and leans down to whisper something in her ear, which distracts her from her wave.

"Who's that?" I ask.

"Jodie."

"Your friend?"

"Yes."

"And the guy? Is he her boyfriend?"

"Yes. That's Flynn. They met when she and I went to the hotel for dinner. He works there."

"So they haven't been together very long?"

"Not long at all."

"You'd never know. They look really happy together."

"And so do we," she says, gazing up into my eyes, as I smile down at her.

"Hey... stranger?"

I turn at the sound of a familiar voice, as does Robyn, and we both startle slightly at the sight of Clark, standing just a few feet away. Beside him is Cerys, who I recognize, even though she's changed her hair. It's still dark brown, but is shorter than I remember. Clark's got his arm around her, and being several inches shorter than him, she fits neatly against him. Just like Robyn does against me... a fact which hasn't escaped Clark's notice.

"Is there something you guys wanna tell me?" he says, frowning at Robyn before he turns a darker scowl on me.

"No." We all move closer together. "You didn't tell me Robyn was a woman."

"And you didn't tell me Spencer even existed," Robyn says.

"So why would we need to share anything with you?" I add, tilting my head at him.

"No reason," he says, keeping his eyes fixed on me rather than his cousin. "But does this mean you're thinking of settling down?"

"No," I say, and he pulls himself up to his full height. That still leaves him a little shorter than me, and even if it didn't, I wouldn't feel intimidated. There's no need. "I'm not thinking of it. I've already done it."

He relaxes, a smile touching at his lips. "You have?"

"Yeah."

"So you don't need to get all protective," Robyn says.

"I wasn't."

"Yes, you were."

"But like she says, there's no need," I say, and he nods his head.

"When did this happen?"

"A week ago."

"And when you've finished with the questions," Robyn says, "would you mind introducing me to your girlfriend?"

"My fiancée," Clark says, and my mouth drops open.

"Fiancée? When did that happen?"

"Not last weekend, but the one before."

Cerys holds up her left hand, offering the evidence of their engagement, in the form of a sparkling sapphire and diamond ring.

"Congratulations," Robyn says, giving Clark a hug, before he finally makes the overdue introductions.

"If it's not a rude question, what are you doing here?" I ask.

"We flew into Boston a couple of days ago to tell my mom and dad about our engagement, but…"

"It all got too much for you?" Robyn says, and Clark smiles, rolling his eyes.

"You could say that. Mom's thrilled, as you can imagine. She insisted on throwing a dinner for all the family, and between them, they're already trying to work out where we're gonna get married."

"We're thinking of eloping," Cerys says, and we all laugh.

"I would if I were you," Robyn says. "Although I'm surprised my mom hasn't called to tell me the good news."

"I think she said she was gonna call tomorrow… so for heaven's sake act surprised."

"I will, don't worry."

"How long are you staying?" I ask.

"Just tonight. We've booked a room at the hotel, and we're driving back to Boston tomorrow afternoon."

"When you get there, you must promise not to tell Mom anything about Spencer," Robyn says, sounding worried. "Don't tell her I've got a boyfriend, or even that I'm living with a man… will you?"

"Do you mean you haven't told her you're sharing the apartment?"

"Of course I haven't."

"You haven't?" I say, turning to face her.

"No." She looks up at me. "Trust me, if I'd told Mom about you, she'd have been sizing you up for a tux from the moment I mentioned your name, and if she knew we were actually together, she'd have ordered the goddamn flowers by now."

I'm surprised by how little that worries me, but I don't say a word… not about that, anyway. Instead, I suggest the four of us get together for dinner.

"That sounds like a great idea," Clark says. "We can catch up properly, and you can tell me everything you've been doing since I left."

"Not everything," Robyn says, looking up at me, and we all laugh.

*

"It was good to see Clark again," Robyn says as she lies in my arms, both of us gazing up at the bedroom ceiling.

"And to meet Cerys. You've never met her before, have you?"

"No. Have you?"

"Yeah. She came for a visit."

"Just one?"

"Yeah. Clark preferred to go there. She doesn't share her apartment, and I think I cramped his style."

"Clark doesn't have a style," she says, making me chuckle. "She's lovely, though, isn't she? And just right for him."

"They're right for each other," I say.

"Which could be why they're getting married."

"Maybe." I turn to face her, pulling her close against me. "It's not such a bad idea, you know?"

Her eyes widen. "Marriage?"

"Yeah."

"Really? I was raised on it, and it's caused me nothing but trouble."

"I realize that, but what you're talking about is the fantasy," I say. "The reality won't be the same."

"Oh?"

I shake my head. "I'm no Prince Charming for one thing."

I roll onto my back, bringing her with me, and as she straddles me, I lower her onto my cock. She feels incredible, and I take a moment to absorb how good this is… how good she is.

"No… I—I see what you mean," she says, stuttering out her words and letting her head rock back just for a second. "Although I think you've forgotten something."

"No, I haven't." I raise my hips just to prove the point. "I realize I'm not wearing a condom, but we're okay for now… and I have to say, you feel so damn good."

"So do you," she says. "It's completely different without a barrier between us."

"It's so much better." She nods her head, moving just a little faster. "And in any case, that's something I wanted to talk to you about."

"It is?" She looks confused, and I sit up, holding on to her, smiling as she rocks against me, flexing her hips.

"Woah, babe. Can you try to remember there's nothing between us… and take it easy?"

She chuckles, which doesn't help in the slightest, and I take a breath, just to get some control… or try to. Robyn takes pity and slows her movements, and I reach up and caress her cheek with my fingertips.

"Thanks," I murmur, and she nods her head.

"What was it you wanted to say?" she asks.

"It was a question, really."

"What about?"

"This morning, when we were talking about going to the Easter egg hunt, we were saying how it was something for kids, and I said we didn't have any. That seemed to make you kinda sad, and I wondered… did I miss something?"

"Like what?" she asks, halting her movements completely, her eyes locking with mine.

"Like the fact that maybe you wanna change that set of circumstances… that you want us to have kids?" I say, holding my breath as I wait for her answer.

"Does it make a difference?" she says.

"To us?"

"Yes."

"Of course it does."

"Then tell me how you feel about it. Do you wanna have kids?" she asks.

I remember being surprised that Clark and Cerys had the children talk so early in their relationship, but now I realize how important it is, and I lie back down, bringing Robyn with me, holding her along the length of my body, one hand behind her head, the other on her ass, our eyes locked.

"If you'd asked me that question six months ago, I'd have said 'no'. Even two weeks ago, I think I'd still have been unsure. I didn't know where I stood with you then, and to be honest, I was more concerned about us than anything else."

"And now?" she says, biting her bottom lip.

"I want everything with you," I say as she sits up and rests her hands on my chest, staring down at me.

"Everything?"

"Yes."

"Including children?"

"Yes." Her smile makes my heart sing, but as she grinds on to me, I hold her still, my hands on her hips. "Wait a second…"

"Oh… sorry," she says, biting her bottom lip again. "We should probably be more sensible, just for now, shouldn't we?" She goes to raise herself off of me, but I pull her back down again.

"To hell with being sensible. That's not why I asked you to wait."

"Then why?" she asks, looking confused.

"Because I told you I want everything… which means I need you to answer another question."

Her brow furrows, and I rest my hands on her thighs, my heart fluttering in my chest.

"What's the question?" she asks, getting impatient.

"Will you marry me?"

Her face clears, but rather than the smile I'd hoped for, she just stares down at me. "Are you serious?" she says.

"Absolutely. I just told you I thought marriage wasn't such a bad idea. Why are you so surprised?"

"Because I just told you it's caused me nothing but trouble."

"Yeah… in your mom's fantasy world. But this is our world, babe. We can do what we like. We can let your mom go wild and plan the wedding she's always wanted for you, or we can elope to an island in the middle of nowhere and tell everyone about it when we get back."

"My mom would kill me if we did that."

"Then we'll find a compromise. Like I say, the how doesn't matter to me. All I care about is you, and spending the rest of my life making you happy."

"You mean that?"

"You know I do." I pull her back down, holding her against my chest. "I just need a one-word answer, Robyn… and if you love me as much as I love you, it's the one with three letters, not two."

"Yes," she says, and I pull back from her as far as the pillow will allow.

"Yes?"

"Yes, I'll marry you. There's nothing I want more."

I raise my head, pulling hers down at the same time, our lips clashing in a bruising kiss as I flip her over onto her back, nestling between her parted legs. We writhe together, rolling one way and the other, until we finally settle, with her beneath me, and I raise myself to my elbows, gazing down into her beautiful face as I flex my hips, making her gasp.

"I told you I was no Prince Charming," I say, and she nods her head.

"I don't need one… not anymore."

"I can still make your dreams come true… if you want me to."

She smiles, her eyes locking with mine as I dip my head to kiss her again, and she makes my heart burst when she whispers, "You already have."

The End

Thank you for reading *Sharing with Spencer*. I hope you enjoyed it, and if you did, I hope you'll take the time to leave a short review.

Printed in Dunstable, United Kingdom